FAREWELL TO YESTERDAY'S TOMORROW

ALEXEI PANSHIN

PHOENIX PICK

an imprint of

ARC MANOR

Rockville, Maryland

ISBN: 978-1-60450-264-0

Sky Blue, Lady Sunshine and the Magoon of Beatus and *Farewell to Yesterday's Tomorrow* coauthored by Alexei and Cory Panshin

www.PhoenixPick.com
Great Science Fiction at Great Prices

Visit the Author's Website:
http://www.panshin.com/

Published by Phoenix Pick
an imprint of Arc Manor
P. O. Box 10339
Rockville, MD 20849-0339
www.ArcManor.com

Printed in the United States of America / United Kingdom

For Ted White and Terry Carr

Contents

Preface

The twelve science fiction and fantasy stories and the final essay that make up this book are printed here in the order in which they were originally written. They were first published between 1966 and 1975, a turbulent time in this country, and a time of great changes in my own life. These stories are both a product and a reflection of their time.

These stories have been a means for me of wrestling with the enigma of being alive. Over and over again, each in its own way, they ask the same childish question: What does it mean to be an adult human being?

So many questions that we ask when we are children are never answered. They are indefinitely postponed. This question—a child's question—was mine. And it was never answered for me to my satisfaction.

What is it to be an adult human being?

It still seems to me to be as urgent a question as it ever was. In view of the desperation of the present human condition, a desperate question. If we human beings are to survive, we must know who we are and what we may become.

The question is deliberately posed in the form of science fiction. Science fiction is a means of stepping outside ourselves and our present condition in search of new perception. If we already knew how to be truly adult, if we already knew how to be truly human beings, we would not be in our present difficulties.

Is our personal future and the future of mankind limited and cloudy? The answer indicated by science fiction and by these stories is: only if we are unable to change ourselves.

If we could change ourselves, what might we not become?

So here these stories are, from "What's Your Excuse?" to "Lady Sunshine and the Magoon of Beatus." A record of change and a promise of possiblity.

—Alexei Panshin
ELEPHANT, PENNSYLVANIA

What's Your Excuse?

Wooley's beard and manner were all that you would expect of any psychology instructor, particularly one who enjoys his work. He leaned back in his swivel chair, his feet on his desk, hands folded behind his neck, and looked at the graduate student who had been sharing his partition-board office for the past two weeks.

"I'm curious about you, Holland," he said. "By my conservative estimate, ninety-five percent of degree candidates in psychology are twitches. What's your problem?"

The room was only about eight feet wide. Holland's desk faced the back of the cubicle, Wooley's faced the door, and there was a narrow aisle between the two. Holland was a teaching assistant and was busy correcting a stack of papers. He looked warily up at Wooley, who had a certain reputation, and then returned his attention to his work.

"No," Wooley said expansively. "On the face of it, I would have said that you had a very low twitch rating."

Wooley's reputation was half for being a thoroughgoing son of a bitch, half for being fascinating in the classroom. He had a flamboyant, student-attracting personality that was great fun for those he didn't pick for victims.

Holland finished marking the paper and tossed it on the stack he had completed. Then he said, "What is a twitch rating?"

"Don't you know that neuroses and psychoses are old hat? They need a scientific replacement, and for that purpose I have devised the twitch rating. Radiation is measured in curies, noise is measured in decibels—now psychological problems are measured in twitches. I'd rate you about five. That's very low, particularly for a psych student."

Holland flipped his red pencil to the side and leaned back. "You mean you really think that psych students are more . . . disturbed . . . than . . . "

"They're twitches," Wooley corrected. "That's why they're psychology students. They're not twitchy *because* they're psych students. What they want is to learn excuses for the way they act. They don't want to change it or even, I think, understand it. They want to excuse it—you know, 'Mama was a boozer, Daddy was a flit, so how can I possibly help myself?' They learn all the reasons that there are for being twitchy and that makes them happy."

Holland cleared his throat and leaned forward to recover his pencil. Holland was a very serious fellow and not completely sure just how serious Wooley was, and that made him ill-at-ease.

"Isn't it possible that you are mistaking an itch for a twitch?" he asked. "Then if somebody scratches, you think he's crazy. But what if their reason isn't an excuse, what if there is a genuine cause and you just can't see it? If you want a crude example, is a concentration-camp inmate a paranoid if he thinks that people are against him?"

"No," Wooley said. "Not unless he's a graduate student in psychology. In that case I wouldn't make any bets."

"Well, what are you doing here?"

"I'm observing humanity, what else? Look, I'll give you an example of a genuine, make-no-mistake-about-it, ninety-five-rating, excuse-making twitch from right down the hall. Do you know Hector Leith?"

"No. I haven't been here long enough," Holland said. "I don't know everybody's name yet, and I haven't observed anybody twitching in the hall."

Wooley shook his head. "You'd better be careful. You've got the makings of a very sharp tongue there. Come along." He swung his feet to the floor and led the way out into the hall.

Holland hesitated for a moment and then shrugged and followed. The corridor ran between a double row of brown partition-board cubicles. On the walls of the corridor were photographs, a book-display rack, notices, and two plaques celebrating the accomplishments of the department's bowling and softball teams. One of the photographs was of the previous year's crop of graduate students. Wooley pointed at the shortest person in the picture.

"That's Hector Leith," he said.

"I guess I have seen him around."

"How old would you say he is?"

Holland looked at the picture and tried to remember the person he'd seen briefly in the hall. "Not more than eighteen," he said finally.

"He's twenty-seven."

"You're kidding."

"No," Wooley said. "He's twenty-seven, he looks eighteen or less, and he is a genuine twitch."

The person in the photograph was only a few inches more than five feet tall, smooth-cheeked, fresh-faced, elfish-looking. He might possibly have passed for a junior high school student except for his air of tart awareness, and he certainly seemed out of place with the others in the picture. Wooley was there, too, with his beard.

Back in their shared office, Holland returned to his swivel chair while Wooley sat on the edge of his desk.

"Now," Wooley said, "he was drafted by the Army and tossed out after four weeks for emotional instability. I don't hold too much with the Army, but I'd still give him thirty twitch points for that. He started out as a teaching assistant here, but he started twitching in front of the class and now he's a research assistant. You can give him another thirty points for that."

"So what's your diagnosis, Doctor?" Holland said.

Wooley shrugged. "I don't know. Manic-depressive, maybe. One day he'll overflow all over you, try to be friends—try to be buddies and ask you out for a beer. You can't imagine how funny that is between his trying to get into a bar in the first place and the fact that he can't stand beer. He'll tell you all his problems. The next day he won't talk to you at all, hide his little secrets away. And when he's unpleasant, which is more than half the time, he'll leave three-inch scars all over you. Give him fifteen points for that and the last twenty points for his excuses."

"All right. What are they?"

Wooley paused for effect. "He thinks—he says he's finally figured it out—that he's living at a slower rate than most people, and he really isn't grown up yet. He still has to get his physical and emotional growth. He's where everybody else his age was years ago."

"Why does he think that?"

Wooley smiled. "Well, he thinks he is growing. He thinks he's gaining height."

Holland said seriously, "You know, if it were so, it would really be something, wouldn't it? I can see why it would make somebody twitchy. To be that far out of step, not know why, and be incapable of doing what people expect of you would certainly be a burden. You'd be bound to think it was you and that would only make things worse."

"Perfect excuse, isn't it?" Wooley asked drily. "There's only one problem and that is it's just wishful thinking."

"Well, if he's growing . . ."

"He isn't growing. He just thinks he is. Come on and I'll show you."

He led the way down the hall to another cubicle that was similar to their own except that there was only one desk. The extra space was taken up by bookshelves. Wooley flipped on the light.

"Come on in," he said to Holland, and Holland stepped inside.

Wooley pointed to the wall at a point where a wood strip connected pieces of particle board. There were a few faint pencil ticks there, the top and the bottom marks being perhaps an inch and a half apart.

"There," Wooley said. "That's the growing he thinks he's done."

"Only he hasn't?"

"No," Wooley said, chuckling. "I've been moving the marks. I add them on the bottom and erase the top mark. He just keeps putting it back and thinking he's that much taller."

Holland said, "Pardon me. I have work to do." He turned quite deliberately and walked out, his distaste evident.

Wooley said after him, "It's a psychological experiment." But Holland didn't stop.

Wooley shrugged. Then he turned back to the pencil marks and counted them. He then picked a pencil off the desk, erased the topmost mark, and carefully added a mark at the bottom.

Then he tossed the pencil back onto the desk and turned away. Just before he got to the door, Hector Leith came around the corner and into the room. They almost bumped into one another, stopped, and then carefully stepped back.

Leith looked much like his picture: tiny, boyish-looking, incongruous in tie, jacket, and black overcoat. The briefcase he carried was the last touch that made him look like a youngster playing Daddy.

He gave Wooley a bitter look and said, "What are you doing here?"

"Looking for a book."

"Whatever it is, you can't borrow it. Get out of here. Don't think I don't know the trouble you've made for me around here, Wooley. Out."

"All right, all right," Wooley said. "I couldn't find it anyway."

He beat a retreat down the corridor, relieved that Leith hadn't walked in a minute earlier. When he reached his own office, Holland was piling papers on his desk.

"What's this?" Wooley asked.

"I'm not staying," Holland said. "I don't think we're going to work well together. They've got a desk I can use in the department office until they can find me another place."

"What's the matter with you?" Wooley asked. "Why should you leave?"

"What's the matter with you?" Holland asked. "They told me that nobody would stay in an office with you, and I can't stomach you, either. And I'd advise you not to pull any of your tricks on me."

Leith, somewhat strained, closed the door behind Wooley when he left. He wondered if he should have been less harsh. He knew that all it did was make him sound petulant, and that was something he was trying to break himself of, even with Wooley. But it was hard.

He looked then at the strip of wood marked with little pencil lines, and smiled with slightly malicious delight at what he saw. He picked up the pencil that Wooley had abandoned and replaced the tick that had been erased.

The top tick was on the level of his eyes now, perhaps even a little lower, and he wondered how long it would be before Wooley finally noticed.

He said, quite softly, "I'm growing up, Wooley. What's your excuse?"

The Sons of Prometheus

1. THE COLLIGATIONS OF THE CONFRATERNITY

You don't suddenly appear out of nowhere. The Colonists find that disconcerting. You arrive in a place from somewhere definite. Particularly on Zebulon.

Zebulon? Whatever you do, don't let them know where you come from. They (finger across the neck with an appropriate sound effect, *zit*) Ship people when they catch them. Remember the Sons of Prometheus—they being the ones who had gotten it in the neck. Of course they were from *Puteaux* and not nearly so bright as we.

It was nice of Nancy to remind Tansman of that and tell him to take care of himself, especially since it was her idea for him to go to Zebulon. It was nothing he would have thought of himself. Zebulon was not really the place for a chromoplastician with no experience in adventure, with no taste for do-gooding, with an active indifference to everything but the tidy definite sufficiency of chromoplasts.

Tansman arrived in North Hill, where he had been told he would be met by Rilke. A solid-wheeled, leather-sprung public coach was as concrete an arrival as he could manage. The rough ride over rougher roads had given him a stiff neck and a headache. He had tried to study local scripture, *The Colligations of the Confraternity,* but finally gave up, put the book back in his bag, and thereafter looked out the window or at his feet.

He was the only passenger. The talk of the megrim had been enough to empty the coach. He'd taken no notice of the rumors of plague when he bought his seat for North Hill, since he wasn't affected. But he was grateful. He didn't relate easily to other people, even Ship people. He had no idea what to say to a Colonist, people who died, people who killed.

It gave him the chance to study the *Colligations,* since that was what Zebulon killed and died for. If the subject came up, he wanted to be ready.

As they rattled through the rutted streets, Tansman looked through the coach window. There was little traffic—none to speak of. There was less noise—stony quiet. Nobody to be seen. It was a strange queer place, this North Hill. Most of the adobe houses they passed were shut and shuttered.

Arriving, Tansman felt more tense than he had since that first moment when he had been set down here on Zebulon and put on his own. It was only the third time he had been on a planet, the third time in his life that he had left *Daudelin,* though he could million his light years. Once in practice for Trial when he was thirteen. Once for thirty nervous days on Trial when he turned fourteen. And now.

Here he was, a chromoplastician in a world ignorant of chromoplasts, an incognito prince amongst sharp-toothed paupers, an uneasy rider in a coach that was now, at last, coming to a stop in a dusty street under a lowering sky. And he was afraid. He wouldn't have admitted it, but he was afraid.

It was his own fault for letting himself be overridden by Nancy Poate. She was his cousin, one of the few people he knew, one of the few people he let himself know. She was older than he, determined and formidable.

"Phil," she had said, "did you or did you not tell me last week that you were finished with that silly set of experiments you've been locking yourself in with?"

He had told her about the experiments to make her go away. She didn't like to hear about them so he always started talking about chromoplasts when he wanted to be left alone.

"Yes," he said. "But they aren't silly. You shouldn't talk about my work that way."

"Then you need a vacation. This will be a vacation."

"Nancy, I'll grant that after Earth was destroyed we owed the Colonies more than we gave them, but this sneaking around doing paternal good works to people who just want to be left alone doesn't appeal to me."

Tansman didn't really care about the Colonies. They weren't real to him. They were distant and vaguely frightening and he didn't want to think about them. He would grant the premises that Nancy insisted upon—because Nancy was immediate and, in her way, even more frightening. But he would seize on any argument he could find and throw it back at her.

And none of it—the points he granted or the arguments he countered with—was real, none of it was thought through. It was all talk designed to keep the fearsome where it belonged, as far away as possible.

Since this argument seemed to be doing the job, he continued with it:

"You don't dare come out in the open, because you're afraid that they'll wring your necks, but you aren't willing to leave them alone. So what do you do? You prod and you poke, you try to establish trade routes and other silly business, and you hand out propaganda and how-to-do-it books, and that makes you feel good. Well, it wouldn't make me feel good, and I don't want any part of it."

Nancy, bluff and unstoppable, just nodded. Tansman would have had himself remodeled if he looked the way she did. He was convinced that she didn't because her appearance helped her to overwhelm people and get her own way.

She said, "I knew I was right to pick on you, Phil. You won't be tempted to meddle. All you'll have to do is be there for two months keeping an eye on things."

"No," he said.

"Phil," she said. "Don't be stuffy."

So now he was on Zebulon, not quite sure how he had been persuaded to come. He was a reluctant fire-bringer, muttering to himself about a man he had yet to meet named Hans Rilke who was a do-gooder with an undurable liver. They might call themselves "The Group," but Nancy Poate's people were low-visibility Sons of Prometheus.

It seemed appropriate that Rilke should have a liver complaint. That had been Prometheus' problem, too. He wondered if it were an occupational disease of meddlers, and he wished Nancy Poate had found a better way to occupy herself than coordinating the activities of do-gooders—including the replacement of their innards.

He took a deep breath and descended from the coach, satchel in hand. He was a tall, youngish man. Not young—he disowned his youth along with all other potential folly. He was a thin man, narrow of face and large of nose. If it had ever mattered, he might have had it altered, but the chromoplasts didn't care and if anyone else did, they had never bothered to tell him.

He was wearing a slouch hat, jacket, breeches and leggings that he had been assured were seasonable and stylish here. He felt like the sort of ass who dresses up for costume parties. He'd never worn a hat before in his life, and he kept reaching up to adjust the clumsy, uncomfortable thing.

The wind under the flat, cold, gray sky was chill and biting. It tugged at his silly hat as he stepped down from the coach, and slapped Tansman in the face with the most overwhelming, pungent, unpleasant odor he had ever smelled. It was an eye-burning, stomach-churning reek that drowned him in singed hair and charring flesh.

The driver of the coach could smell it, too. He didn't wait for Tansman. He gave a sharp whistle and his horses lurched forward. Raising dust, open coach door banging back and forth, the stage rattled to the right and around the corner and was gone between the mud-walled buildings, leaving only a dust-whorl memory.

And Tansman stood alone at the edge of the square of North Hill. Fifty yards distant across the square was built a great bonfire. There may have been a base of wood beneath, but the primary fuel was human bodies. Some of the bodies were clothed, the fire licking at the cloth, lines of flame running down arms and legs. Most of the bodies were naked, marked by great purple bruises like port-wine scars.

Three determined men in gloves and white cloth masks worked by the fire. One did his best to hold a maddened horse still. The other two worked as a team to unload the cart. They grabbed arms and feet and heaved bodies like logs onto the fire. They were fast, silent and clumsy, impersonal and afraid.

One body, a female, was thrown so carelessly that it rolled down the pile and slapped at the feet of a fourth man, a white-suited, white-cowled, black-belted friar. He took no notice but continued his benediction, adding his single note of dignity to the crude and ugly disposal of the dead.

Tansman turned away. It was more than he could stand to watch. It was the closest he had ever been to death, that rarity on the Ship, and it was too close for his mind and stomach. He was not afraid. Before he left he had been given proofs against the accidents of Zebulon, including this hemorrhagic fever. He could have afforded a scientific curiosity. But one look at the burning pile of ephemeral human animals on the cobbles, one sickening whiff of their mortality, was too much.

He gagged and smothered his face in his hand. He gagged again, and ran. He ran down the street the coach had traveled into town, and he did not look back at a heavy rattle that pursued him like a nightmare of death. His bag banged heavily against his legs as he ran, and his breath came shortly.

Then he tripped and fell and lay panting in the dust. The rattle grew louder. A horse whickered. The thought flashed in his mind that he had been discovered. They knew him here on Zebulon. He had been brought to the place of death where they disposed of the true men they detected, and this was the death cart come for him.

He wanted to cry, *Not me! Not me!* He had never wanted to come. When would the nightmare end? Would he wake, safe in his own bed? He wanted to leap up and lock the door.

And then a wheel stopped by his head. He looked up at a gnarled little old man sitting on the seat of a flatbed wagon. The old man was dressed in brown leather, worn and soft, that might be seasonable but could never have been stylish. There was a gold-spot earring set in his right ear and a broad-bladed knife with a curved point at his belt. He had curly muttonchop whiskers and dirty brown hair, both shot with gray, and his last shave must have been half a week past. He was a monkey man.

"Mr. Tansman?" he said, grinning down as though he enjoyed the sight of Tansman lying on his face in the street.

Tansman said, "You aren't . . ." and then stopped, because it was clear that he wasn't. The pictures of Rilke that Nancy had shown him were nothing like this man. He had to be a Zebulonite, one of them, part of the nightmare.

"I'm from your uncle, come to fetch you to Delera. Hop in, boy, and let's be off. I've no mind to catch the megrim."

Tansman pushed himself to his knees and snatched up his fallen hat and bag. He stood and dropped them in the bed of the wagon and then began to brush the dust away.

"Ah, you are a dandy, aren't you? City people! Climb aboard, damn you. I'm not waiting."

Tansman stepped on the wheel hub and then up to the seat. The quick little man shouted to his horses and off they jounced through the dry, rutted streets. The old man didn't slow the pace until the last flat-topped roof of North Hill had been left behind.

He brought the team down to a walk, resettling himself on the hard wooden seat and taking a great sigh of air, as though it were only now that he really dared to breathe.

"You're lucky I stayed for you, boy. I wouldn't have spent another ten minutes in that charnel house. I haven't lived all these many years to end me days being sizzled in the town square, and I don't fancy walking around with half me mind leached should I survive the megrim, neither."

He shuddered and cast an eye at the blank and leaden sky. "I should have known. I should have stayed at home tucked in me bed. The megrim is no more than you'd expect with five moons full and the shippeens walking."

The dirt lane they followed ran parallel to a series of small hills rising away at the left. Down the slope at the right was flatland that stretched away level as a table as far as the eye could follow until it was lost in the grayness of the sky, cracked mud merging with muddy sky at the horizon. The road angled down from the town to meet the closer grayness.

With surprise at himself for venturing to speak, but because he had to know, shippeen that he was, Tansman asked with the haughtiest air he could assume, "How do you know the Ship people are about?"

"How do I know? Heh! Ain't it obvious to anyone with his wits?" The monkey man held up his hand and ticked off his evidence on his fingers. "There are five moons full, right? And then there's the plague. Do you expect a shippeen to tap ye on the shoulder and announce hisself?"

The dust roiling up from the horses was too much for Tansman. He reached into the back and found his slouch hat and began to fan the dust away with it.

The old mortal man snickered. He pointed ahead. "The dust will ease when we reach the flats," he said.

Tansman resented the snicker and the contempt he thought he detected in it. "You work for my uncle, do you?" he asked in a tone designed to settle their relationship.

"Yea. Garth Buie is me name. Old Garth, they call me. And you're Mr. Tansman."

"That's right. *Mr.* Tansman."

With that established, Tansman sat back, stiff and upright, determined to say no more than he had to. This strange, quick, ignorant, and superstitious old man made him nervous. He continued to fan away the dust, but only when he had to and then in quick surreptitious little flicks of the hat.

After ten minutes they reached the flatland, and here the road continued, still parallel to the line of hills, almost straight, almost level, and as Old Garth had promised, almost dustless. Tansman brushed the dust from himself and from his hat, wiped his face, grimacing at the grime on his handkerchief, and set the hat in place on his head.

In another mile they came to a crossroad. There was a sign that read Delera and pointed toward a break in the hills. Old Garth slowed the wagon and guided the horses through the turn.

"Do ye see the brothers? Bound for the monastery at Delera, I'll warrant."

Trudging up the first rise beyond the turn were two men in white-cowled suits, the match of the man who had stood without flinching by the fire in the town square in North Hill. One, short and broad, carried a pack on his back. The other, a tall man, carried a bag like Tansman's, switching hands as he walked. A small wolfish dog with a bushy tail curled high over its back frisked at their heels. The friars took no notice of the wagon clattering up the slope behind them, but the dog held the center of the road and yapped threats until the wagon was closer than the walkers. Then it turned, a rear guard whose moment to retreat had come, and hurried to catch up.

It occurred to Tansman that Old Garth intended to offer them a ride, and he wanted to forbid it, but didn't dare. What could he say to them? He was suddenly angry at Rilke for not having come himself, for putting him in this uncertain position. He didn't say anything. He bit his lip and sat the straighter, thinking of the *Colligations*.

They overtook the friars at the top of the rise, the dog circling away to the far side and pressing close to the friar carrying the bag. The short friar looked up as Garth brought the wagon alongside and reined the horses.

Garth saluted and said, "Good afternoon, Brothers. Will ye honor us by riding along?"

"Well, bless you, son," the friar said, throwing back his cowl. He had a red face and a bald head with just a fringe of hair, a plebeian snapping turtle. "A ride is just the thing for weary feet."

He had his pack off in no time and the tailgate of the wagon lowered. And that quickly, after two short sentences, Tansman knew he found him dislikable. The friar radiated an abrasive self-confident pushiness, as though he expected things his own way and expected you to realize that it was his right. He took the tailgate down and hopped aboard as though he owned the wagon.

The other friar, whose suit was cinched with a black belt to the short one's belt of red, had yet to look up. He turned and knelt, setting his bag down, and while the short one was making a backrest for himself out of his pack and Tansman's satchel, he called the little dog close with a waggle of his finger and a pat on the ground, and caught it up.

And then he turned and looked up at Tansman just as the red friar was saying, "I am Brother Boris Zin. And this is Senior Brother Alva Abarbanel."

Tansman was caught by the penetrating glance. The Senior Brother's face was long and lean and intelligent, a face that Tansman might want to wear when he was old. His brows were bushy and white and his eyes beneath were deepset and clear. It was a face that Tansman liked as instantly as he disliked the other, but the gaze was so sharp that he could not bear to meet it lest he lose all his secrets and stand revealed. So Tansman looked away.

Garth said, "Brother Asmodeus!" And there was such fear in his voice that Tansman could not help but look back at him. And indeed, Old Garth was frightened, edging away on the seat toward Tansman.

Brother Boris held up a hand. "Aye, Brother Asmodeus. But have no fear if your hearts be pure. He is in my charge and he stands under an interdict of silence. Until the Questry completes its accounting and calls him forth from Delera, he is bound neither to teach, nor to write, nor even to speak. You are safe."

"Must I give him a ride?" asked Garth.

"You forget yourself, my son," said Brother Boris. "Whatever Brother Alva's errors may prove to be, he is still a Senior Brother of the Confraternity, and as such, he is entitled to your respect. Errors in faith are not for such as you to judge. They are the business of the Questry."

"Yes, Questryman," said Garth, and he saluted him.

Tansman sat silent. The less said, the better.

"Besides," Brother Boris said, plumping Tansman's bag as though it were an out-of-shape pillow, "Brother Alva and I travel together, and you would not have me walk."

"Yes, Questryman. I mean, no, Questryman."

"Please. Call me Brother Boris. Simple Brother Boris."

Simple Brother Boris gestured to his companion, who still stood beside the wagon. After an unrevealing glance at Garth, Brother Asmodeus the Fearsome set his bag and his white dog within the wagon, bade the dog stay with a silent finger, then walked to the rear, climbed up, and raised the tailgate after. Then he sat cross-legged, one hand on his bag, the other on his dog, smiled and nodded to Garth to proceed.

After they had traveled the road for some minutes Brother Boris said, "What are your names, please?"

There was no real politeness to the interrogative, no hint of personal interest. It was a pure expression of the right to know everything. It was just what Tansman had anticipated and feared when Old Garth, the ignorant monkey man, had first shown his intention to stop. Tansman could only wish that Garth felt as uncomfortable with his gesture as he did.

"Old Garth Buie. Mayhap you've heard of me. They know me up at the monastery. I went up in a balloon once."

Garth fell silent, and Brother Boris did not seize the opportunity to pursue the details of that adventure, so after a moment Tansman said, without turning, "Philip Tansman."

"Effects are a certain sign of their cause, as I'm sure Brother Alva would tell you were he free to speak. The Men of the Ship are about, for heresy, evil, and disease are to be seen around us. Infection of the body, infection of the mind, and infection of the spirit. Why is it that you travel at such a dangerous season?"

Garth said, "It's as I told the lad. I should have known enough to stay at home in me bed. When all moons stand full, the shippeens are abroad."

"No, my son," Brother Boris said. "You must not believe that. What you have said is rank superstition. The Confraternity has kept careful records—as I may say, having spent a year assigned to the task when first I aspired to the Questry—and the phases of the moons have nothing to do with the comings and goings of the Men of the Ships. During the year I labored at the records, a nest of Shipmen, openly proclaiming themselves in all their rottenness and calling themselves the Sons of Prometho, were blotted by the Confraternity. At that time Aleph and Veth were full, Gimel was in the last quarter, and Daleth and Beth were new. Only once in fifteen turns of Aleph are all moons full together. Heresy, evil, and disease, and the men that spread them, are to be found in any month. Is that not true, Brother Alva?"

Tansman did not want to look, but the edge in Brother Boris' voice made him turn. And he saw nothing, for Brother Alva sat steadily, expressionless, one hand still on his bag, the other still resting in the ruff of his little dog. The only difference was that now the dog was lying instead of sitting.

Brother Boris looked up at Tansman with his red bully face. Overbearing. Not unintelligent. But if Brother Alva was heresy, was the red brother evil, or was he disease?

Brother Boris said, "And why do you travel with the megrim abroad, Mr. Tansman?"

For want of a better, Tansman assumed a modified version of the tone he had used with Garth. Lofty, but not disrespectful—anything but that with a Brother of the Confraternity, a Questryman. He hid his fears behind carefully measured speech.

Through tight teeth he said, "I'm to mind the interests of my uncle, who keeps a store in Delera. I didn't know of the danger of megrim when I set out. By the time I came to North Hill, it was easier to go on than to go back."

"Aye, yes," said Old Garth. "You should have seen him running like a hound-driven cony through the streets of North Hill."

He laughed. Tansman smiled stiffly. He felt caught in a guessing game with no clue to the right answers and his neck at stake.

"Why cannot your uncle mind his own interests?"

"His parents are old and ill and not expected to live," said Tansman. "He goes to visit them."

"I misdoubt he'll be stopped by the megrim, neither," said Garth, to Tansman's gratitude. "He's talked of nothing but Mr. Tansman's coming this turn of Aleph. Fragile as the old folk are, he'll only be hurried by news of the megrim."

"A dutiful son," said Brother Boris.

Struck by inspiration, Tansman turned again on the seat before Brother Boris could level another arrowed question.

He said, "It must be uncomfortable for you to ride so long back there, Brother Boris. May I offer an exchange of place?"

The offer was instantly taken with a "Bless you, my son." In making the change to the back, Tansman let his hat be caught by the wind. It fell to the road and rolled. Tansman scrambled after it, the little dog rising and barking at him.

By the time he caught up to the wagon again, Brother Boris was firmly established on his seat beside Old Garth. And he, Tansman hoped, was firmly established as a hound-driven cony with pretensions. Let him be laughed at by these ignorant mortal men. He was safer that way, and he knew who he was.

He still had to ride facing Brother Alva in the back of the wagon, Brother Asmodeus, but whatever Brother Alva saw with his penetrating eyes he was bound to keep to himself. It was not comfortable to turn on the seat and speak, as Tansman knew, and Brother Boris learned. So on they rode to Delera, as they were, and Tansman leaned against his bag—not Brother Boris' pack—and lived with the rising cold.

It was well after dark when they reached Delera. The road came down a steep grade to the town. Halfway down, at a bend, another road led back up the hill at an angle. There the monastery stood at the crest, a great bulk looming in the uncertain light of the full moons that shone through the breaking clouds.

Brother Boris said, "We thank you for the ride."

"Our honor, Questryman," Garth said.

Brother Alva lifted his dog down, and then his bag and Brother Boris' pack. He looked up the road to the monastery and then to the road behind them. And stood waiting.

"I may be down to see you soon," Brother Boris said. "I must see to the state of faith in Delera and a beginning is a beginning. What is it that your uncle sells?"

Tansman said, "Sundries. But I am no clerk."

Garth threw off the brake and lifted the reins.

"What are you, Mr. Tansman?" asked Brother Boris.

But the wagon was in motion then, and Tansman was spared the explanation of chromoplasts. He doubted that Brother Boris would have understood.

2. THE POSSIBILITY OF NEW COVENANTS

The town of Delera was dark, and Tansman feared for a moment that the plague had outstepped them and silenced the town. It was a strange sort of fear, not of plague or the pains of death, but a child's fear of the unknowns that dwelt in blackness. The planet of Zebulon and the town of Delera were places of night. There was even a curious sense of relief in Tansman's fear—if the megrim had struck like wild lightning, leaving death and silence behind, he wouldn't have to play this game anymore. He could go home. It was an attractive thought.

But Garth seemed untroubled and the relief and the silence were broken by a street dog. It raced out of the night and fell in beside them, barking and playing tag with the horses' hooves. Then the town became another place, merely sleeping.

Old Garth pulled into an alley between two adobe piles and the dog fell away, self-satisfied. Then Tansman could see lights on both left hand and right, invisible from the street.

Garth reined the horses by a door on the left. It opened and there was a figure in the doorway holding a lamp.

"Aye, Mr. Rilke," Garth said. "Here we are and lucky to be here. There's megrim in North Hill. Hop on down. I'll see to the horses and wagon."

"Philip, my boy!" said the man in the doorway. He had a pointed chin and long wispy hair. His face was pale in the lamp glow.

Tansman threw his bag down and jumped after it. Under Garth's eye he said, "Uncle!" with all the appearance of enthusiasm he could muster. His travel-befuddled legs were unsteady under him.

"It's good to see you," he said, improvising. Then Garth and the wagon rattled on toward the stables in the back.

"I take it you're Rilke," he said then in considerably less friendly tones. "You don't look that much like your pictures."

The man in the pictures was barely more than his age and looked like anybody. This man was older and didn't look like anybody—he looked like a Zebulonite.

"Save it for inside," Rilke said tiredly. "People live in the next house. Unless you want to give them a life history."

Rilke closed the door behind them and led the way inside. A curtain separated the living quarters from the store at the front of the building and Tansman got only a glimpse of darkness and an impression of things hanging—sundries. They passed on into the kitchen.

"I imagine you're hungry," Rilke said. "I don't suppose you know how to cook. Garth will come in and do for you while I'm gone. I've prepared him. I told him you were a society boy and don't know how to wipe your behind."

His tone was short and sharp and he didn't look at Tansman. He crossed to a hanging kettle over an open hearth fire and gave it a stir.

Tansman said, "I expected you in North Hill. I should have been warned that you weren't coming."

Rilke turned. "I didn't feel up to it, sonny. And you're here just as soon as if I'd made the trip."

He didn't look well. He looked tired and sick. His hair was sparse and had only a tenuous connection to his head. His skin was papery.

That was the price of fourteen years on Zebulon. It turned you into a sick old mortal man. No one would have thought Rilke and Tansman of an age. Tansman was young—youngish. And Rilke had to be his uncle. Never a brother or a cousin. Tansman hadn't understood the reason for their nominal relationship before.

He set his bag on the table and opened it, found a bottle made of glass and threw it to Rilke, not caring particularly whether or not he managed to catch it. He managed to catch it.

Tansman said, "You had a Questryman resting his back against that half the distance from North Hill. If Old Garth hadn't come to my aid a couple of times, I would have had real trouble with his questions. Does Garth know about you?"

Rilke drank from the bottle, closed his eyes, and then took a weak step to a chair. After a moment he looked up and said, "What was a Questryman doing in the wagon? What did he pump out of you?"

Tansman rose and walked to the kettle and gave it a stir. Then he looked around for a plate. He felt an obscure joy. He didn't like Rilke and his air of moral superiority. If they were on the Ship, where opinion knew Rilke and his kind for sentimental fools, Rilke would never have dared to take this tone. Tansman was a scientist, a useful man, a credit to *Daudelin*. Here on Zebulon, Rilke felt free to exercise his contempt. Well, let him. Tansman knew who he was and he knew who Rilke was. He didn't mind finding Rilke sick—that was justice. And if he knew the answers to Rilke's questions, he was ready to let Rilke sit and whistle until he was ready to give them.

He said, "What do you have to drink?"

Rilke indicated a pot. Tansman lifted the lid and sniffed.

"Is that what you ruined your liver with? What else do you have?"

"Water."

"All right, I'll have water. You know, I'm not one of your people. I'm not part of this Group of yours."

"I know," Rilke said, the hostile note in his voice plainly evident.

"I agreed to help Nancy Poate. I'm already sorry, but I agreed and I'll do it. I'll sit in your chair for two months, and I'll do my best to see that you aren't discovered when the Questryman comes down here and checks over this store. But I don't like you any better than you like me. I'll thank you for a little civility. And I'll thank you for a plate."

Rilke handed Tansman a plate.

"Thank you," Tansman said. He began to serve himself stew.

Rilke pointed a finger at his back and said angrily, "I know you, too. I've heard all about you. You're an ice skater. You never did anything real in your life. You skim along on the surface of things. I don't thank Nancy Poate for sending you. I mean to tell her so."

"Tell her so, and be damned. If you were more persuasive and less meddlesome, maybe you could attract someone more to your taste than I seem to be. As it is, it seems that you are going to have to make do with me."

Tansman sat down at the table with his stew. Rilke looked at him fiercely and Tansman looked steadily back. At last, Rilke sighed and dropped his eyes.

"Water," said Tansman. "And a fork."

"You don't understand, do you?" said Rilke. But he rose and drew Tansman water and found him a fork. "Tell me about the Questryman."

"Garth picked him up at the first crossroad outside of North Hill. He said that he means to investigate the state of faith in Delera, including this store."

" 'There's little enough to worry about," Rilke said. "All of our books have been checked by the Questry and given an overmark. The rest of the stock is innocuous."

"He discounts me in any case," said Tansman. "He believes me to be a society boy who doesn't know how to wipe my behind. It's the other one that Garth was afraid of, the one Brother Boris was escorting to the monastery. Brother Asmodeus. If he hadn't been under an interdict of silence, I believe Garth would have run from him."

"Alva Abarbanel? Here?"

Tansman nodded. "That was his name."

Rilke buried his face in his hands and began to cry, suddenly, loudly, shockingly. Tansman was so taken aback at this fall into weakness and defeat that he almost ceased to eat. He took another bite. But Rilke continued to cry, shoulders heaving, so at last Tansman dropped his fork. The stew was not so good anyway.

"What is it, Rilke? What in hell is it?"

Rilke lifted his head and shook it. "He shouldn't have written the book. *The Possibility of New Covenants.* I told him not to. He defended the *Sons of Prometheus.* And now he's under interdict."

"You know this man? This Zebulonite?"

"He was our best hope. He is a man of intellect and honor and he followed his mind to conclusions that other men will not dare. He said that new Godly Covenants were possible, that purity and the Ships were not a contradiction in terms. If he had kept his silence, he might someday have led Zebulon into a better state of understanding of the Ships. We were in correspondence."

"Did you tell him who you were?"

"He knows what I am—a liberal, truth-seeking man. And that is all. But what are we to do now? I must talk to Nancy. Oh, God! All these years. I'm so tired."

Then Rilke raised his head and wiped his eyes. "And you must be tired, too. Let me show you the way upstairs." He blew his nose to regain his composure and dignity.

Rilke picked up Tansman's empty plate and set it on the sideboard. "There's so much to show you before I leave tomorrow. You'll need a good night's sleep. You won't be able to ask anything of Garth. He knows nothing. He's worked for me for thirteen years, but if he thought I was from a Ship, he would be off to the monastery in no time to fetch the Questryman."

"If you can't trust him, why don't you get rid of him and find somebody you can trust?" Tansman asked.

Rilke shook his head again. "You really don't understand, do you? 'Old Garth' is the reason I do what I do. He's had a life five times as hard as I have, and he'll be dead a good sight sooner. He's five years younger than I am."

"You must be joking!"

"Because he's younger than you, too? He is. Things need to be evened, and I mean to spend my life trying to see that they are. Even though I despair. Come along now."

As Rilke led Tansman up the stairs, Garth came in through the door from the alley, dusting his hands.

"Well, lad," he said. "All squared away?"

Tansman stopped with a foot on the stair and looked at him, stared as though he could pierce the mask of monkey wrinkles and find beneath a man as young as himself. After a moment he said, "Yes, thank you."

Rilke said, "There's stew waiting in the kitchen."

"Ah, thankee."

The bed in the spare room was hard. The room was bare and close. It was the farthest that Tansman had ever been away from home and he slept badly. He dreamed, something he never did in his safe bed in the Ship, something he never remembered doing. His dreams were ugly and frightful.

A horse screamed in terror. It plunged in the heat and stink, frantic to be free.

Smoke, acrid smoke, rose in a smothering stinging billow.

It was hot from the fire, but Tansman felt cold, felt alone. Helpless.

He lay head down in the cart of bodies, unable to move. He was not dead. He was not sick. He couldn't be. But he could not protest. He was helpless.

The men in gloves and masks stoking the fire pulled the bodies free and flung them on the pyre. And all he could do was slip closer and closer to their hands. He wanted to protest, but he couldn't. He was alive! It wasn't right. He didn't want to burn. He didn't want to die. Not yet. Not with so much undone, so much left of his life to live.

But he couldn't stop them. There was nothing he could do.

And suddenly he recognized the men behind their masks. Brother Boris. Simple Brother Boris, smiling behind his mask and enjoying himself. And Hans Rilke.

"Into the fire," said Rilke. "Into the fire."

And Brother Boris said, "A beginning is a beginning. You take the arms, I'll take the legs."

Tansman wanted to protest. No. No. But they lifted him up and went, "One, two, three."

And then rattling across the town cobbles came a wagon.

Garth! Old Garth! Good old Garth!

Just as they threw Tansman up in the air toward the fire, he came rolling past and Tansman landed in the back of the wagon.

"He's too young to die," Garth called. "He's too young. Too young. To die."

"But he'll be the better for it," called Brother Boris.

And Rilke yelled, "Don't trust Garth! Don't trust Garth! Come back, Tansman."

And on the wagon rolled toward the far side of the square. And Garth was laughing.

That was when Tansman woke in the dark, on the hard bed, sweating, trembling, but alive, safe and alive.

Ah, but still on Zebulon.

3. THE SECRET OF THE SHIPS

One week after Rilke's departure to visit his dear old parents, leaving his store in the care of his flighty young nephew down from the city, Brother Boris came out of the monastery and began his examination of the state of faith in Delera. He did not begin with Tansman. He did not begin with Hans Rilke's store.

Oh, but Tansman did hear all about it. It was his introduction to the town. They came to have a look at the city boy turned clerk and to talk of the progress of Brother Boris through the town as he hunted infection of the mind and infection of the spirit, the better to save Delera from the infection of the body, the megrim. Tansman stood behind his counter and listened.

He heard who was in trouble, and he heard who would be in trouble. He heard what Brother Boris was asking, and he heard what he should have been asking. It was an education in human nature. At first he was shocked by the talebearing, for men would come and confess their confessions and smile and be patted on the back. Only gradually did he realize that what seemed craven self-service and shameless subservience to the superstitions of the Confraternity was really a deep and universal fear of the megrim. The megrim killed half those it struck and left another third witless. Reason enough to welcome Brother Boris and his apprentices.

Tansman sold many copies of the *Colligations of the Confraternity*, fewer but substantial numbers of the *Teachings* and the *Commentaries*, and almost no other books. When he might have been observing the floggings in the town square, he stayed in the store and studied his own copies.

He studied as though he were back in school again. He studied as though he were readying himself for Trial. He despised every moment he had to spend in learning this ignorant nonsense, cramming information into his head that might be useful, might be essential, or might never be asked, knowing that once his examination was over he would forget every bit of it. But he was determined not to fail, for the sake of his neck. He did not want to suffer the fate of the Sons of Prometheus. He had no desire to be "blotted." He didn't even care to be flogged for the health of the town.

Garth didn't study. He was an ignorant old fool and would freely admit it. Ignorance is a privilege of stupid old men who live in stables. He proved his piety, as much as it needed proving, by attending the floggings religiously.

Tansman would lie awake in bed on nights when he had bad dreams and think about the questions he thought Brother Boris would ask and the questions that he might ask. And sometimes, when the dreams were bad enough, the questions that he could ask. He wished he had gaiety enough to be blithe and superficial, but he was a hound-driven cony with pretensions and was necessarily stuck with scholarship.

He checked the store a dozen times. He leafed through every book that Rilke had in stock looking for danger. There were encyclopedia distillates and self-help books couched in half-mystical terms. He left those. There were books like *The Secret of the Ships* that purported to tell all and in reality told nothing. They were written by some poor idiot like Rilke to temper prejudice by substituting gray lies for black, as though that were the way to do it. He could picture the well-intentioned firebringer sitting up late night after night, weeks leading into months, to fashion these compromises. But he left them on the shelves.

What Tansman removed were two books by Senior Brother Alva Abarbanel. He did it even though they looked innocent enough, at least to his eye. They said nothing about the Ships or the Sons of Prometheus. They even carried the overmark of a Superior Brother, attesting to their freedom from corruption. But they were theology, and he felt them to be dangerous. He was willing to let Rilke be the one to sell them if Rilke wanted them sold. He wasn't going to do it.

Then he had nothing to do but wait for Brother Boris to come and either pass or fail him. While he waited, he counted his discomforts. You could make a list of them: rain, cold, mud, filth. Strangeness—strangeness is a basic discomfort. A hard bed. Garth's cooking. Bad dreams. Between the bed, the cooking and the dreams, he slept badly. When counting the discomforts ceased to put him back to sleep, he turned to Abarbanel's theology and that served. The motives behind *The Possibility of New Covenants* might be admirable, but the arguments that demonstrated that one might even be from a Ship and be pure were knotted.

Tansman knew how many days he had served on Zebulon and how many more he had remaining. In his spare moments he thought about chromoplasts and the door he would lock himself behind when he was safely home.

It threatened rain on the afternoon that Brother Boris finally came. Tansman knew that Brother Boris was coming—the store had had no business all day. Tansman recognized the meaning of that, but he didn't attempt a last-minute cram. He was either prepared or he wasn't, and there wasn't much that he could do about it now.

It was Garth who pointed out the imminence of rain. Tansman helped Garth wrestle barrels off the porch and inside the store. His hands were tougher now than when he had come. He'd found a certain satisfaction in showing that a city boy with a fancy coat and soft hands could work.

Tansman was tamping down a lid on a pickle barrel when Brother Boris, even more florid than he remembered, stepped up on the end of the porch followed by two young aspirants to the Questry.

"As I promised, Mr. Tansman," he said, "I've come to look at your store."

"My uncle's store, Brother Boris," said Tansman, offering him a respectful salute. "Would you care for a pickle?"

He had tried the pickles himself and found they made him ill, but Garth Buie loved them and would eat three in an afternoon, piercing and pungent though they were.

Brother Boris said, "Thank you."

There was sweat on his forehead though it was a cool afternoon. Pickle in hand, he turned to the younger brothers who followed him.

"Mind," he said. "It is perfectly in order to accept offers of privilege, hospitality and tokens of esteem. You may learn much in this fashion. You simply must be determined that your judgment shall not be affected."

And he bit into the pickle until the juice ran. He closed his eyes at the sharpness of it.

To Tansman he said, "This is Brother David and Brother Emile. I teach them what I know. Brother Emile already lays a very pretty stripe."

They nodded and Brother Emile smiled faintly. Both brothers were very young and aspiring to greater dignity than they could easily carry.

Tansman saluted them. "A pickle, Brother David? Brother Emile?"

Both shook their heads.

Brother Boris finished his pickle and wiped his juicy fingers on his suit. Around the last of his mouthful he said, "Come, let us go inside. We have much to discuss. Time grows short, many are yet to be examined, and already the megrim has struck a black sinner in Delera. We must see to the state of your soul, Mr. Tansman."

Tansman rolled the barrel inside the store on its lower rim, wheeled it across the floor, and slammed it into place beside its fellows. The three brothers followed him inside.

Garth looked up as they entered. He saluted the brothers and made a ducking motion as though he would withdraw.

"No, no. Stay, my son. We may wish to make question of you, too, Garth. Even the least among us may fall prey to the corruption of disease."

"Would you like to go into the living quarters?" Tansman asked. "It's more comfortable there."

"We can inspect your living quarters later. Indeed, we will. We will begin with the store now. Don't try to direct us, Mr. Tansman. We are quite capable of directing ourselves."

"Your pardon, Brother Boris," Tansman said.

Brother Boris blinked and shook his head as though he were trying to rid himself of mind-flies. He wiped his forehead and looked at the sweat on his fingertips.

"It's dim in here," he said. "Let us have light."

Tansman gestured to Old Garth who hurried to light lamps. It didn't seem that dark to Tansman, but he was determined to make no trouble for himself by crossing Brother Boris. He seated himself on his pickle barrel and waited. As the lights came up, Brother Boris began to circle the store like a hound cruising for scent. Brother David and Brother Emile stood together, watching Brother Boris, watching Tansman.

Brother Boris circled the counters examining merchandise, picking up this and that and then setting it down. At last he stopped in front of Tansman and pointed a finger.

"You haven't attended the floggings in the town square, Mr. Tansman. You have figured in my prayers since I first noted your absence, but you have continued in your failure to appear." He shook his head. "You make me fear for you."

Brother Emile smiled again as though already anticipating another opportunity to practice his lessons. Tansman swallowed, but kept his composure. It was a question that had occurred to him in his hard restless bed, and he had an answer of sorts.

Watching his words, he said, "I am of tender stomach, Brother Boris. It's a fault of my city breeding."

He sat straight, knees together, attempting to offer as little offense as possible. His answer was only a guess, and each word was only an uncertain approximation, spoken in fear and trembling, spoken in the knowledge that it could not be recalled and altered for the better. He stilled one hand with another in his lap.

Into the silence he said, "While others were at the flogging, I remained here, studying the *Colligations*."

He opened his mouth to speak of the superiority of his sort of piety to the other, but then did not dare. Who could know what Brother Boris preferred? So he left his mouth hanging open and then slowly closed it. The silence remained and he sat uncomfortably under Brother Boris' eye. He could not look away at Brother David or Brother Emile or Old Garth hanging the last lamp.

At last Brother Boris said, "I am to believe that *you* are a scholar of the *Colligations?*"

"Oh, aye," said Old Garth. "He's always at his scripture, one good book or the other. Every spare moment."

Tansman felt a rush of gratitude for the ignorant old monkey. It seemed he was always coming to his aid when a proper word was needed with Brother Boris.

Tansman said, "It is nothing I am used to speaking of. There are many in the city who would not understand."

"That is true!" said Brother Boris vehemently. "And the city will suffer for its corruption and disbelief. Many many will die. The megrim is God's knife to cut down the sinner."

He paused then and sucked in a sudden breath. "Oh," he said. "My head. It spins. Your pickle, your pickle, Mr. Tansman. It does not seem to agree with me." And he wiped more sweat from his forehead.

"Your pardon, Brother Boris," Tansman said. "In the *Teachings,* Elder Osgood says that a rest at the proper moment redoubles the strength for holy work." He rose from the pickle barrel. "May I find you a place to rest?"

Brother Boris waved him away. "The work will not wait. The work will not wait. There are questions yet to be answered. I am told by most reliable communicants of the Confraternity that you have for sale here the works of the heretic Brother Alva Abarbanel. He is confined to a penitent's cell, but all the mistakes of his misbegotten lifetime continue to spread."

"I did not know that he had been declared heretic."

"You were not at the flogging this morning."

"My most grievous fault," said Tansman. "But while it is true that my uncle did have the early writing of Brother Alva for sale, knowing no better and judging the matter, I'm sure, by the Superior Brother's overmark, as soon as I discovered the books, I removed them from sale. You may ask Garth."

But that was an error. Garth might be relied on to volunteer a helpful comment, but he couldn't be asked for one.

He hung his head and said, "The truth is that I do na read so well. I did na know that Mr. Rilke kept the books of Brother Asmodeus for sale. Is it true?"

Brother Boris said, "You continue to surprise me, Mr. Tansman. I would like to meet this uncle of yours. Where are the books he sells?"

Tansman pointed to the shelves at the rear of the store and Brother Boris started to move toward them. Then he caught at a counter suddenly and leaned on it. He turned and beckoned to Brother David and waved him to the books. Brother David hopped to the job. He hurried back through the store and began to look over the books. He pulled out one and then another and replaced them, and then he pulled out a third, looked at it briefly, and hounded back with it to Brother Boris, still leaning on the counter.

Brother Boris took the book and began to glance at it. As he read, his natural redness increased.

"How do you explain *this*?" he cried, his voice rising.

"What is the book?"

Brother Boris held it up. "*The Secret of the Ships*. If you love the Confraternity, why do you peddle this filth? Evil is *corrupting*. Is profit so important?"

Tansman said, "But the book carries the personal overmark of a Senior Brother. I saw that."

"He doesn't know. He doesn't know!" Brother Boris slammed the book to the floor. Then he raised a shaky hand to his forehead. "I *see* the evil and I know it. But my head—why does it not . . . stop . . . moving?"

He pawed at Brother David with a blind left hand. He banged his forehead with his right, as though he could knock the fog and trouble from his mind. Brother David reached for him, but then Brother Boris' knees gave way and he fell to the floor. Tansman came off his barrel calling for Garth and knelt beside Brother Boris. His forehead was sweaty and cold.

But Brother David stood with Brother Boris' left hand still in his own. The loose white arm of the suit had fallen away. Brother Boris' arm bore the stigmata of the plague. It showed three purple blotches, the sign of corruption. Brother David stood looking at it with horror. He pointed silently, mouth agape, mouth working, and then he dropped the arm, which struck the floor with the damp slap of a dead fish.

"The megrim," he said. "It's the megrim."

He backed away toward his twin, but the other young brother did not wait for him, turning and plunging in panic out the door. Brother David, after one more backward glance at the man who had taught him all he knew about the detection of evil, who now lay motionless on the floor, felled by the megrim, the very mark of evil, hurried after, calling, "Wait! Wait for me, Brother Emile!"

Tansman turned toward Garth. The little old man was half-crouched behind a counter as though he, too, would duck and hide if only he dared, if only he could escape Tansman's eye.

Tansman said, "Give me a hand, Garth. We must get Brother Boris to the wagon and carry him to the monastery."

"Oh, na. Na. Don't make me touch him. Leave him as he lies."

"We can't do that. He is still alive. He may recover if he is given care."

"Na, Mr. Tansman. The megrim is death or an addled mind. I'm afrighted. I'm old. I don't want to die. Especial I don't want to die of the megrim and go to perdition."

Old Garth continued to stay his safe trembling distance. Tansman could not bring himself to force the little man. Old as Garth was, he was younger than Tansman. He could not blame the man, and he would not cut his few short years shorter.

"Hitch the wagon," he said. "Bring it to the alley door. I'll take him to the monastery myself."

While he was lugging Brother Boris across the floor, heels dragging, and wrestling him out the door and up onto the wagon bed, Tansman was too busy to think. Garth watched him from down the alley, nervously, skittishly, as though ready to run for the sanctuary of the stable to hide under the hay.

It was only when he had Brother Boris's head pillowed on a smelly horse blanket, the first thing that came to hand, and was sitting on the seat of the wagon, holding the reins ready, that Tansman became afraid. Not of the megrim. He had no fear of that. He was safe as no other person in Delera. He was afraid of driving the wagon. He didn't know how.

When he was a boy preparing for Trial, he had learned to ride a horse, though they had always made him nervous, but he had put all that as thoroughly out of mind as he would put the *Colligations* now that he was safely through his examination. He didn't remember. And he had never driven a team of horses. One more ordeal in this series of ordeals that was Zebulon.

He sighed, closed his eyes for a brief moment, wishing, wishing, then opened his eyes and brought the reins down. The horses began to move.

He held them to a slow pace down the alley. He felt the first hint of relief when they turned left onto the street at his guidance. He continued them at a walk through the town, heart pounding, muscles tense. He knew he was tenser than he needed to be, but he could not relax. Every moment was uncertain. It was a different sort of fear, but no less real, no less unsettling than the fear he had felt under the eye of Brother Boris. He was aware of nothing but the wagon, the team, and the road, waiting for one or another to do something strange and unexpected. If there were people to witness his passage and see the body of Brother Boris lying motionless in the wagon bed, he could give no accounting of them. His attention was narrow.

They passed through the town and up the hill, still at a slow walk. He knew in his mind that it was the same hill down which Garth had driven him so long before because it could be no other, but in daylight instead of dark, from the new direction, and with the experience of these weeks in Delera behind him, it felt a different place. As though in confirmation, the lane to the monastery was not where he expected it, close to town, close to the bottom of the hill, but much much farther. He could see the dark fortress swimming in the heavy clouds overhead, but only at last did he reach the lane and turn in.

When they came to the gates, the great heavy doors were shut. Tansman climbed down from the wagon and tied the horses to a standing metal ring. He looked for a way to signal and saw nothing. The high, bare, black walls stretched away to the right and the left, rising out of the hilltop. And he was alone on the road.

He called and there was no answer. He called again: "Hello, inside! Hey, hello!" But there was no answer.

At last he pounded on the door with the flat of his hand. He alternated with his fist. The sound was heavy and hollow.

At last a slot opened in the door. A pinchcrack. Tansman could not see who was within.

"What do you want?"

"I have with me Brother Boris Zin, the Questryman. He collapsed in town. Open the gate."

"The gates are shut. The gates remain shut. There is megrim in the monastery."

Tansman said, "I fear Brother Boris has the megrim."

"Where are Brother David and Brother Emile?"

"They ran away when Brother Boris fell ill. What do you wish me to do with Brother Boris?"

There was a silence. The slot closed in the door and Tansman waited. Nothing happened. The wind whipped and a spattering of rain began to fall, the rain Garth had promised. And still Tansman waited. At last the pinchcrack opened again.

The voice said, "Take Brother Boris from the wagon and set him by the door. He will be taken inside."

So Tansman lowered the tailgate and climbed into the wagon. When he touched Brother Boris, the friar moved and said, "I *know* the evil. The Men of the Ships are among us, and they must be found."

But after that he said nothing more as Tansman moved him to the end of the wagon and eased him to the ground. Then Tansman jumped down and closed the tailgate. Finally he took a deep breath, for Brother Boris was a heavy man for all his shortness, and seized him under the arms and set him by the door, as he had been told. Then he untied the horses, unset the brake, and led the horses in a circle. He could not have driven them that tightly. Then he climbed up and started the team back down the hill at a walk.

The last time he looked back he could still see Brother Boris, white suit against the dark wall. The doors were still closed.

The rain set in before he reached town. It drenched him. It turned the road to mud and sent streams crying through the roadside ditches. It was never like this on the Ship. None of it.

✦

With the megrim in Delera, Tansman closed the store. There was no business. Houses were boarded, just like the houses he had seen when he arrived in North Hill. There were those who fled the town, those who believed they knew places of safety. But who was safe if a man like Brother Boris could be stricken?—though there were even whispers about Brother Boris in those days before people stopped talking to one another.

And a pyre was laid in the town square. First logs, then bodies. And the smell rose above the town, saturating the town, penetrating everywhere, reaching into even the most tightly closed room. It was a constant reminder of the transience of life and the permanence of death. At least for mortal Colonists.

It was not Tansman's problem. There was nothing he could do about the megrim short of breaking out Rilke's medical kit. That would reveal him as a shippeen. That would ruin all of Rilke's slow and careful work. As the number of dead mounted in the town and the bonfire burned, he wondered if revelation and ruination might not be better than this.

But it wasn't his job. His job was to safeguard Rilke's secret. So he closed himself in his room and read the works of the heretic Brother Alva Abarbanel and did his best to sleep. His bad dreams continued. Zebulon, his nightmare, continued. And there was no end to it.

One of the first nights, when he was sitting in his room listening to the one noise of the night, the neighborhood problem dog yelping and skittering through the alley below, there was a knock on his door. It was Old Garth.

Garth was nervous and diffident. Very nervous.

He said, "You won't be wanting me tomorrow, will ye, Mr. Tansman?"

He didn't say "boy" or "lad" much anymore. He said "Mr. Tansman."

Tansman had closed the store by then. He had nothing for Garth to do. There was nothing he wanted for the old man but survival.

He said, "No, I won't. Do you want to leave town until the megrim is past?"

Garth shook his head. "May I borry the wagon and team? They need someone to haul for the fire. I said I'd do. I know it was presuming. May I? Is it all right?"

"Garth, no!" said Tansman. "You don't have to do it."

Garth held out his hand, rough-backed and corded. It was trembling.

"Aye, I'm scared. I don't deny it. But it has to be done. I watched ye the other day with Brother Boris. Ye were scared, but ye went ahead. It's the same for me now."

Tansman shook his head. How could he tell Garth of what he had really been frightened? There was no way, none short of admitting who he was, what he was. He couldn't do that. The best he could do was . . .

He said, as firmly as he could, "I'll deny you the wagon, Garth. This is a job that I should do."

"I thought ye might say that. Na, lad, do na stay me. I've thought about this and me mind is determined. Somebody has to do the job, and when they asked me, I said I would. I do na want to die. But better me who's had me life than somebody young who has his life yet to live. I'll fight ye, boy, but I'll na give in."

They argued, and in the end it was Tansman who gave in. He could do nothing else. He had no argument to counter with and win except the truth, and he could not speak the truth. So finally Tansman gave Garth his permission to use the wagon and team, and in the morning Garth began his work of finding and collecting bodies and carrying them to the fire.

Tansman felt ashamed.

4. ALL-PURPOSE HOUSEHOLD HINTS AND HOME REMEDIES

Tansman awoke suddenly from a doze, unsure, and disoriented. For a moment he did not know if he were truly awake or whether this was another dream. A single oil lamp lit the room. A book, *All-Purpose Household Hints and Home Remedies,* lay open in his lap. It allowed no cure for the megrim.

Then he heard a noise outside in the alley again. He closed the book and set it aside. He picked up the lamp from the table and went downstairs. The air was cool outside.

The horses, well-trained, stood quietly in their traces, shaking a head and blowing, lifting a hoof and setting it down *clack* on the brick. Garth barely maintained his seat. The lines were slack in his hand, his eyes were shut, and he weaved on the wagon box. There were yellow streaks of vomit on his legs and between his feet.

He opened his eyes blearily at the light and said with care, "I'm sick, Mr. Tansman." Then he fell forward out of the wagon.

Tansman untangled him from the lines. There was no question of taking him to the stable. He hauled him inside. He was lighter than Brother Boris, this little monkey man. Tansman carried him upstairs, undressed him, and put the old man in his own hard bed. Garth was marked by the megrim.

Then he went outside again and led the horses and trailing wagon to the stable. He unhitched the horses. He knew nothing of the gear so he left it in a careless heap, but he was able to remember how to rub horses down. The motions were automatic—his muscles remembered what his mind had forgotten.

His mind was on other things. What was he going to do? What did he owe Garth? This wasn't the first time he had asked himself these questions. This moment had been foreseeable. This moment had been foreseen. But only now was an answer required of him.

Tansman told himself that still he did not know what he was going to do. But when he was finished with the horses, he walked slowly back up the alley, went upstairs to Rilke's room, and opened the heavy chest. He took out Rilke's medical kit. He looked at the kit, and then he closed the chest and left the room with the kit.

His mind said that it had no idea what he was doing, but his muscles knew. He was going to save Garth if Garth could be saved.

Tansman had led a quiet life, an isolated life. He had never truly liked another human being before, but in his heart he knew that he liked Old Garth Buie, this simple, ignorant old mortal.

In all his life he had never done another man damage. He had added some small knowledge to the human store, even added some years to the human lifetime. His lifetime, his sort of human.

But to know the quality of life on Zebulon, short and mean, and to know that in *Daudelin* there was an easier, simpler life, and then to choose the suspension of pain in the Ship, was to be guilty. He was guilty. He was a man of the Ships, and he would not give up *Daudelin* for Zebulon. But he would temper that guilt in one small way. He would save the life of Garth Buie.

Garth's little gnarled body thrashed uneasily under the blankets Tansman had covered him with and brought Tansman awake in his chair. The lamp was low as he had left it. He turned it up and carried it close to the bed.

Garth was mumbling and moaning to himself. Tansman reached over to touch his forehead. It was feverish, as before, but possibly a bit cooler. Tansman fetched broth that he had been simmering over the fire and spooned it down Garth's throat. Garth swallowed, but his eyes did not open.

Then it was afternoon. Tansman kept the windows covered, and the light was just a glow along the walls. It was time to give Garth another injection. As Tansman bent over, Garth's eyes rolled open and looked blankly at Tansman. Tansman slid Garth's sleeve up, placed the blunt tip against Garth's arm as the eyes flickered, held the less strongly blotched arm steady, and pressed the button, Then he turned away and replaced the injector in his little medical kit. When he looked again at Garth, the wiry old man was resting easily, his eyes closed again. Tansman sighed—his tense muscles ached. He took soup for himself, made with the advice of *All-Purpose Household Hints and Home Remedies.* The book kept figuring in what he dreamed.

Tansman sat watching Garth in the last orange of the daylight. He nodded in his chair and fell asleep. Strange shapes lumbered through his mind. He was threatened, questioned and pursued. And with the light dimming in the room he looked to see Garth gone from the bed, dressed and vanished.

He went out to the patio roof of the warehouse. There was a new film of wetness underfoot. The air was damp and heavy and the smell of the fire was part of the dampness and weight. It was a sticky elastic that couldn't be peeled free.

Tansman went down the uncertain stairs to the alley, hand on the railing, one step at a time. When he reached the bottom, he wiped that hand dry on his pants and looked both ways. One way was the closed courtyard and stables, the other the street. Light moon gleam on unmortared brick, wet slick.

It was a strange silent uncertain moment. The alley was a lean foggy echo, dim, damp, and empty. He turned from the closed courtyard and walked slowly up the alley toward the street.

There was a sudden explosion of movement by the wall. It ducked into the building across the alley. Tansman followed, moving easily. There was no light there as there usually was. Tansman went up the stairs.

He heard Garth's voice but couldn't make out the words. He found the latch at the top of the stairs.

Garth said, "A shippeen, to be sure! He follows me! You must give me help. You know me—old Garth Buie. I was the one that went up in the balloon. Save me soul and body from perdition!"

The room was dark. Tansman could see that Garth was addressing a circle of faces. Garth looked around as he came in and gave a shudder of horror. He shrank away.

"But it's me," Tansman said.

"It's him! It's him! He's a shippeen! Mr. Tansman is a shippeen!"

Tansman put out a hand but Garth could not be mollified with a gesture. He lifted a heavy, hand-pegged wooden chair as old as Zebulon and brought it over the shoulders of Tansman. It was only at that moment when the chair crashed into his shoulders, whipped his neck, and sent him down with consciousness draining that Tansman was sure this was a waking nightmare and not another dream. It was so hard to tell the difference sometimes.

His head ached. His neck was wrenched. His back ached. He had tensed just before the blow when he realized that he was going to be struck. Strangely, he knew he was awake and not asleep, but he was disconcertingly unaware of where he was or how he had gotten here. He could recognize reality now if only he could find it somewhere.

The circle of faces stared at him. From his knees he looked back from face to face. All were dead. Rotting dead. Dead and unfound.

He went down the stairs gaining greater sense of self with each step until in the alley again he had snatched the dream back from the place where dreams unrecalled are stored. He knew. He thought he knew.

Garth was at the corner when he reached the alley. He turned left out of sight. Tansman tried to run and skidded dangerously on the cobbles. An ankle became tender for a step or two. When he got to the street, he called, "Garth, Garth. Come back. I won't hurt you."

But Garth was running, clear now in the moonlight. He was screaming, "The shippeen! Help, save me!"

No windows opened. There was no response to his cry. If there were witnesses, they were not telling. Garth, the old man, fled through the town. Tansman ran after him.

Neither man ran well. When Garth reached the end of the paving, he left the road and began striking out directly up the hill. The road switched back on its way up the hill to the monastery. Garth scrambled up the hillside.

Tansman, following, saw there was a footpath. In spite of being struck by the chair he was able to follow without scrambling. That and the fact that Tansman was able to continue at all after being struck with the chair were testimony of Garth Buie's weakness.

Tansman stumbled and lost sight of Garth. He followed the path as best he could up the slope in the uncertain moonlight.

He stopped at one point and said, hoping to be heard, "Look, Garth. Come back. I really mean you no harm."

Then he took a long shuddering breath of cool black air, almost free of the town stink, and stopped stark and listened. He heard nothing. He moved on, following the path.

He was struck again, this time by no chair, but by the full wiry weight of a small body. Tansman went off the edge of the path. Garth was on his shoulders, and he felt a small sharp hurt in his side, and before he could be curious about it, it hurt much more than that. He knew he had been stabbed.

Garth said anxiously, "And you a *shippeen*, Mr. Tansman. You a shippeen."

Tansman fell on his side and back and rolled with the slope. Garth landed astride him and was thrown as Tansman rolled. They rose and Tansman would have spoken, but he thought better of saying, "I'm really all right." He didn't think that Garth would be convinced. This was serious. He couldn't let Garth reach the monastery.

Tansman launched himself forward and Garth protected his purity against this monster with his broad knife blade. The knife sliced Tansman's arm, but Tansman's superior weight brought Garth down. Tansman used his knee to knock Garth's breath away. He then shifted it to nail Garth's knife hand and wrested the knife away.

Garth tried to struggle free, heaving his body under Tansman's weight, trying to free his pinned wrist, but lacking the strength. Tansman was stable, easily controlling Garth, but breathing hard. Then Tansman stepped off, rose and let Garth rise.

"I'm really all right," he said now. "Please, Garth. Come back with me."

Garth was indomitable. He said, "The Brothers will blot you, Mr. Tansman." And he bolted up the hill.

Tansman ran after Garth and jammed the knife into him to make him stop running to the monastery. It wasn't right. Garth should have been grateful.

Garth gave a cry and fell dead.

Tansman rolled away and came to his feet. He threw the knife as far away as he could. He was bleeding and a collection of bangs and bruises. He was sick and unsteady and he threw up, the taste hot and sour in his mouth. And retched again, and then again.

Then at last he turned and looked for Garth. Garth was not there. Fear rose again in Tansman.

Limping, he came on Garth's body on the path. Garth was crawling. Tansman seized him by the leg. Garth cocked his other leg and kicked Tansman in the face. Tansman let go and Garth continued to crawl up the hillside.

Tansman pried a muddy rock out of the hillside. It was just larger than his hand. He crawled after Garth, grabbed and held him with one hand and hit him in the head with the rock. He did it several times and the rock was bloody.

He threw the rock away and rolled the body over. Garth was dead. His cheek was broken and his left eye hung loose from its socket.

Tansman wept. It was the first time since he had passed Trial and become an adult citizen of *Daudelin* almost forty years before that he had cried. He cried for himself and his innocence. He had murdered a man and knew it.

At last Tansman put the body on his shoulders and started down the footpath. He found it hard going, moved slowly, and stumbled frequently. He weaved as he walked. Twice he set the body down in the mud while he caught his breath and rested his aching shoulders.

The street was empty. He could see the glow of the fire, the muted smolder. The shutters remained closed. The street was his. The dog came shooting out from between two houses to sniff and snap, but he paid it no attention, continued to plod on, and finally it fell away and left him alone again. He was walking in a trance, forcing himself to finish what he begun, mind in a state of suspension. He stopped and put the body down while he rested. His right arm was caked with blood, and the wound in his side made him gasp when he put Garth down.

Garth grunted in pain. His pain was so intense that his face screwed but the noise was only half-uttered. The worst of it was the silent part. His hand groped at his face and his broken eye.

Tansman made an inarticulate cry. This was by far the worst nightmare that he had had on Zebulon. He was no longer afraid, so that what he did cost him more. Tears of pain and pity in his eyes, knowing what he did and acting deliberately, wanting to be sure, he killed Garth for the third time. He put his hands around Garth's neck and squeezed until he was certain that Garth was truly dead. The neck gave way under his hands and then he continued to hold it too long until he was sure, sure beyond any doubt that Garth was truly dead.

Garth! Garth! Old mortal peasant fool. Colonist. Mudeater. Fellow victim.

He ignored the overpowering reek of singed hair and burned flesh. He added wood from the pile that stood at hand until the fire blazed. Then he added Garth's belated body.

He stood as it burned and watched. He tried to think, tried to phrase things right in his mind, but he could not. He could not see to the bottom of his nightmare. All that he knew was that it existed and that it continued.

5. THE COMMENTARIES

The plague swept over Delera, washed back through, and was gone. People returned to town and unboarded their houses. They counted noses and restored life. When other stores reopened, Tansman reopened, too.

Tansman's first reaction to killing Garth was to wait. But no one called on him to chat about strange cries in the street during the height of the megrim, so he was forced to think about what he had done. He wasn't used to that. He was used to staying in his rooms and playing with chromoplasts. But now he had to think about himself.

He was a bewildered child. He couldn't make sense of it. He felt he was wrong, but he didn't think he was wrong, and he couldn't reconcile the difference.

He had done exactly what he had been left on Zebulon to do—he had kept the Prometheans a secret. He had saved them embarrassment by keeping their modest good works modestly unacknowledged. But he could not find any satisfaction in it.

He did not think he was guilty. He had tried to save Garth's life, and Garth had hit him with a chair and then stabbed him. And would have done worse.

But he did not feel justified, either. Strange thoughts came welling up as possibilities: He had killed Garth to get the old man to take him *seriously*. He had killed Garth to show him that he had the power to do it. He had killed Garth to stop the nightmare.

All he was certain of was that he was a child, and the old man had been younger than he. He was a child. He didn't know what would become of him, and he didn't know yet what he would become.

Young Brother Emile came down with an order for supplies from the monastery. Tansman remembered his face but could not remember either his name or Brother David's. Tansman was deep in his labyrinth and there were names in other lost corridors that he could not easily locate.

Brother Emile helped him by supplying the names. Brother Emile was much cheerier than he had been in company with Brother Boris. He had been raised on a farm and he hitched the wagon for the city boy. They drove the supplies up to the monastery.

Tansman asked about Brother Boris.

Brother Emile said, "Oh, he's not so well, I'm afraid. He lives but I think he will spend his life in corners. His mind was blurred by the megrim. And lucky for me, too. I have a vocation. I like the monastery. But I haven't found my spot yet. If it hadn't been for the megrim, I would have joined the Questry, but now I know it's not for me. There's too much chance of becoming contaminated. Brother Boris was a strong and willful man, and see what happened even to him. I'll guard my purity, I think."

Tansman asked about Brother David—"The other one, your friend."

Brother Emile said, "Oh, Brother David does not have a vocation. He did not come back to the monastery. He was not as good at flogging as I was, either. I don't know why they chose to give him a chance at the Questry."

When they rolled within the monastery, the gates standing wide open, Tansman saw Senior Brother Alva Abarbanel at walk in the courtyard. He asked about Brother Alva.

Brother Emile said, "He is not declared heretic yet. Brother Boris was saying many strange things that last day. It has only been recommended that Brother Alva be found a heretic. It will take months or a year to settle it. Brother Alva has been a true brother during the megrim. I wonder when the Master will return him to his cell?"

"Is he still under his interdict of silence?"

"Oh, yes. He utters no word to any Confrere."

Tansman wanted to tell someone of what he had done, but who on Zebulon would understand what he did not understand himself? Could he tell Brother Alva? Brother Alva with the fathoming eyes, Brother Alva the heretic, Brother Alva the silent?

He found Brother Alva walking with his dog. He was alone in a corner of the garden looking at a moon over the high massive wall. There was always a moon, even in daylight. The little dog made no sound as he approached and then, when Tansman spoke, startling Brother Alva, lowered its head and made an uncertain sound between a growl and a whine.

Tansman said, "You remember me. My name is Philip Tansman. Brother Alva, I am from the Ship *Daudelin*. Will you listen to me?"

Brother Alva nodded and quieted the dog with his hand. And he spoke. "Are you an apparition? I command you, announce it if you are."

"I am a shippeen."

"I am forbidden to speak to Confreres, but not to apparitions or shippeens. But if you are an apparition, the product of my pride, my own dearest wish fulfilled, I would rather that you left. Vanish!"

"No," said Tansman. "I'm no apparition. I am from *Daudelin*, the Ship that brought you all here to Zebulon."

Brother Alva said, "I know that. I know that." His voice was full and rich, though not low. He spoke quietly, but almost joyously. His face celebrated.

He said, "I have waited these many years to see you. You are so late. I thought you would be sooner. To think that it should be now. To think that it should be here. Will you answer my questions? There is so much I need to know of you."

Tansman said, "Please, brother. Will you listen to me?"

Brother Alva said, "Forgive my impatience. Of course I will listen. But give me hope."

"I will talk, and then I want you to tell me something."

"Ah, a riddle."

"I killed a Zebulonite. The old man, Garth Buie. I nursed him when he was sick of the megrim and I saved his life, and he discovered I was from a Ship. He hit me with a chair and he stabbed me and then he would have come here to report me to the brothers. He said he would see me blotted.

And I killed him with his knife . . . and a rock . . . and . . ." Tansman looked at his hands. "And I put his body on the fire in the square. I wanted to help him and I killed him. Tell me what I should have done?"

"You ask me?"

Tansman nodded. "I want to do what is right, but I don't know what it is. Everything is mixed in my mind and I can't sort it out."

Brother Alva, taut, caught in this moment, said, "Tell me, then, Man of the Ships, do you mean us good, or do you mean us ill?"

"I don't know," Tansman said. "I don't know. Good! No, I don't know. How can you know how things will turn out? I want to become whole, that's all I know. And I'm split in half."

"But you can never know," Brother Alva said. "All that a man can do is make a Covenant and live by it and live through it. Have you made a Covenant? You can, you know. Yes, you can."

Tansman shook his head. The last answer to his dilemma was to become a Zebulonite and join the Confraternity. Even a man like Brother Alva was diminished by the Confraternity. Or did Brother Alva mean that? Tansman had the sudden surging hope that he meant more.

"Make one! Make your own Covenant!" Brother Alva spoke insistently, but his tone was not hectoring or critical or self-righteous. It was open and joyful. He was calling Tansman to transcendence. It was as though Tansman's hesitant and qualified endorsement of good had been a fulfillment of all that Brother Alva had dreamed and lifted him to a final height. And now Brother Alva was turning and beckoning to Tansman, not because Tansman deserved it, not for any reason, but because it was what was done from that height. It was the nature of that height.

Brother Alva said, "Even you can make a Covenant."

"With whom?" Tansman asked in agony. "How? How?"

Brother Alva said, "You are the only man who can answer that. It may take your lifetime to make, but it is the only thing your lifetime is for."

✦

When Rilke returned, looking more like a cousin than an uncle, he asked Tansman where Garth was. It was something that Tansman could only admit once, and he had done that. He said, "He died of the megrim."

He also said, "I learned one thing while I was here. You do what you are doing for *yourself*. Not for them."

"You're wrong. You don't understand at all," Rilke said. "I'm not selfish."

Tansman wasn't sure he hadn't been mistaken. He had said what he meant to say, and meant to say it, but now he was no longer sure of the meaning of what he had said.

"Why are you here?" asked Tansman.

"Not for me. For them. To end ignorance on Zebulon. To bring Zebulon up to our standard. To save good men like Brother Alva Abarbanel. To make this planet a place where Ship people can walk openly. I don't expect it all to happen in my lifetime. And I don't expect to be noticed or given credit. It's enough to be part of it."

"Would you kill to keep what you do a secret?"

"Yes, I would," Rilke said. "I've done it."

"'Was that for them?"

"It wasn't for me. It was for the sake of others."

"It's all a waste," Tansman said. "You hurt people for no reason!"

He burst into tears. It was the difference between herding people like sheep and beckoning from a height that made him cry.

Rilke said, "Tansman, you're still a fool."

Tansman went back to the Ship. He tried to forget Zebulon, Rilke, Brother Boris, Garth, and Brother Alva, but they all kept coming back into his mind and talking to him. He buried himself in his room and locked himself in his work, but his room was a cell and his work was suffocating. He felt numb. He only existed.

After a year he went to Nancy Poate and asked to be sent back to Zebulon. He threw up first. The only place he could imagine himself never killing again was on the Ship. If he went to Zebulon, he might kill, and the thought made him sick. It had kept him away for a year. At first he thought he might ask to be sent to another Colony, but he couldn't be sure he wouldn't kill there, either. If he wanted to live, to be alive, he had to leave the Ship and accept the possibility that he might kill.

He did know that he needed to make a Covenant. He wanted to make a Covenant. He could not make one on the Ship. The one place he was sure he could begin to look for one was Zebulon.

So he went back to Zebulon. By the time he came again, Senior Brother Alva Abarbanel, loyal to his own Covenant, had refused his last chance to recant, repent, and retract, and been blotted by his brothers.

The Destiny of
Milton Gomrath

Milton Gomrath spent his days in dreams of a better life. More obviously, he spent his days as a garbage collector. He would empty a barrel of garbage into the back of the city truck and then lose himself in reverie as the machine went *clomp, grunch, grunch, grunch.* He hated the truck, he hated his drab little room, and he hated the endless serial procession of gray days. His dreams were the sum of the might-have-beens of his life, and because there was so much that he was not, his dreams were beautiful.

Milton's favorite dream was one denied those of us who know who our parents are. Milton had been found in a strangely fashioned wicker basket on the steps of an orphanage, and this left him free as a boy to imagine an infinity of magnificent destinies that could and would be fulfilled by the appearance of a mother, uncle, or cousin come to claim him and take him to the perpetual June where he of right belonged. He grew up, managed to graduate from high school by the grace of an egalitarian school board that believed everyone should graduate from high school regardless of qualification, and then went to work for the city, all the while holding onto the same well-polished dream.

Then one day he was standing by the garbage truck when a thin, harassed-looking fellow dressed in simple black materialized in front of him. There was no bang, hiss, or pop about it—it was a very businesslike materialization.

"Milton Gomrath?" the man asked, and Milton nodded. "I'm a Field Agent from Probability Central. May I speak with you?"

Milton nodded again. The man wasn't exactly the mother or cousin he had imagined, but the man apparently knew by heart the lines that Milton had mumbled daily as long as he could remember.

"I'm here to rectify an error in the probability fabric," the man said. "As an infant you were inadvertently switched out of your own dimension and into this one. As a result there has been a severe strain on Things-As-They-Are. I can't compel you to accompany me, but if you will, I've come to restore you to your Proper Place."

"Well, what sort of world is it?" Milton asked. "Is it like this?" He waved at the street and truck.

"Oh, not at all," the man said. "It is a world of magic, dragons, knights, castles, and that sort of thing. But it won't be hard for you to grow accustomed to it. First, it is the place where you rightfully belong and your mind will be attuned to it. Second, to make things easy for you, I have someone ready to show you your place and explain things to you."

"I'll go," said Milton.

The world grew black before his eyes the instant the words were out of his mouth, and when he could see again, he and the man were standing in the courtyard of a great stone castle. At one side were gray stone buildings; at the other, a rose garden with blooms of red, white, and yellow. Facing them was a heavily bearded, middle-aged man.

"Here we are," said the man in black. "Evan, this is your charge. Milton Gomrath, this is Evan Asperito. He'll explain everything you need to know."

Then the man saluted them both. "Gentlemen, Probability Central thanks you most heartily. You have done a service. You have set things in their Proper Place." And then he disappeared.

Evan, the bearded man, said, "Follow me," and turned. He went inside the nearest building. It was a barn filled with horses.

He pointed at a pile of straw in one corner. "You can sleep over there."

Then he pointed at a pile of manure. There was a long-handled fork in the manure and a wheelbarrow waiting at ease. "Put that manure in the wheelbarrow and spread it on the rose bushes in the garden. When you are finished with that, I'll find something else for you to do."

He patted Milton on the back. "I realize it's going to be hard for you at first, boy. But if you have any questions at any time, just ask me."

A Sense of Direction

Arpad woke quietly in the night. Without moving, he looked around: the fire was low, a lapping yellow and red in a sheltering half-circle of rocks; the wind was a cool transparent fingertouch; the circle of the scout-ship to his left, one ramp lowered, was a blot against the sky. Around him, wrapped securely in the quiet of the night, were the others, sleeping. Standing guard were David Weiner and Danielle Youd. Arpad smiled to himself because he didn't like either of them. He had reason not to.

He would have smiled as wickedly had anybody else been on guard. He didn't like any of them, and he had reason.

The camp, set up just hours ago to serve for three nights, was pitched in a valley of short grass, of rocks and hillocks, of water following a Sunday afternoon course. The hills that framed the valley were high and unfinished, rough shoulders and hogbacks. They were covered with short grass, too, green turning to late summer brown, and dotted with granite extrusions.

Arpad was thirteen, a wiry, dark-haired boy, competent, unhappy, able to bide his time. After two early unthoughtout attempts to escape had been turned back with easy laughter, he had learned to pretend, learned to wait. Now they thought he saw himself as one of them. Now escape was no longer expected. He wondered what they would think when they found him gone. He hoped things would be unpleasant for David and Danielle.

With a silent invisible hand he checked the knife at his belt, fingers testing the snap for security. Then he leaned back and worked his arms inside the straps of the filled knapsack he had been using for a pillow. He moved slowly. He took fifteen minutes to do it, one eye on the boy and girl walking the periphery. They were gazing into the dangerous might-bes of the darkness as they went, not at the circle of sleepers. They saw no more than they expected to see. Blinkered minds.

Four feet away from Arpad was a cut bank, a sharp slope. He had picked the spot. He breathed twice and then like a ghosting cat he was down the slope and lost in the grass that nodded and lied and hid him from view. Hands and knees he crouched. No one here. No one here. In a moment no one was.

At a distance, in the simple light of day, the valley might have seemed all of a piece, even and undifferentiated. Open. In the reality of night it was far from even. It held gullies, mere dips in daylight, that could conceal in the shadows of night. Rocks, scrub, grass, depressions—all gained character in the darkness.

Arpad had paid close attention to every word that bastard Churchward had said about the use of terrain through the past months. He had hated him for his abuse and listened to what he said as gospel. During the hours of fading light since the landing of the scoutship, when his attention was supposed to be on his part of the labor of establishing the camp, supposed to be on food, Arpad had tried to think as Churchward had taught him, as Churchward might think if he had a free moment.

He had picked the best line to the shelter of the river bank, his true and final concealment, his line of escape. He silently followed his line.

Then, while still on his hands and knees only ten feet short of the river bank, face low in greenery, there was suddenly a looming shape in front of him in the night. Not again! The same old sinking feeling when freedom seen was snatched away with a laugh. Before he moved he should have found Churchward, fixed him firmly in place.

But there he was, off on a midnight prowl, scouting the land by night so as to be all the more omniscient tomorrow. He'd ask questions he knew the answers to and take his secret delight in every embarrassing moment of delay: *What's the matter,* Mr. *Margolin?*—a sneering emphasis on the "mister" that was there for nobody else. *Sharpen up, there. You aren't on New Albion now. This is the real world.*

Real enough, painful enough. Arpad knew that it wasn't New Albion. If only it were. And what would Churchward do and what would Churchward say when he collared him?

But then Churchward continued to move toward him and Arpad realized with a sudden joy that flat against the ground he couldn't be seen. He waited no longer. He didn't lie still to be stumbled upon and he didn't announce himself. He flipped the snap on his sheath, pulled his knife free and went for Churchward's throat.

Churchward gave a gratifying grunt of surprise and followed his own good advice. He threw himself backward, falling on his shoulders, and Arpad did his part, just as he had been taught, and landed on top of him, using his knees like pounding rocks to lead the way for the rest of his weight.

There was a moment, exactly the sort of moment Churchward taught you to take advantage of, when Churchward lay helpless under the knife. But. But. Arpad had never killed and even an eyelash blink of petal picking—*should I? shouldn't I?*—was too much. Churchward flipped him over his head and Arpad landed on his back halfway down the angled little slope to the river. The knapsack was a hard cushion, a backbreaker, and Arpad's breath was knocked out of him with an explosive pop. He held onto the knife, slid to the bottom of the slope and pushed himself to his feet. He held his breath against the ache in his back. He turned to face Churchward.

Churchward, his mentor, his enemy, looked down at him. "Ah," he said. "*Mis*ter Margolin—my favorite Mudeater. You didn't learn your lessons very well."

Arpad wanted to say something about lacking an effective teacher, but as always he couldn't articulate his answer, as always he couldn't retort effectively. Anything he said would only be turned, twisted or topped with a memorized cleverness. It was an incapacity that had made him the frequent grinning witness to his own humiliation since he had come to the Ship. The grin was the face of frustration.

He did manage to choke out, "You never saw me."

Churchward said, "You could never pass me in the dark. If I didn't hear you, I'd smell you."

Tempted by the sound of that cutting, rubefacient voice, Arpad almost chanced a throw in the dark with the knife. He regretted his missed opportunity to plunge the knife in again and again. But he couldn't dare.

"I'm leaving," he said. "Don't try to stop me."

"Stop you? I wouldn't dream of it. Go and be damned. It's an excellent idea. I told them they should never have wasted their sympathy on you. This simplifies matters. I'll just tell them that you decamped in the night. I must say, I don't mind being proven right about you, you little beggar. So much for the sentimentalists."

Arpad's teeth were set so hard against each other that a tooth chipped under the pressure, startling him. He would learn the power of words, he would, and use them as weapons to club and cut. He spat the fragment of tooth out, and then turned away.

He could hear Churchward's laugh as he took a deep aching breath, but the breath was free. The breath was of cool clear night air, and the way was open. That was enough, even though, as he began to trot away along the side of the river, he could hear the insulting sound of Churchward making water.

Nobody followed him. That was good, even though it meant only that nobody cared.

By the time he was out of sight of the fire glow around the first hill curve, the camp, the scoutship, Churchward and the Ship no longer existed for him. Erased. This wasn't New Albion, but it would do. The last two years had never happened. Life was beginning again.

◆

The windhovers rode the sun and wind like so many bird-shaped kites on leading strings, floating high above the hills. But were they free? Could they be pulled back to earth, reeled in at will? Who were they? Who were they? Arpad thought he knew.

The hills were eternal. The hills were home. Arpad walked through the green-brown short grass that covered the fingers and fists, elbows and shoulders. The grass whispered against his legs. He had an eye for country, a talent for finding his terrain, a pace to carry him forever, and a sense of direction that could take him across the miles and bring him home again. His spirits were high. The country was a delight. He felt at home. He felt as though he were home again.

These past two years had been his punishment for dreaming himself a Shippie. He'd taken pride in a father who was better because he had once traveled between the stars. He had felt set apart.

And he had been properly damned for his pride. He had been kidnapped and carried off to the Ship of his father, *Moskalenka*. Magicked and turned into a windhover.

Windhovers always come to earth again. They flit and fly, but in the end they always touch down again.

What plans did they have for Arpad? To prove themselves worthy, the windhovers have a puberty rite. They drop their children on a colony planet to survive like a common Mudeater for a month. They give them training first, but if the fledglings fail, small loss to the nest. It was from his Survival Class, here on Aurora for three days under the eye of its flightmaster, young Mr. Churchward, that Arpad had taken his leave.

Why wait another year? All that one year could offer was the opportunity to become a full-fledged kite—or to take up real life once more. He could do that now. He was doing that now.

This wasn't New Albion, to be sure, but there was no way to return to New Albion. Windhovers never light in the same place twice—they sail above life. But Aurora would do. It was solid earth. It was real.

Arpad could make a life here. And if all went well, in time he might discover a way to clip wings. Churchward might yet learn what was the real world.

At sundown he stood at the top of a hill looking down on a cluster of wattle-and-daub buildings set in a valley bowl. They were a far cry from the sturdy board buildings he remembered from home. The buildings, thatched-roofed, looking like so many broad-capped mushrooms in the twilight below, squatted in the bare brown dirt. The lowering sun colored the far rising hillside a dull red. A haze of smoke hung above the roofs in the evening cool, and children raced in and out among the houses. He could hear them calling.

Arpad paused on the hillcrest, a stranger, a thin boy in red shirt and brown shorts carrying a pack on his back. Then he found the well-beaten path that took the easiest course to the bottom of the hill and made his way down to the gathering of huts. He was hungry and tired, but here he was. Finding. Found.

When he was halfway down the hill, he was seen by the children, who piped and pointed and then disappeared. One moment there were people to be seen in the village. The next, there was only smoke.

But when he reached the bottom of the hill, there was a three-man delegation walking toward him. Two of the men carried spears, short-handled, leaf-bladed. The three walked in a fashion that gave them an over-precise, affected appearance to Arpad's eye. When they stepped, it was on the balls of their feet first, rather than down on the heel like most people. All three men wore knee-length pants and loose shirts and beards without mustaches. Arpad touched his face. He had no beard yet. No mustache, either.

Two of the men wore flat-crowned hats. The one without a hat was also without shoes, as though he had been stretched out for an after-dinner snooze in his mushroom and had only had time to grab a spear and come out to greet company. Arpad didn't feel he rated spears, and he wondered what he should do to give a properly peaceful impression.

They brought a variety of odors with them from the village—smoke, food, and the gallimaufrous smell of strange people. When Arpad was close enough, he stopped. They continued to move, too close, looming, uncomfortably close, frighteningly close. Their spears looked all too real and deadly. He would have bolted if he hadn't been so tired and hungry.

The man without a spear, the middle man, the youngest but clearly the leader, said flatly and brusquely, "What do you want, boy?"

"My name is Arpad Margolin. I need—" He stopped then, taken aback by the sounds of shock and dismay that the spear carriers made.

The one without a hat said, "Have you no sense of propriety? Oh, the shame! What your ancestors must think of you!"

The leader held up a silencing hand, and then in the same flat tone asked, "What do you want?"

His accent was strange but intelligible.

Arpad tried again. "They've been keeping me on one of the Ships for the last two years. *Moskalenka.* I've left now. I've run away and I'm ... looking for somebody who will take me in."

He gave them an anxious pleading look. He was, after all, only a thirteen-year-old boy. He might walk a full day into the unknown. He might make totals of his enemies and subtract and divide them in his mind. But his resources were limited.

"One of the Great Ships?"

"Yes." Arpad nodded. Then he said, "Yes, sir."

"And you left them?"

"Yes, sir."

The three looked at him and then at each other. Then the leader pinched his nose between thumb and knuckle, snuffled, and pursed his lips judiciously. He rubbed his chin and then he said, "Stay here," and beckoned to the other two.

They moved off about ten feet and huddled together in close conference. Arpad caught only fragments of the conversation. Something about, "We know his name. He's committed us." And "He *is* wearing red. Maybe it would be lucky to listen." But none of it made sense to Arpad. It was just words.

At last they broke their huddle and surrounded Arpad again.

The leader nodded and said, "All right. You can stay. We will listen to your litany. We'll have the accounting in an hour. For now, go along with this Bill."

He pointed at the hatless, shoeless man. The man nodded and grinned, but it wasn't quite a friendly expression. It reminded Arpad of the state of his stomach.

"Can I have something to eat?" he asked. He was sorry he asked it if it jeopardized his position, and he was ready to say so. Otherwise he really meant it.

"Go on," said the leader. "Go on."

And Arpad uncertainly trailed after Bill. Bill was a big, balding, broad-nosed, broad-shouldered, splay-footed fellow. He walked on precisely placed toes through the village. Arpad walked behind, at first on his heels as he was used to, then in an imitation of Bill. The effect was approximately the same as he would have achieved walking on bare feet over sharp pebbles. Arpad wasn't sure he had it right, but he wanted to please.

Bill ducked his head at the door of one of the mushrooms and disappeared inside. Arpad looked left, looked right, then followed him inside, ducking under the thatch.

There was only a single room inside the hut. It was a theater stage, a basically empty area that with the aid of props might be turned to any purpose. The property boxes were precisely placed around the room. The floor was hard-packed dirt broken by a fire pit and a larder hole.

A woman past her youth was scraping food out of a black earthen pot onto a large limber leaf. She set the pot down and began to fold the leaf like a cloth. Food. Arpad's mouth watered.

Lying on a mat at the right of the door was an old man, head on a pillow, bird-eyes sparkling. His dirty bare feet stuck out of the cover. Almost automatically as he entered, big Bill kicked the sole of the old man's right foot hard enough to make him suck for breath and pull both feet out of range. A resentful kick, a spiteful kick.

"Hold on with the food there," Bill said to the woman. "The boy is hungry."

Arpad nodded.

The woman found a small bowl and shoved some of the suspicious mess from her leaf into it with her hand. She passed it to Arpad with a smile that lit her face briefly and then was gone with an apologetic nod. There was no eating implement. Bill brought out a long piece of bread, looked for a knife, and then started to tear off a hunk. Arpad drew his all-purpose throat-cutter and handed it over, receiving a cut of bread in return.

Bill took a piece, too, shared a swipe into Arpad's bowl and stuffed bread and mess into his mouth. He seemed to be harboring a secret excitement. His face kept almost twitching into a grin.

He continued to hold the knife for a long moment, testing the heft and balance. Around the food, he said, "Are all knives on your Ship of this quality? This is a fine knife." But he didn't seem inclined to keep it. He admired it and handed it back. And almost grinned.

Arpad began to eat. The food was strange in taste and stranger in texture. He might have had difficulty in getting it down if he had not already had the experience of learning to eat and like the range of food he had found aboard the Ship, from bland and mechanical stuff produced in vats to exotica from a dozen colony planets. This mess was comparatively palatable. He only had trouble with the lumps.

As Arpad was eating, Bill beckoned to the woman of the hut. She picked up a pot and they stepped outside behind Arpad's back. There they spoke to each other excitedly for a moment and then their voices died away.

Arpad began to have the insistent feeling of being watched. Finally he turned abruptly and found the old man sitting up on his pallet and watching him with small, overly bright eyes. Arpad had forgotten about him.

He fluttered a hand weakly at Arpad. "Come here, boy."

Arpad didn't want to. The old man was thin and bony and hungry-looking, and Arpad didn't want to share. The old man looked ill, and Arpad didn't want to catch anything strange.

The old man said, "Come over here and talk."

With an unadmitted, unemitted sigh, Arpad rose and crossed the room. He would do the things he didn't want to do. He would adapt. He would do what was done here. He sat down by the old man, but he carefully kept his bowl and the remainder of his meal in his farther hand.

"Don't be so standoffish," the old man said.

Reluctantly Arpad skrinched closer, up to the very edge of the thick grass mat. That wasn't close enough for the old man. He heaved himself halfway off the pallet the better to bathe Arpad in his sour old breath. Arpad felt overwhelmed. He moved his bowl and then shifted after it.

The old man edged after. "What are you doing here, boy?" He scrabbled at Arpad with a hand. "Tell me who you are."

The sound of the old man's yells of outrage brought big bald Bill charging into the hut. Arpad was ducking away. The old man was ineffectually trying to strike him, flailing at the air. The bowl of food lay spilled in the dirt.

"What's going on here?" Bill asked as he boosted the old man back onto his pallet with the tip of his toe. He shook an admonishing finger at him.

In indignation, as though to vindicate himself, the old man said, "He told me his name! He told me his name!"

Arpad said, "But he asked me."

"I never did! I only asked who he was and what he was doing. I didn't ask his name. I'm too old to take on any more debts. You know I wouldn't do that."

Bill looked down at him with an expression that said that much as he might like to believe the old man, he wasn't really sure that he did. Sneaky old men are capable of almost anything. But then he reluctantly acknowledged that perhaps this time, just this once, it might not have been his fault. Well, not entirely.

Bill turned to Arpad and shook his head, "You just don't know any better, I guess. Coming from a Ship the way you do, I guess you wouldn't. Nothing I ever heard about the Ships made me think they had any sense of what is fitting. You seem like a good boy at heart, and I don't think you mean any harm. We forgive you. You'll learn what's proper."

He turned to the old man and said somewhat resentfully, "What difference would one debt more or less make to you now? We probably don't owe him anything, and maybe he'll take over some of your debts."

The old man's eyes brightened. "He will?"

Arpad said, "But I don't understand. Why shouldn't I tell you my name? You told me your name."

Bill managed to look both puzzled and affronted. "I never did. I wouldn't do a thing like that."

"You said your name was Bill."

He tried to confine his laugh, and it came out in an amused snort. "Bill isn't my name," Bill said. "You really don't know anything, do you? Bill is the Village Name. We're all Bill until we decide about you. Then, if all goes well, you'll be Bill, too."

◆

All of the men in the village were assembled in the largest mushroom, fifty men named Bill sitting cross-legged in the dirt of the Council Hut, when Arpad was brought in for judgment by the Bill that he knew best. His Bill had put on his shoes this time, but left his spear behind. Like all the rest of the Bills, he was wearing his flat-crowned hat, and he'd produced an extra for Arpad so that the boy could make as positive an impression as possible.

It was dark outside, and a bright fire burned in the center of the circle of men. No women were present. The leader waved Arpad to a place at the center of the circle, close by the fire.

"Stand there, boy, where we can all see and hear you," the leader said. "Look him over well. Turn around, boy. Does anyone have objection to hearing his name?"

The fifty Bills were silent.

"There you are, boy. We've talked things over among us, and we've decided to let you tell us who you are. Are you willing to trade names, accepting all consequences, debting and paying as one of us?"

"May I say who I am now?" Arpad asked, and he heard someone murmur, "The boy is well brought up."

With food in his stomach, some food, Arpad felt less tired and less helpless, but he still had no clear idea of what was happening. He wasn't sure that he wanted to accept all consequences, or he wouldn't have been if he could have thought about it, but now, in the middle of things, he could only let things happen as they would and make his decisions later.

Arpad said, "I don't really understand your customs. Why can you tell your name some times and not others?"

The leader looked puzzled as though he were being asked to put things into words that had never before required explanation. He seemed overwhelmed in his struggle to work out a proper answer.

At last he said, "Well, if you know a man's name, you have to discover whether you owe him anything or not. Naturally. So you both have to agree that you are willing to accept the burden of each other's names. I mean, that's only right, isn't it?"

Arpad nodded. He supposed it was so, though he didn't see the point where he was concerned. He knew he hadn't ever seen any of these people before. What could he possibly owe them?

"Tell us your name, then."

"My name is Arpad Margolin," he said, and stopped.

The leader said, "Go on."

"Go on?"

"What about the rest? Recite your generations. Tell us your family."

"Well, my father was named Henry Margolin. He was from *Moskalenka*, but they put him out. My mother was from New Albion. She was named Nesta Hansard. I don't know if she's still alive. My father died."

He stopped again.

"Don't you know your family?" the leader asked, and the fifty Bills shook their heads. "Can't you name them all in their generations?"

Arpad echoed the Bills with his head.

"How very odd. Our children know their generations to the founding of Aurora." The leader shook his head, too, and thought. At last he said, "Well, let's see if we can find a way around."

He questioned Arpad shrewdly. It helped that New Albion had been settled after Aurora and no one there present had ever heard of the place. It helped, too, that *Moskalenka* was not the Ship that had carried men to Aurora.

"Do you have any relatives aboard *Jaunzemis?*"

Arpad shook his head. "As far as I know, I don't have relatives on any other Ship. People don't seem to cross from one Ship to another much. It takes permission."

"I guess that's all, then," the leader said. He polled the circle formally. "Does anybody here present claim or acknowledge debt or obligation?"

One man at Arpad's left toward the back of the circle stood and said, "My grandfather three times removed, Nobuss McCarthy, was a shippeen of this Ship, *Moskalenka*. He named to his son all his debts, and his son to his son, and so to me, and he named among the men who cast him forth from the Ship one Oscar Margolin. A debt was judged against him in this village and the debt was never paid."

"Do you acknowledge this debt, or do you have a counter-debt to charge?" the leader asked.

Arpad said, "My father was cast out, too. Doesn't that make it even?"

The leader looked at Arpad and shook his head slowly. His manner said plainly that no weaseling was allowed and that this was definitely weaseling, and he had hoped for better.

Arpad said, "I don't know. I suppose he must have been an ancestor of mine." He couldn't help adding, "But I don't know anything about it."

The leader raised his eyebrows and gave his head a last little shake. He said, "Do you acknowledge the debt?"

"I guess. Yes."

The leader said, "McCarthy, what will you settle for."

McCarthy looked at Arpad. Arpad waited without knowing what he waited for, and was frightened.

"Oh." McCarthy shrugged. "I guess that knife of his will cover it."

The leader held out his hand to Arpad for the knife. Arpad undid the snap and handed it over. The leader examined the knife closely. He sighed.

Then he said, "It's worth more than that debt, McCarthy. Are you prepared to take on another debt of your own?"

"For that knife? Yes."

"All right. Go ahead, take the knife. But I'll mind the boy's interests until he can mind them for himself. I'll see to it that you pay the debt back."

McCarthy said, "Well, maybe we can let the knife go."

"No, take it."

McCarthy reluctantly came forward and took the knife. Arpad had unbuckled the sheath and gave that to him, too. McCarthy looked at the sheath in one hand, knife in the other, seemingly not sure whether to be happy or not. Finally he smiled ruefully and returned to his seat, showing the knife to his interested neighbors, each one of them making his own assessment.

The leader said, "Well, now that is settled. Now, Arpad, tell us about your Ship and why you came to leave."

So Arpad told his story. He had never told it before—people on New Albion and in *Moskalenka* had always known who and what he was, and though their ideas of him had been different, in both cases they had been definite. He was no more practiced in explanation than the village leader, so his account was halting and often broken into by requests for clarification. But soon enough he warmed to the telling, encouraged by their willingness to hear and care.

Arpad's father had been a Planetary Agent for the Universal Heirs of Man. With noble intent he had gone to New Albion determined to do good works to them, to dispense largesse and knowledge of a better way of life. It was to be a temporary thing, several years spent in honorable puttering until he decided what he really wanted to do in life.

But he had let his head get away from him. From improving the lot of the colonists, he had passed to improving the breed. But since he was noble about things, he'd married the girl.

Twenty years before, he would have been as abruptly and thoroughly disinherited as McCarthy's ancestor had been for his earlier-day transgression. But things had changed. People were more generous nowadays, if not that generous: *"It's one thing to* help *the little people, but you've lost your sense of proportion, Henry. Marriage?"* If it was no longer against the rules, it was still a breach of propriety, the social equivalent of marrying a Negro, an Untouchable, or a Christian in times past.

Margolin was not actually Expelled, but in the interests of all his stay on New Albion was indefinitely extended. His family and friends were saved the embarrassment of his company. Henry Margolin was not Expelled, but he was left to sit on New Albion until his premature death.

At that point his associates decided they just might have treated poor Henry a bit shabbily. By that time a few more people belonged to the Universal Heirs of Man, and Henry was beginning to look a bit less shocking and a bit more romantic. They owed him something.

They accordingly proceeded to repair to New Albion, remove young Arpad from the altogether unsuitable care of his mother, and return with him to the Ship. That Arpad's mother resisted the idea, was, of course, to be expected from one of her background. New Albion was not the most advanced of the Colonies. That Arpad himself resisted only served to demonstrate how badly his father had served him and how much he was in need of a proper education and exposure to a finer way of living.

When they returned to the Ship, they found Arpad a place in a dormitory with twenty other youngsters. They arranged for a tutor and scheduled his life, and rested content, more than satisfied that they had done their duty by Henry and his issue. Now it was up to Arpad to take advantage of the multitude of opportunities that Providence, in their persons, had presented to him. If Arpad failed, that was Arpad's fault.

And, of course, Arpad failed. He lacked any background in the ways of the Ship beyond stories from his father that had swelled his head and given him illusions of superiority without telling him much that could be of real use after his kidnap. He knew much of the once-played game of Saluji, but it had taken him a full year to learn to satisfy Ship notions of propriety, a year of pain and humiliation.

After the first moment he lacked sponsorship. He lacked friends and he never discovered the way to make them. His fault—ask anybody. Most important, as a Mudeater he encountered hate and contempt in quantities that he could not cope with, hate and contempt that found easy confirmation in his flaws, lacks, and inabilities. People like Churchward were unlikely to discard their laboriously constructed pictures of the proper ordering of the universe for the sake of one scruffy little boy.

So, given the opportunity to decamp, an opportunity that could not be eternally denied, Arpad had split in search of a life more closely resembling the one he had formerly had. He was a beggar who had rejected the society of kings to seek out more comfortable company. Churchward had not been surprised.

And Arpad's search had brought him here.

✦

When he was done, the leader, obviously speaking for every Bill in the house, said, "It's just as I thought. The people of the Ships have no sense of fitness or decency. They treated you shamefully."

He put his hands on Arpad's shoulders. "You have come to the right place. It is well that you did not land by accident in the next village. Those Ralphs have a less secure grip of these things. We will feed you and house you and treat you as one of our own." He kissed Arpad on the cheek. "My name is Yoder Steckmesser."

And all the Bills nodded and called assent. One by one they filed up and made Arpad a present of their names, acknowledging thereby that he was *people* and not a Ralph, someone they could and would stand in a relation of owed-and-ower with. The Bill that Arpad knew best was named Henry Heineman. He remembered that one and Yoder Steckmesser and Jorma Mc-Carthy. The other names passed in a blur, and Arpad couldn't help but wonder when it was clear that he couldn't hold the names in mind whether or not he was committing a breach. The one thing he was sure of when all the men had taken their places again was that none of them had been named Bill. Or Ralph.

Then Yoder Steckmesser motioned for Henry Heineman to stand. The bald man was smiling. He seemed relieved and pleased.

"Come here, Henry," Steckmesser said. "Henry, you need a son, don't you?"

Henry nodded. There were nods, grins, and remarks made around the circle. Apparently it was a well-recognized fact that Henry needed a son.

"Well, we have a well-informed, intelligent boy here without any debts." He turned to Arpad. "Henry Heineman is an unlucky man. His ancestors have left him burdened with debts, the weight of years, and his father has only added to the burden. His father has been a loose and flighty man. Henry has no son to follow him. He will have to wander the world forever after death under the pain of his unpaid debts. Unless he has a son to lighten his weight. Now, if you are willing, you can be his son. His name and your true father's name are the same, and that is a lucky sign. It is a good sign for the future. Will you take him for a father?"

Arpad said, "Yes."

"Henry?"

"Oh, yes, " Henry said. His eyes filled with tears. He grabbed Arpad and kissed him heartily.

Then his wife was called within the Council Hut. When she heard that her hopes were fulfilled, that she had a new son, she smiled and cried at the same time, and held him with a grip so tight that he needed to fight for breath.

They didn't delay. They had an adoption ceremony on the spot. The other women in the village came flooding into the hut with food and poteen. Everybody kissed everybody. Congratulations were lavished on Arpad—and on Henry Heineman. Arpad's claim on Jorma McCarthy was used to cancel one of Henry's obligations. Then everybody settled down to eat and drink. The party went on for hours.

Late, late in the night, the end of a long, long day for Arpad, he and his new parents were escorted with torches through the village to their home. He had tried some of the poteen, only a little, and his mind was fuzzy and he wanted to sleep. He accepted one last round of slaps on the shoulder and kisses.

When they were inside and it was suddenly much quieter, Sara, Arpad's new mother, pointed at the old man asleep on his pallet, cover tightly held under his chin like a dreaming three-year-old.

"What about the old man?"

Heineman said, "Oh, no. It's too late to think of it tonight. Wait until morning, and then Yoder will give me a hand."

"Another debt?"

"No, I went out with him on Welcome." Heineman put an arm around Arpad's shoulder and pulled him in to the standard uncomfortably close distance. "Don't be so cold, boy. Arpad, Arpad." He savored the name.

"You know, I never thought I'd have a son your age who didn't even know how to walk normally. You're a good boy, though. I couldn't have asked for better. You'll learn."

He was burbling and bursting. He was happy.

Arpad was simply sleepy.

In the morning when he awoke, Sara immediately rose from the fire and brought him breakfast. She bent and kissed him. She was so eager to please. It was such a difference from the Ship. They cared about him.

The old man lay silently on his mat, the cool bright morning sunshine lapping through the door and bathing his ankles. He wriggled his dirty withered toes.

Arpad's new father was nowhere in sight. The day seemed well under way, and Arpad wondered if he should have been up earlier. But the night had worn so late and he had been so very tired. He didn't remember everything. He reviewed the names he did remember: Jorma McCarthy, Yoder Steckmesser.

His new mother went out for water, pot on her head. As Arpad ate, he could catch occasional glimpses of children playing tag around the mushrooms, yelling and calling. He wondered who he would find of his age. Friends?

He hurried to finish. He hurried so fast that he couldn't even say what he ate. Just as he finished his last bite, his father entered the hut. Heineman's short breeches were stained with dirt, and he was sweaty and tired.

"Ah, good morning, Arpad," he said, and came over and gave him a hug. "I thought you'd sleep forever."

Sara returned with her water. "All done already?"

Heineman nodded and said, "I can use a drink. As cool a day as it is, that's hot work."

Sara got him a cup and drew water from her pot.

"Ah," he said, drinking deep. "That's good. Yoder will be here in a few minutes and he'll help me finish."

"Is there anything I can do?" Arpad asked.

"Don't fash yourself. Have some more breakfast. We need to get some weight on your frame. We'll be back in no time. We're just going to bury the old man."

Startled, Arpad shot a look at the old man. He got an alert bright-eyed look in return.

"But he isn't dead," Arpad said.

"Of course he is," Heineman said. "Ask anybody. Since we adopted you last night."

Arpad looked at the old man again. The old man didn't say anything, but he nodded agreement.

Yoder Steckmesser cleared his throat at the door to announce his arrival. "Hello there, Arpad. How are you today?"

"All right, I guess," Arpad said.

"Grab the other end there," Heineman said.

He reached down and picked up the head end of the old man's pallet. Steckmesser reached down to take the other corners.

"Oh, wait," said Sara. "Save the coverlet. Arpad can use it." And she smiled at her son.

With the coverlet removed and folded, Heineman and the village leader lifted the mat and the old man, maneuvered for clear passage through the door, and carried him out. The old man said nothing. He lay quietly, not objecting, passively accepting. He did seem to take pleasure in observing. His bright bird-eyes moved and sparkled.

As they disappeared into the street, Arpad stood and looked after them.

"Would you like some more breakfast, Arpad? . . . son?" Sara asked.

59

Arpad shook his head.

"Run along, then," Sara said. "The children are playing. Don't contract any debts, now."

Slowly Arpad went outside, ducking under the overhanging thatch, into the gentle sunshine. Heineman and Steckmesser carried their burden along at a right good pace. Nobody found their progress strange. The children continued to play. The old man did raise himself on an elbow, the better to see where they were going.

Arpad trailed along behind them as they passed through the village and out into the valley bowl along a well-trod path. They carried the old man to the foot of the hill that Arpad had descended the evening before. Only the evening before. There they came to a cluster of round little grass-covered mounds.

Beside the mounds there was a new hole, freshly dug, and beside it a pile of friendly brown dirt still unfaded by the sun. They set the old man down there and conferred about the hole. Then Arpad's new father hopped down into the hole and dug it out a little deeper.

Arpad hung back. He didn't come close but watched at a separating distance.

He watched as Heineman stepped out of the hole again. The men picked up the pallet again and straddled the hole, then carefully lowered the old man into the grave. The grave was shallow and rounded and when the old man was sitting in it on his pallet, his head was still above the ground. A bit of pallet trailed over the edge of the hole onto the ground. Steckmesser tried to push it down into the hole, but it refused to fold until the old man cooperated by pulling it into the hole with him and then reseating himself.

Then Heineman and Steckmesser seized shovels and began to fill the hole. Arpad watched for a moment, and then turned away. He couldn't continue to watch.

He turned up the hill, walking the angle of the slope. When he reached the crest of the hill, he looked back again. He expected the village to look very different from the way it had the evening before, but except for the light it was the same. Mushrooms inches high springing up in a little verdant bowl after a rain. Children like elfin dolls playing.

But then there was a difference. He hadn't seen the mounds last night. And there were two men shoveling dirt around a bright-eyed old man's shoulders.

He wished he knew what to do. He didn't understand these people any more than he had understood the Ship when he was first brought there, kicking and screaming. Could he grow used to this? If he had thought of the Ship as a place whose ways were not his ways, then what of this place?

He felt agitated and uncertain. He began to walk aimlessly through the grass, trying to think. Not happy. Not as happy as he had been yesterday when he had hoped to find the life he had left behind. His mind was a tangle.

And then in panic and horror he began to run. He galloped. What he was running from, he wasn't sure, but he ran until he could run no farther. There he fell on his face in the grass and panted.

He wanted to lie there forever. He wanted never to get up again. This quietness was what he most desired.

But after a time of lying quietly under the moving sky, listening to the brush of the breeze, something stung his ankle. He sat up.

Where was he? What was he to do? He was hungry.

And so he made up his mind.

It was night before he found the camp again, guided by a sense of direction that did not fail him. He was traveling slowly then, hungrier, leg-weary.

He came over a gentle hill and there the camp was. It was across the valley, on the far side of the slowly moving river, marked by the great fire glow.

Arpad went to ground on his side of the river. He wormed his way to a place from which he could see the camp clearly. The scoutship still in place. The people, the others, the familiar strangers, were asleep. He marked the movements of the guards. He couldn't recognize them at this distance. He did recognize Churchward as he left the fire and prowled out into the darkness.

Then Arpad remembered what Churchward had said about never passing him in the night, and the idea came to him. He smiled to himself and made a determination.

After a time he moved upstream until he was out of range, out of sight, and there he found a quiet place to cross. The water was shallow and cold and pulled at him to follow it away, but he ignored it. He knew where he was going.

He moved with infinite care back toward the camp. He circled wide, moving from one bit of shelter to another. He moved slowly and he kept a constant eye open for Churchward, the creature of night.

When he saw him, Arpad was about to cross from the shelter of a scrub tree to a dry gully. The motion was from an unexpected direction, and Arpad caught just a flash of movement from the corner of his eye. Cold fear exploded in his stomach. Heart pounding, he froze to the ground, hoping he hadn't been seen, wishing there were some way to be invisible, praying. Praying. Like a bad odor on the wind, Churchward passed him by and cruised on out of sight, bent on his own games, and never saw him at all.

In ten more minutes, Arpad was in the same grass that had hidden him two nights before. Above him was the cut bank, the fire circle, the sleepers, the ship, and two drowsy children on guard. The grass surrounding him, shielding him, nodded and lied again, as grass will. Then Arpad slipped up the bank, crouching low, into the circle, and was one more quiet sleeper, quickly, silently, cleanly. No one saw him move at all.

He relaxed, and this time he hoped Churchward would be embarrassed. In any case he felt good. He felt free. He felt equal to anything. He had decided to deal with one set of problems at a time, and this had been the first. Tomorrow would bring others, but he would cope with each in its turn. First things first.

He was tired, and he fell asleep quickly.

How Georges Duchamps Discovered a Plot to Take Over the World

Georges was making love to Marie when he made his discovery. She was, in truth, a most piquant thing with black hair and black eyes and skin of pale ivory. But, it cannot be denied, she had a button in a most unusual place.

"What is this?" Georges said. "A button?"

"But of course," she said. "Continue to unbutton me."

"No, no," he said. "This button."

He touched it with a finger and she *chimed* gently.

"You are not human," he said.

She spread her hands, an enchanting effect. "But I feel human. Most decidedly."

"Nonetheless, it is apparent that you are not human. This is most strange. Is it, perhaps, a plot to take over the world?"

Marie shook her head. "I am sure I do not know."

Georges touched the button and she produced another bell-note, quiet, bright, and clear. "Most strange. I wonder whom I should inform? If there is a plot to take over the world someone should know."

"But how could I be unaware?" Marie asked. "I am warm. I am French. I am loving. I am me."

"Nonetheless . . ." *Ding-g-g.* "It is incontrovertible."

Marie frowned. "Pardon," she said. "Turn again."

"Turn?"

"As you were. Yes." She stretched an inquiring finger, and touched. There was a deep and mellow sound like a pleasant doorbell.

"And what is this?" she asked.

"Mon Dieu!" he said in surprise. "Is that me?" He got up and went to look in the mirror, twisting somewhat uncomfortably, and sure enough, it was. He rang twice to make sure.

"In that case," he said, "it no longer seems important."

He kissed Marie and returned to the point of interruption. Skin of smooth pale beautiful ivory. I understand that if Georges receives the promotion he expects they are thinking of marriage in a year, or perhaps two.

One Sunday in Neptune

Ben Wiseman and I were the first people to land on Neptune, but he doesn't talk to me anymore. He thinks I betrayed him.

The assignment to Triton Base, an opportunity for me, was for him simply one final deadend. I couldn't yet see the limits of my life, but he could see the limits of his. His life was thin, and he had a hunger for recognition.

He was a man of sudden enthusiasms, haphazardly produced. He knew next to nothing about biology, but having a great deal of time to stare at the green bulk of Neptune in our sky, he had conceived the idea that there was life on the planet, and he had become convinced that if he proved it, he would have the automatic security of a place in the reference library. His theory was lent a certain force by the fact that we had found life already on our own Moon, on Venus and Mars, on Jupiter, Saturn, and Uranus, and even on Ganymede. Not on Mercury—too small, too close, too hot. Not on Pluto—too small, too far, too cold. But the odds seemed good to him, and the list of names he would join short enough to give him the feeling of being distinguished.

"Life is insistent," Ben said. "Life is persistent."

He approached me because he had no one else. He was an extremely difficult man. At the age of thirty-five, he still hadn't discovered the basic principles of social dealing. On first acquaintance he was too close too quickly. Then he took anything less than total reciprocation as betrayal. The more favorable your initial response to him, the greater wound he felt when he was inevitably betrayed. He had no friends, of course.

I betrayed him early in our acquaintance, something I was unaware of until he told me. After that he was always stiff and generally guarded, but since he found me no worse than the general run of humanity, and since the company on Triton numbered only twenty, he used me to talk to. I was willing to talk to him, and in this case I was willing to listen.

Triton, Neptune's major satellite, is a good substantial base. It comes close to being the largest moon in the Solar System, and it is two fingers larger than Mercury. It's the last comfortable footing for men in the Solar System, and the obvious site for a major base.

With Operation Springboard complete and our first starship on its way to a new green and pleasant land, major activity had ceased at Triton Base. We twenty were there to maintain and monitor. Some of us, like me, were there because we were bright young men with futures. Some, like Ben Wiseman, were there because no one else would have them.

But in general life was a bore. Maintenance is a bore. Monitoring is a bore. Even the skies are dull. Neptune is there, big and green. Uranus can be found if you look for it. But the Sun is only a distant candleflame flickering palely in the night and the inner planets are impossible to see. You feel very alone out there.

I was interested in Ben's suggestion. Mike Marshall, our leader, had dropped the morale problem on me in one of his fits of delegation, and since I was bored myself I was in favor of any project that might give us something to do on Sundays.

I said, "This is a good idea, Ben. There's one problem, though. We don't have the equipment for an assault like that. You know how tight the budget is, too. I could ask Mike."

"Don't ask Mike!"

"Well, I'd have to ask Mike. And he could ask. But I don't think we'd get what we have to have."

"But it's much simpler than that," Ben said. "The Uranus bathyscaphe is still on Titania. It's old, of course, but there is no reason it couldn't be used here. The two planets are practically twins. Opposition is coming up. The bathyscaphe could be brought here for almost nothing. I thought you could requisition it through your department."

That was Ben for you. A very strange man. I think he supposed that I would very quietly requisition the bathyscaphe that had been used to probe the atmosphere-ocean of Uranus, and just not say anything to Mike. Then he and I would slip quietly over to Neptune on our weekends. If he could have obtained and operated the machine by himself, I'm sure he would have preferred that.

"If the equipment is still on Titania, we may be able to get it," I said. "I'll ask Mike when I take up department operations with him tomorrow."

"Don't ask Mike."

"Look, Ben. If you want this at all, it has to go through Mike. There's no other way. You know that."

"No," he said. "Just forget the whole thing. I'm sorry I brought the subject up."

Ben was jealous of his ideas. If they passed through too many hands, they lost their savor for him. This was a good idea, or so it seemed to me, but he would prefer to let it lapse than to have the rest of our little colony involved.

I talked to Mike the next day. Mike was another odd one. At some previous time he may have had drive, but he no longer cared very deeply. He delegated as much responsibility as he possibly could. He worked erratically. And he greeted my proposal with no great interest.

"Who cares if we find life on Neptune? We already know that ammonia-methane worlds can support life, and none of it has been very interesting after the novelty wears off."

"That's true," I said, "but do you suppose I care one way or the other if we find another strange kind of minnow? The important thing is that it would give as many of us as turned out to be interested something constructive to do. It's a project I could enjoy."

"Do you think anybody else would?" Mike asked. "How many first landings have there been? If you count everything, there must have been fifty or sixty. Who remembers them all? Who cares?"

"The point isn't whether anybody else would be interested," I said. "This isn't for outsiders. Mike, this morning I got out of my chair and I found that my rear end had gone to sleep. I want something to do."

It took argument, but Mike finally agreed to find out if the bathyscaphe was available. It turned out to be, and it arrived at Triton Base aboard ship some seven months later. That wasn't so very long. We didn't have anything else to do. We didn't have anywhere else to go.

Ben, of course, was hopping mad, mostly with me. I'd stolen his idea. I'd ruined his idea. I'd betrayed his trust. I'd spoiled things.

"It's the last time I ever tell you anything," he said. As he had said more than once before.

The project turned out to be far more of a success than I had ever anticipated. Our job was to keep contact with the starship, which we did adequately, and to keep a large, empty house in order, which we did inadequately. Not that anybody cared.

After the bathyscaphe arrived, however, schedules started being observed. People cared whether or not they were relieved on time. There was less dust in corners, less dirt on people. Minor illness fell off dramatically. And my rear end stopped going to sleep on me. Even Mike, of all people, became interested.

It was all very much like the boat you built in your basement when you were fourteen. It was what we did in our spare time. It was the Project.

Ben was in and Ben was out. Ben worked sometimes and sometimes he didn't. He didn't feel the venture was quite his anymore, but he couldn't bring himself to stay away. So even he wound up involved.

Everybody else cared a lot. There was work to do. The bathyscaphe had to be overhauled completely. That took a lot of spare time. And when we were done, there was every prospect of even more spare time being whiled away in months and months of exploration.

Like all the outer planets except Pluto, which is a misplaced moon, Neptune is a gassy giant. At one time it was expected to have a layer of ice and rocky core beneath its atmosphere. In fact, however, it has no solid surface. It's all atmosphere, a murky green sea of hydrogen and helium and methane and ammonia. There are clouds and snowstorms, but no place to put your feet.

More than anything else, it is like the oceans of Earth, and the vehicle we intended to use to explore its unknown depths was a fantastic cross between a dirigible and the bathyscaphes of Piccard and his successors. Neptune was no well-tended garden, safe and comfortable, but in fact it was more easily accessible than are Earth's hostile ocean deeps with their incredible pressures.

The planet was only a step away from us on Triton, closer than the Moon is to Earth. It was possible for the bathyscaphe to reach Neptune under its own power, but not for it to return up the gravity well. Consequently we decided to use a mother ship, like a tender for a helmet diver, that would drop the bathyscaphe and then recover it. In a way I was sorry, because I found the idea of a hydrogen-fired balloon chugging its way through space amusing.

In time we were ready to make our first probe. The question then became one of who would be the two of us to go first. It was a painful question. Should it be settled by rank? Should it be settled by amount of work contributed? Should it be settled by lot? As the day of readiness came closer, the issue became more acute. Each method of choice had its champions. By and large we were polite about the subject, but there was one fistfight between Arlo Harlow, who had worked particularly hard, and Sperry Donner, who was second-in-command, which was terminated when both participants discovered they actually had no particular enthusiasm for fistfighting.

Mike finally settled the issue. The first trip would be Ben and me because we were responsible. After that it would be alphabetically by pairs. He told me later that he had been intending to be strictly alphabetical, but that would have thrown Ben into the last pair, which was one problem, and would have made Ben the partner of Roy Wilimczyk, which was another.

"This seemed the best solution," he said. "If anybody can cope with him, it's you."

"Thank you," I said, and he understood that I didn't mean it.

Ben was frankly mellow that week—mellow for Ben. This means that about forty percent of the time he was his obnoxious ingratiating self instead of his normal obnoxious uningratiating self. He even forgave me.

Finally, on a Sunday that was as brisk and bright and sunny as a day ever gets on Triton, four of us set off toward the great green cotton-candy boulder that filled a full ten degrees of sky. Ben and I didn't wait to see it grow. Long before the ship was in a parking orbit, Ben and I were in the cabin of the bathyscaphe and the whole was enclosed in a drop capsule.

I was piloting our machine. Ben was to supervise the monitoring equipment that would record our encounters with the planet. We weren't lowered over the side in the tradition of Earth's oceans. We were popped out like a watermelon seed. We were strapped in and blind. I had my fingers on the manual switch and had no need to trigger it. The rockets did what rockets do. The drop capsule peeled away automatically.

Then when our lights came on, we were deep in a green murk. It wasn't of a consistency. There were winds or eddies, call them whichever you choose. Our lights probed ahead. Sometimes we could see for considerable distances—yards. Often we could only see a few feet. We had the additional eyes of radar, which looked in circles about us and saw nothing except once what I took to be an ammonia snowstorm and avoided. Other sensors listened to the sound of the planet, took its temperature and pulse. Its temperature was very, very cold. Its pulse was slow and steady.

I feathered my elevators and found that the bathyscaphe worked as I had been assured that it did. The turboprops drove us steadily through the green. I was extremely glad to have my instruments. They told me I was right-side up, a fact I would not otherwise have known. And they kept me connected to our mother ship.

"I hope you are keeping in mind why we are here," Ben said.

"I am," I said. "However, until we know the planet better, I think one place will be about as likely as the next. I haven't seen any whale herds yet."

"No," said Ben, "but it doesn't mean they're not out there. They may simply be shy. After all, the existence of the Great Sea Serpent wasn't definitely established until the last ten years. I'd settle for something smaller, though."

We had collecting plates out. They might well demonstrate the presence of the same sort of soupy life that was found on Uranus. Ben kept busy with his monitoring. I kept busy with my piloting.

I had helped on this venture because I was bored, thoroughly tired of doing nothing in particular. I had come to Neptune with only the mildest interest in proving Ben's case. Now, however, I began to feel pleased to be where I was. The view, as we drove ourselves through the currents of this gassy sea, was monotonous, monochromatic, but weirdly beautiful. This was another sort of world than any I had been used to. I liked it. It may sound funny, but I respected it for being itself in the same way that you respect a totally ugly girl who has come to terms with herself.

I was pleased that men should be here in this last dark corner of the Solar System, and glad that I was one of the men. There is a place in reference books for this, too, if only in a footnote with the hundreds of people who have made first contacts.

It was a full five hours before we were back aboard our mother ship. Arlo Harlow helped us out of the bathyscaphe.

"How did it go?" he said.

"We won't know until we check through the data," Ben said. "We didn't see anything identifiable. Not where he drove."

I said, "You'll have to see it for yourself. I don't think I can describe it for you. You'll see. It's a real experience."

Arlo said, "Mike wants to talk to you. He's got news."

Ben and I went forward to talk to Mike back at Triton Base. The satellite was invisible ahead of us—with Neptune full, Triton was necessarily a new moon, and dark.

"Hello, Mike," I said. "Arlo says you have news. Did the starship check in?"

"No," he said. "The news is you. You two are a human-interest story. The last planet landing in the Solar System. Hold on. The first fac sheet has already come through. The headline is, 'NEPTUNE REACHED.' It begins, 'In these days of groups and organizations and institutions, in these days when man's first ship to the stars casts off with a crew of ten thousand, stories of individual human courage seem a thing of the distant past.' And it ends, 'If men like these bear our colors forward, the race of man shall yet prevail.'"

"I like that," Ben said. "That's very good."

Mike said, "There's also a story that wants to know why money was ever spent on such pointless flamboyance as this landing."

"Tell them in the first place that there wasn't any landing," I said. "We were in Neptune, not on it. Then make the point that the bathyscaphe was left over from the Uranus probe and that we put it in shape ourselves."

"I did that," Mike said. "They got it in the story. The first one. The writer applauds your courage in chancing your life in such a primitive and antiquated exploratory vehicle."

"Oh, hell," I said.

"Listen. They have some questions they want answered. They want to know why you went. Why did you go, Bob?"

"Tell them that it seemed like a good idea at the time," I said.

"I can't give them that."

"We wanted to find out whether there was life on Neptune," Ben said.

"Did you find any?"

"As far as we know, we didn't," I said.

"Then I can't give them that. Try again."

I thought. After a moment I said, "Tell them that we didn't think it was right for men to go to the stars without having touched all the bases here."

As "touch all the bases," that line has passed into the familiar quotation books.

Ben and I are in the history books, too—in the footnotes along with the hundreds of other people who made first landings. If you count the starships, that list would run into the thousands.

Ben isn't happy buried in the footnotes, and he and I don't speak anymore. He's mad at me. He never discovered life on Neptune, and nobody, it is clear, is ever likely to. On the other hand, I'm the author of one of history's minor taglines. He finds that galling.

It isn't a great distinction to bear, I'll admit, but there have been dark nights in my life when I've lain awake and wondered whether or not I would leave any ripples behind me. That line is enough of a ripple to bring me through to morning.

Now I'm Watching Roger

Now I'm watching Roger. Roger is hanging facedown in his ropes overhead and looking at me. He isn't saying anything and I'm not speaking.

I wish I had the time to spare in relaxation that he does, but I'm kept constantly busy. There are a million things here to do. If I had Roger's free time, I'd know how to put it to good use. I wouldn't idle.

I wonder about Roger's experiments. The only time he ever seems to work on them is during our regular telecast to Earth. I asked him about his experiments once, but he didn't take notice. He jumped up into his ropes. He's very well practiced at it now. If I had more time, perhaps I could make flying leaps to the top of the dome, too.

Roger is too silent. He never speaks up when Jack does something to annoy me, and this encourages Jack to take more advantage. Roger will never settle anything, and I've saved him from Jack I don't know how many times. But how do you ask a man to back you? He either sees the need or he doesn't. It isn't proper to ask, so I don't.

On the other hand, if he's going to play the silent game, there's no reason why I shouldn't play it, too. The only time I'll speak is when I stir from my silent work to drag Jack off his back. But I don't expect he will notice.

✦

To taunt me Jack takes off his black hat during our telecasts. He's charming and plausible. If you believe him, we would be happy to stay another eight months on the moon. I'm not sure I could juggle things that long, though I'll grant that Jack might.

When it is my turn, I nod and wave to Earth. I tell them we're keeping busy. Roger works away at his experiments in the background. He waves to the camera but he doesn't say anything.

When the telecast is over, Jack puts his black hat back on again. He spent an entire evening making it out of paper and coloring it black with ink. I didn't watch because I was busy working. Jack knows the black hat annoys me, but I'm not saying anything or taking any notice.

He may be plausible in public, but Roger and I know him better. He only eats the good parts of things and leaves the rest. I imagine he was indulged.

69

And he's a glutton. I pointed it out when he left the rind from the Christmas fruitcake and his antics lasted for a month. He started by leaving crusts and bits of cracker on my plate and grew even more blatant when I refused to take any notice. At the end he was gobbling with both hands and flinging food about.

I do have an audio of several episodes but it isn't easy to tell what is happening.

I have a number of recordings of Jack. None of Roger except for background.

In one recording I say, "Jack, you haven't been sterilizing." It is a point I am particular about.

"It's true, Clarence 'Clancy' Ballou, I haven't been. I've decided to give it up. I'll take my chances with the moon. Let the moon take its chances with me. I wouldn't mind giving it a dose of something."

"That's against policy," I say.

"Screw policy, Clarence. Maybe you're too nice for this work. There's the universe, as regular as a clock. Then there's us, life, an out-of-place accident. We're anarchy, disorder. No matter how tough the universe makes the rules, life will survive and spread. The moon is only the first step. Someday we'll spread to the stars and take over everything. We'll rip the guts out of the universe. We'll stripmine the stars. Life will prevail. It's our destiny to crap up the works."

"You make us sound evil. That's what the regulations are for, to ensure that we don't contaminate other worlds."

"You don't understand, Clarence. We are evil. And it's up to us to make the most of it."

"But I'm good. I've always been good."

"Learn better.

It was after that that he made his black paper hat. It's supposed to be a reminder to me, but it isn't really necessary. I know which of us is which.

Jack is outside. I've been counting our sacks of garbage. I believe that two are missing. I fear the worst.

Was it sterilized? Not if he didn't sterilize it.

I fear the worst.

Just before the telecast I say to Jack, "What about the garbage?"

"What garbage?"

"I know about the garbage. Unless you stop burying it outside, I'm going to have to tell them back home."

He takes off his black hat. He combs his hair and practices his smile.

"I've been counting," I say.

On the telecast I'm cautious. I say that some garbage is missing.

They ask Jack about it. Jack is in charge of accounting for the garbage. He says that it is all there.

I call on Roger. Roger smiles and waves from the background for the camera.

Jack smiles and tells the audience about garbage accounting procedures. He is very plausible. He thanks me for raising the question.

After the telecast he says, "I have a higher loyalty." And he puts his black hat back on.

What can I do?

◆

Another sack of garbage is missing.

I don't know what to do.

Roger just fell off the bench. Since I enforced safety regulations and made him stop sleeping in his ropes, he has taken to biting his fingernails and falling off the bench.

I've been thinking about Jack. I've been thinking about the moon infected with life. I've been thinking about people like Jack overcrawling the universe.

Jack is larger than I am.

I've just made myself a white hat.

Another sack of garbage is missing. Sometimes I think Jack is not completely sane.

◆

I have taken charge of garbage accounting. I think I'll rest easier now that it is in my hands.

In future I think that the answer must lie in unbreachable refuse containers. And a tight check system to see that everything gets deposited. But even these cannot be enough if the irresponsible aren't weeded out beforehand. The power of life must rest in hands that respect it. I'm not sure how that can be ensured, but I will think about it until the rotation changes.

This new job means one more intrusion on my time, but it's necessary. Those who can do are condemned to do to the limit of their strength.

I explained on the telecast to Earth tonight as best I could. I told them the problem and how I solved it. I'm sure I didn't tell it well—Jack was always the raconteur—but they seemed to understand. Roger looked up from his work long enough to nod and wave to the people back home.

I think things are under control.

◆

Things are much smoother now. The change in Roger has been amazing. He is more active now. He works with greater concentration. He listens to my advice and nods. He has even been outside the dome for the first time in months.

That is the good side. On the negative side he has taken to his ropes again. I haven't the time or the heart to speak to him about it.

I'm very busy.

✦

I just counted and counted again to be sure. One of Jack's fourteen sacks is missing; I believe a foot. I don't know how it could have happened. The right foot, I think. We must get unbreachable refuse containers.

Now I'm watching Roger. Roger is hanging in his ropes and watching me.

Arpad

don't expect to live past sixty. Not on my life-style. Somebody will see me killed, I'll attract lightning, or I'll shock and thrill the world by dropping dead some Sunday. In the meantime, my style has advantages.

Sixty is early middle age by Ship standards and careful Shippies pace their lives accordingly. I don't. I play go for broke. I shatter the common clown by enjoying everything he's afraid would kill him by sixty, and I blind him with my speed. I act while he thinks about acting. I invent problems on the moment and dazzle my way out of them, and he merely invents problems.

I relish the thought of dying at sixty. I want to find out what I'm able to do with plastics, do it, do it big, and get out. I don't want to hang on. Shakespeare and Napoleon, who did their own separate work in plastics, both died on the eve of fifty-three as bare young men. But they had tested their limits. I don't yet aspire to die at fifty-three, let alone at thirty-three. Right now I'll settle for sixty years to find my limits.

I haven't found them yet. Understand that.

I was brought up a Shippie against my will and only gradually grew to enjoy it. My father was a disinherited Shippie, Expelled, or the closest thing to it, for marrying down. He lived at the tepid tempo of a Shippie to the day of his death.

I was born on the planet of New Albion. On the basis of my father's stories of my fine heritage and the strength of my imagination I fancied myself a cut above my friends, but I had the same dirt between my toes.

My father died at the premature age of eighty-four. Some of his cronies in the old Universal Heirs of Man gang took their remorse out on me. I was rescued, saved from myself, saved from my mother—and what an operation that was—and restored to *Mother Bertha,* their Ship, to be made a first-class heir of Earth and Man, as was my due. They held their noses, told me of my luck, and abandoned me to a dormitory to make the most of my new opportunities.

Twice I was prevented from escaping. The third time I changed my mind and returned.

I decided I would show them that I could beat them on their own terms. At the age of fourteen in the Ships they turn you out on a colony planet—

73

some hellhole like New Albion—to survive on your own resources. If you do survive, you are an adult citizen.

Well, that's my own home jungle. I figured that if I could cope with New Albion—and I was doing all right there—and survive Ship civilization, I could pass Trial snickering. After that I could walk away—either pick myself a colony planet to my taste or act badly enough, after my fashion, to get ejected like my father before me.

By the time I did pass Trial, and I sailed, I had changed my mind. I no longer ached to leave. I'd been looking around the Ship, and it was clear that there were many more opportunities than anybody in sight was taking advantage of. I couldn't walk away from that.

The Ships were launched just over two hundred years ago to carry survival colonies away from an overpopulated and depleted Earth on the hysterical edge of self-destruction. Seven Ships founded some one hundred colonies. And now, all these many years later, the only movement between the stars is the seven Great Ships on eternal motherly rounds to disapprove of their children. They are *good* mothers.

There are only 28,000 people in *Mother Bertha*. The Ship is a small world full of fat, slow, lazy, democratic gods. Sheep. Clowns. The democracy is in direct relation to the fatness, the slowness, and the laziness. But a colony planet, even the best and biggest of them, is only one world. A Ship gives access to a hundred worlds.

Or a hundred plus seven.

There's a certain joy that comes in thinking about the possibility of affecting a hundred and seven worlds. That's a lot of plastic to shape, however you like best to mold plastic.

My father died at eighty-four, still trying to decide what he wanted to be when he grew up. Admittedly I haven't yet made my final decision, but I've got it narrowed down—stun, dazzle, damn the consequences, and die at sixty leaving plastic shapes behind me for people to wonder about for a hundred or a thousand years. The more unused opportunities I see around me the higher goes my estimate of how long I can keep my name in conversation. Whatever may have become of Earth, people still do talk of Shakespeare and Napoleon, and will.

Not that I seek admission to their company yet. I've just been trying my experiments for the last little while, each one a bit more expansive than the last. If I hold my pace, at sixty I will have explored my limits.

Each of the Great Ships follows its own separate schedule, and one Ship will meet another two or three times in a year. The people who matter exchange information. The people who don't matter don't pay much attention. I'm constantly amazed by the amount of attention a Shippie can sink into quad sports. Seizing that attention is one of the opportunities that nobody is taking advantage of. But I have never claimed that it is easy. You must strike them a thunderblow between the eyes.

When I was twenty, *Mother Bertha*—that is, the home of my fathers, *Moskalenka*—met *Sara Peabody* at a time when I was primed to start a new experiment. I made petition to change Ships.

I was met by a young girl recently enough a Citizen still to talk of it. She was an attractive young chub, a pretty bit of plastic, a blonde in a yellow striped jersey like a butterflower. Her name was Susan Smallwood and she had been sent to guide me.

After introducing herself, she said, "Are you sure you want to transfer here? Really?"

"I think so," I said.

"Are you in the Sons of Prometheus or anything like that?" she asked.

"No." I have a lingering prejudice against people of that sort, but I didn't express it. I was satisfied to say no.

"Then you shouldn't have much trouble. My mother's Mobility Officer. You'll have to talk to her."

I needed a guide. The innards of a Ship are a scramble. It took me fully two years to learn my way around *Mother Bertha*. If I wanted to touch Ship-pies in that particular way—and I'm thinking about doing it—I'd write about deep, hollow, safe earthwarrens. Mother badgers tight in their dens. It would be a safe set of symbols to play with.

Susan Smallwood took me through runs and tunnels to my appointment. She was curious about me and showed it. "Why do you want to transfer?" she said.

"Oh, there's opportunity here," I said.

"I don't see much."

She had met me in *Sarah Peabody's* scout bay. We had stood dominated by the line of scoutships—*Sarah's* links to other Ships and other worlds. It isn't much of a jump to call them opportunities. Ship people think in bland and figureless prose. They see only scoutships and the absence of scoutships.

Butterflower was a nice girl, the sort I wanted to take notice of me before I stopped caring. Now what I wanted was someone to speak in tongues with.

"I'm going to be chela for Heriberto Pabon. That's an opportunity."

"Oh, but he's dirty," she said.

"My teachers said that he was. But he is supposed to be brilliant."

"I wouldn't change Ships to serve somebody like Heriberto Pabon," she said.

"There are too many Margolins in *Mother Bertha*. That's reason to change ships."

"Where?"

"*Moskalenka*."

"Oh," she said. "That's kind of good. We have families like that here. But not many Margolins."

"That sounds like opportunity," I said.

"I guess."

Mrs. Smallwood, *Sarah Peabody's* Mobility Officer, was a harder and less attractive version of her daughter. People like her are ripe for molding because they are so certain that they cannot be molded.

Though Butterflower was a Citizen, her mother presumed, ordered, and dismissed. There was strain between them. When Susan left, her mother made some remark about wishing her daughter would show more initiative, just as though she hadn't been grinding her heel into every bud of initiative the girl had poked up. I tucked that away to think about.

When I have tempo in chess and the force of attack is with me, I take little notice of my opponent's game. I just play like a tide. But when I'm moving initial pawns and the rhythm of the game has yet to be established my way, I keep track.

Mrs. Smallwood assumed her cap of office, fixing it into place to demonstrate the new and official woman I had to deal with. She sat down and straightened papers.

She said, "We must be quick to decide about this. I don't know how you run your Ship, but this one is going to be on its way in five hours. We have a schedule."

Ships do have schedules, keep them, and live by them. *Mother Bertha* and *Sarah Peabody* have the times and places of their meetings scheduled for twenty years.

"Oh, I understand," I said.

I understood that being quick to decide would mean doing things at her pace and in my best imitation of her style. I was patient—which I can be when I must, having had practice enough—I did things in her pace and style, and I watched her.

"You wish to study with Heriberto Pabon?"

"Yes, ma'am. He was recommended to me by my teachers. And he agreed to accept me."

"Do you know anything about him?"

"Not really, ma'am. Not at first hand. We haven't met."

"That seems irresponsible, young man," she said. She sorted paragraphs in front of her. "Heriberto Pabon may have found a safe hole for himself, he may consider himself above ordinary rules and standards, but should you care to ask anyone, you would be told that he is a fast and unsocial man."

I didn't smile at the description.

"I have your approvals here. What could they have been thinking of?"

I said, "I believe my advisers think me too narrow, too concerned with public work, and not concerned enough with other areas of my development."

"But you have doubts about this?"

I spread my hands. "I'm in the hands of my teachers."

"I suppose that must be respected," she said. "But we don't encourage immigration, Mr. Margolin. And it would be three years before you could be returned to *Moskalenka*. We don't prevent anyone from leaving us, but frankly we do make some selection about whom we allow to join us. We have the lowest population of any of the Ships and, we like to think, the most select. But don't think of us as exclusive. Still, let me ask you one thing. Are you a member of the Sons of Prometheus or any other reconciliationist group?"

"No," I said. "There's enough to do within the Ships to satisfy me. So many things to do. But, tell me, if I had belonged, would that be reason for exclusion?"

"Not for that alone," she said, but her tone seemed to indicate that it would be close to sufficient.

"I didn't realize there were rules against belonging to the Universal Heirs of Man or your Sons of Prometheus."

"It's my duty to see that troublemakers are not permitted to disturb *Seirapodi*. We have a nice safe stable Ship here, and we want to keep it that way. It's been my observation that reconciliationists are troublemakers. Not all of them, but too many."

"Ah, yes," I said. "I've had my own bad moments with them."

"You have?" she said. "But look here. You did spend your early days on a planet. On New Albion." She checked the name.

"Heaven knows, ma'am," I said, "that's true. It was an accident I'd like to be forgiven. I've spent all these years since I was restored to *Moskalenka* trying in one way after another to make up for it. I've done one thing after another. I would never think of the colonies until I had thought of the Ships first."

"That's only proper," she said.

"There's so much to do, so much left to be done."

"So few feel that way. I don't think I like your advisers. Why would they want to change you?"

"I don't always do as much as I feel I should," I said modestly. "But I do try."

Mrs. Smallwood said, "I can save you from all this Heriberto Pabon nonsense by rejecting your petition."

"I must respect my teachers," I said, and lowered my eyes.

"I suppose," she said, and reached for her stamp.

I said, "This could even be an opportunity. It's a matter of attitude."

Bang, she went. "I suppose if you choose to see it that way, it might be."

I left Mrs. Smallwood in her office. Perky little Susan Smallwood was waiting for me outside. I had been wondering if she would be, and was pleased to find that my guess had been correct.

I still needed a guide.

"Well," she said, "are you allowed to stay?"

I nodded.

"See, just as I said. As long as you don't belong to extreme organizations, you're all right with Mother."

"I have an appointment to see someone about my choice of a place to live. What would you suggest I ask for?"

"Oh, I wouldn't know about that," she said. "A thing like that can make a big difference. People can set store by who you live among."

"Yes," I said. "I know that can make a difference. Who do you live among?"

"Oh, nobody. Just new Citizens. We aren't anybody. Mostly we haven't found other neighborhoods yet, I guess." Then she offered, "Do you want to stay in my apartment until you decide? Or will you want to talk first to Heriberto Pabon?"

I smiled. "I'll call him from your apartment," I said.

✦

I don't pretend to subtlety. If I were roundabout, I couldn't cram everything in. I don't have that kind of time to waste. When push comes to shove, I do. Anything that gets lost in the shove I never miss.

I set to work directly. The secret to moving people is to touch their hearts. It isn't as difficult as it might seem. Shippies are amazingly local and have such secret hunger for the marvelous.

I set up court in Susan Smallwood's apartment while I was still living with her, and recruited my first converts. Kids they may be, but they are also voting Citizens. Older people sometimes lose sight of that. And there are advantages to a retinue.

I began by making muscles for them. I came on slightly dangerous. I was from off-Ship. I was associated with Heriberto Pabon. Man of Mystery, me. I knew answers they had no questions for.

I told them tales of wonder. I told them of the League of Shiphoppers, for one. This was a group of unknown invisibles, unbounded by Ship custom.

"On the move all the time, using Ships and Colonies as indifferent resting places, they go where they like, when they like, as they like."

The young ones asked young questions:

"Where do they come from?"

"How do they do it?"

"Really? You're not telling stories?"

"From Ship to Ship? Oh, that would make me feel giddy."

I said, "It's a secret floating life. Unwatched, unnoticed. They use the Ships as indifferent stepping stones."

A sceptic, a boy named Joe Don Simms, said, "And we're expected to believe this is happening all around us?"

Sceptics are almost always burly people, I have found. They add bulk to a retinue.

"Yes," I said.

"Even here? Even here? Do you claim that these Shiphoppers can and do pass through *Seirapodi?*"

"Maybe *Sarah Peabody* has gotten left out of the game," I said.

"But you said they go everywhere."

"So I did," I said.

"But now you say they don't 'hop' here." His voice added the doubting quotation marks. If his voice hadn't, his expression would have.

I included the ten of them in the sweep of my arms. "Of us here tonight in this room, around this candle, at least two."

They showed awe. Simms demanded, "Who?"

"You expect identifications?"

"I suppose you will say yourself, since you are from another Ship."

"I'm not from another Ship," I said.

"What do you mean?"

"I was born on the planet of New Albion and I go where I please."

Simms said, "I don't believe you!"

I said, "If you were clever enough, it could be checked," and turned the conversation to other things. Saluji, primarily.

But at the end of the evening Simms stayed behind with Susan and me when everyone else had left and demanded to know whether the Shiphoppers were "real" or "only a story."

"That's all right, Joe Don Simms," I said. "It's not too late. There's still time for you to start. It isn't all done before you. You can be anything you want to be. We'll let you play."

He burst into tears. I let him cry.

When he was done, he said, "Who is the second Shiphopper?"

"You," I said.

And he cried again.

For those primed to be touched by it, the prospect of unending rolling meadows can be just as potent as mother badgers in their dens.

I set up my own apartment after a few days. Not among the kids. I didn't bar them. In fact, I encouraged them to visit. But I gave them a little distance to travel to come to me. Not among any group of similars of my own age, interests, or ambitions. I feel no need to copy the limitations of a faction. And not near Pabon, of course. We might have embarrassed each other.

I decided my best part was presumption, and so I settled among a gang a hundred years my senior, where I stood out conspicuously. These people were the last memory of the vogue for a peculiar game called Saluji that had swept the Ships before my father was yet a Citizen. Old as they were, these people still had their courts and their competition.

They sent their ax to deal with me—a hard old Saluji player named McKinley Morganfield. But better than anything, better than impressionable young girls, or officials, or sceptics, in all the world I deal best with crotchety old Saluji players. I remember who they were.

McKinley Morganfield began by asking who I thought I was, elbowing my way in where my presence was not appreciated. But my following admired him, and I spoke to him of my father's friend, Ira Ayravainen.

"There was talk of the two of you meeting once, wasn't there?"

"Egh, talk," he said. "Nothing came of it. Nothing ever came of it. When there was interest, nobody did anything like that. It might be possible now, but nobody plays Saluji anymore and there isn't any interest."

"There's interest," I said. And my people nodded.

I said, "And you never met Cropsey."

"You know about Cropsey, too?" He was impressed with me against his judgment.

"Of course," I said.

"He was a first-class pecker in Saluji. By report."

"You may meet them yet in a Seniors match," I said.

"Where?" he asked. "How?"

I had my own people's attention, too. I had introduced them to the pleasures of Saluji, and named the names—like McKinley Morganfield's—but I had not told them anything of this. I don't believe in wasting my marvels and miracles.

"Sixteen months from now, all of the Ships will rendezvous at the South Continent of New Albion. Games will be held. You will have your chance at both Ayravainen and Cropsey."

"Is this possible?" McKinley Morganfield asked.

"There's never been a rendezvous," said Simms. He still had moments when he wondered, but that was good. It helps to have a variety of notes in a claque. It sounds less claquish that way.

"The Ship men gather to play their games, down on the worlds of men," I said. "They pitch their tents and fly their pennons."

"I've never heard of any of this," said McKinley Morganfield.

"It's still in the organizational stages," I said, "but it will happen. It isn't being widely talked about until it has been completely coordinated. But in sixteen months there will be a rendezvous. The first one. And there will be Senior Saluji matches."

"But what of the Ship's schedule? That can't just be abandoned."

"The Ship's schedule can be modified," I said. "A Ship can go anywhere its Citizens decide to take it."

And that was a new thought to them.

During the next few months I spent my spare time talking constructively to people. At first you enlist individuals and it all seems painfully slow. You think nothing will ever happen. But then the individuals add their own associates, just as a poet starts with one or two words that ring brightly and watches them accumulate company.

I did nothing but talk. I do it all with my hands behind my back.

I didn't talk much with Heriberto Pabon about what I was doing. He once asked whether there was anything to the talk he was hearing about a Rendezvous on New Albion—"Rendezvous in '32" was the slogan he had heard.

I said, "Yes."

"Are they really going to have the first Universal Saluji Championships?"

"I believe so. Yes."

"Amazing. I remember the pylongs used to last for hours when I was a boy. And the young people are playing Saluji again. I'll have to get out my batons."

He walked off practicing hand shifts. And hand shifts out of style in Saluji for eighty years. Those were the early crude days before the game was refined.

My sturdiest opponents were the Sons of Prometheus. Not at all the way you would think. But we were far from natural allies.

They were originally chapters of do-gooders. If you belonged, you promised to bring light to the colony planet on which you passed Trial. Eventually they broadened and shallowed to become an entrenched pro forma Opposition. While one might think they would be ready for an opportunity to abandon the schedule, that wasn't at all the case. They were in business to squabble about the schedule, not abandon it. The schedule was their tie to their people handing out bandages on the colony planets.

I went in to talk with them. I asked for a quiet conversation with two of their leaders. I took a small herd of supporters along, but I left them at the door.

After I listened to them I said, "The very best of all possible reasons—information. One very interesting fact emerged when this Ship and *Moskalenka* recently met. I bring it with me and I have permission to tell you. On your vow of secrecy, of course."

"What?" said one. He was the less sympathetic. The other responded to my smile, or I thought she did. A short, slight, dark woman.

I looked at them both, one face to the other, and smiled at her. Then I nodded as though I believed I had their agreement.

"Earth was never destroyed. That was a story that was given out, but it isn't true. It isn't true."

"I've heard that rumor," she said.

"What proof do you offer," he said.

"None," I said. "But if you looked into it, you might find that we have only assumed that Earth was destroyed. Or that we have been deliberately misled. It's easier for them that way. You know they dislike the acceptance of responsibility."

That was a favorite charge of the Universal Heirs of Man. "It's true," she said. "They do sometimes lie to us."

"Only rarely," he said.

"If there were a Rendezvous, maybe someone would go back and see if Earth really is only a cinder," I said. "It's worth knowing, isn't it, Mr. Dentremont?"

"Abandon the schedule?"

"To find ourselves."

"Leave the Colonies who depend on us?"

"Let them swim."

"Give up the chance of power?"

"Seize power. When seven Ships meet, new revelations should be had for the asking. Turn them to use. Kill with a word."

She said enthusiastically, "If we did abandon the schedule, I'd like to take a Ship and travel to the heart of the Galaxy. I want to know what company we have."

He said, "You've said that before."

Ah, the yearnings of Shippies. Well, I understand that one.

I took her aside afterward and introduced her to some of my people. Some of them were toying with that dream, too.

She came. He followed.

When I first discovered that I was able to move people, I sometimes did it just to see myself do it. It is little short of amazing what hoops people will leap through if they are encouraged. It was the arrogance of discovery. Now I'm more restrained and more purposeful.

I don't move people gratuitously. Well, seldom. When I do move them, however, it gives me a true pleasure.

The mythless are easy. Those who believe come harder. What it takes is a better myth.

◆

Heriberto took up Saluji for several months, but then abruptly one day he put his batons away again. I asked him about that.

"It was fun," he said. "My shifts are as sound as ever. But I haven't time for that now. Three new projects came to me today, and I must begin them and see which is worth the pursuit."

"You won't be playing at Rendezvous?"

"Oh, I may watch a match or two if I have time," he said. "Right now it looks as if all my time will be tied up in association meetings."

"Mm," I said. "Meetings?"

"I've been solicited by three and absolutely barred from two. They find me disturbing. I believe I'm chairing one series."

"Oh," I said. "Well."

The opportunity for conspiracies of all sorts had occurred to me, but I hadn't actually plotted them. Let everybody have the fun of making his own story.

◆

82

Mrs. Smallwood, Ship's Mobility Officer and mother of my old friend Susan, said, "It seems I was too hasty in allowing you aboard, young man. Don't think we're not aware of what you have been doing. We are aware of you."

"Yes, ma'am."

"In the old days, and not so long ago, you would have been Expelled from the Ship. When I was a young Citizen, I voted twice with the majority to Expel. If you were brought up now, I'd vote you out. You are a troublemaker."

Mrs. Smallwood had called twice when I was out. She wanted to talk to me. Having seen me once, she might have preferred to keep vid distance between us. I'm not sure what she was thinking of.

I went to her office, finding my own way. I took only two warm bodies as sideboys. I left them in her outer chamber.

I said, "As far as I know, I haven't done anything quite that serious."

"You've been lying to people," she said. "You know as well as I that this Rendezvous is all a lie. *Moskalenka* said nothing of this. And when we meet *Jaunzemis* next month, I'm sure neither will they."

"Probably not," I said. "If you ask official sources."

"I should be recording this."

"But one year from now, seven Ships will meet off New Albion. There will be games, meetings, convocations, assemblies, parades, bazaars, and celebrations. All for the first time."

"Stop that," she said. "It's not going to happen. It's not. We won't abandon the schedule."

"You will abandon the schedule if enough Citizens call for it."

"They won't."

"Ah, but they might. They will."

"Nobody will come to this Rendezvous."

"This Ship," I said. "And when it arrives, the others will be there, too."

"No," she said. "No."

"I have a proposal," I said, smiling. "Lock me in my room for eleven months and take away my vid."

"You're laughing at me," she said. "I wish I could."

"Then exile me on the South Continent of New Albion."

"You were born on New Albion."

"Long ago. And on Eastcape, a long distance to swim."

"How would it look if that were brought out?"

"I don't care particularly," I said. "If it weren't too late and if South Continent didn't have such fine weather and pleasant countryside, I'd ask for the site to be changed."

She shook her head. I'd really gotten to her. She shouldn't have asked to see me. I'm no pleasure to officials.

"You are a very devious young man, Mr. Margolin."

That did bring me up short. I think my major shortcoming, aside from the fact that my sense of humor isn't appreciated by everyone, is that I'm excessively straightforward. But after I considered it for a while, I decided that it was all right. If they choose to misunderstand me, it can only be to my advantage.

"Or," I said, "if it met with your approval, I could transfer into *John Thomas* next month."

"I despise these new slangy names," she said. "I'll take it under advisement. Now, if you'll leave, I'm already late for my Saluji afternoon."

"I was admiring your batons," I said. "Very handsome."

When I crossed into *John Thomas,* Heriberto not only recommended me to my new mentor—who, I must admit, had already heard of me—he gave a statement on my behalf to *Sarah Peabody,* which was very decent of him. But then I'd found him a good man.

He said, "He came well recommended to me. Now I find I have nothing more to teach him. I must pass him along to another pair of hands."

I took two Shiphoppers along with me into *John Thomas. Sarah Peabody* stops no one from leaving, and *John Thomas* isn't as sifty about newcomers. One of the Shiphoppers was Joe Don Simms. About a week after we had made the change he came to me in complaint. He claimed that things were neither as exciting nor as heart-lifting as I had described them. As for me, I was feeling pretty good.

"What am I to do?" he asked.

"Swim," I said.

I only have one thing left to settle. I still haven't decided whether I am to be Shakespeare or Napoleon.

How Can We Sink
When We Can Fly?

In the final analysis civilization can be saved only if we are willing to change our ways of life. We have to invent utopias not necessarily to make them reality but to help us formulate worthwhile human goals.

—RENÉ DUBOS

1

Endings of stories come easy. It is the beginnings, when anything is still possible, that come hard.

To think yourself into somewhere strange and someone new, and then to live it, takes the nerve of a revolutionary or a bride. If writers had that kind of nerve, they wouldn't be writers. They would be starting revolutions and getting married, like everyone else. As it is, we tend to cultivate our gardens and mull a lot.

When the beginnings come harder than usual and when the only news that penetrates the Pennsylvania outback is of lost causes and rumors of lost causes, I give a call to Rob to grab whoever he can find between Springfield, Massachusetts and here and come on down for the weekend. The people around here are good people, but all they know is what they hear on the evening news. And they can't talk shop. Rob talks good shop, and he has a completely unique set of rumors. His news is no better, but it isn't the common line.

It does him good to come, too. Springfield is no place to live. In a sense I feel responsible for Rob. Springfield was founded by William Pynchon, who was an ancestor of mine. He wrote a book in Greek called *The Meritorious Price of Our Redemption*, which was burned on Boston Common in 1650 as religiously unsound, and he went back to England. He stayed long enough to found Springfield and a branch of my mother's family, and make me responsible for Rob.

If I ever meet Thomas Pynchon, who wrote *V.*, I intend to ask him how he feels about Springfield, Mass. In the meantime Rob has some leeway with me, which he takes advantage of on occasion.

I was expecting Rob and Leigh, but when we picked them up on Friday morning at the lunch-counter bus stop across the river in New Jersey, they had a kid with them. Leigh is in her thirties, good silent strong plain people. She writes westerns. Rob had collected her in New York. Where he'd gotten the kid I didn't know.

"This is Juanito," Rob said.

The kid was blond as Maytime, dressed in worn blue jeans and a serape. He was wishing for a beard. I didn't know him, but he looked like a member of the tribe.

"I'm Alex and this is Cory," I said, and he nodded. Then the five of us headed for our 1951 Plymouth, our slow beast.

"I'm just as glad to get out of here," Rob said, looking back as we headed onto the bridge to Pennsylvania, "It reminds me of Springfield."

It is a depressing battered little town. A good place to leave behind.

Cory said, "And you know, there are people who commute to work in New York from here every day. Two hours each way."

"It's a long way to come for flaking paint and tumbledown houses," Rob said. "But I suppose if that's the way you like to live . . ."

He turned to look at the brighter prospect of the Pennsylvania hills. "Well," he said, "let's get going. Bring on your sheep and geese and cats."

I said, "There are a couple of ducks now, and Gemma had three kittens."

The only part of the livestock that belongs to us is two of the cats. There are two stray tomcats on the place and some independent bullfrogs. The sheep and their lambs are the farmer's. The rest belongs to our landlady up in the big house.

Leigh said, "How old are the kittens?"

Cory turned and said over the seat back, "They haven't even got their eyes open."

Across the Delaware in Pennsylvania we passed a broad field full of dead auto bodies rusting into the land, crossed the shortest covered bridge in the county, and headed up into the hills.

"Well," said Rob. "How badly are you stuck?"

"Stuck," I said. "I'm doing a story based on an idea of Isaac Asimov for an anthology of new stories."

"You're a hack," said Rob. "You work for money."

"Right," I said. "I work to live, and live to work. No, my problem is that I want to respect Asimov's idea without following it to the letter. I guess the problem is that I can't see any way to get from our now to his future. When I listen to the news, I wonder about any future at all. So I sit in front of the typewriter, but I don't write. I'll find the story, I'll see the way, but right now I'm still trying to find my beginning."

"Don't brood about it," said Leigh. "Sit down and write it the simplest way." Kind advice, because in spite of what Leigh may sometimes say about her own work, that's not the way she writes.

"Seen any movies lately?" Rob asked. Not an idle question.

"None," I said. "The movies they've been bringing around here haven't been the ones I'm planning to catch. Not Anthony Quinn and Ingrid Bergman in a love story for the ages. Besides, I couldn't take the chance of getting that far from the typewriter. Not with the birth of a story imminent."

"I know you've stopped answering your mail," he said.

"Do I owe you a letter?"

"Of course."

"It must have gotten lost in the mail strike," I said, though in fact I hadn't written. "Our mail hasn't yet gotten back to normal. I'm keeping a list of things that haven't come, starting with a check from Henry." Henry is the agent of all of us. Henry is the agent of half the writers I know.

"Hey, you had a sale?" Automatic question.

"My first this year, and just in time, too. We need the money. They were supposed to pay at the end of last month, and today is already the tenth."

"What about letters?" Rob asked. "Have you really been answering your mail?"

"Letters? I'm busy. All my time goes to writing—that is, not writing."

"Travel? Have you been anyplace recently?"

The size of a mental block can be fairly estimated by the writer's list of austerities. It is less a matter of income than an inability to put anything ahead of writing—that is, not writing. If a writer does nothing whatsoever but sit very very still and pretend to think, you know he is up the creek without a paddle.

Cory answered that one. "Not since Christmas," she said.

"Fine," said Rob, like any doctor in possession of a juicy symptom. "Are you able to read?"

"I never stop reading," I said. "I've never been that petrified."

"Name a good novel you read recently."

"Does it have to be good?"

"Name a novel," Rob said. "It doesn't have to be good."

"All right," I said. "I'm not reading fiction. *Creative Mythology*, the fourth volume of *The Masks of God*."

"Is that as heavy as it sounds?"

Cory said, "I lost momentum half through it."

"That one is for inspiration," I said. "Then *Personal Knowledge*, by Polanyi. That's food for thought. And *Heroes and Heretics: A Social History of Dissent*. That's for the times. I pick one or the other up in the morning, read a paragraph or a page, and then I think about the Asimov story."

"Oh, you lucky writers," Leigh said. "Your time is your own."

Rob finally let me off the hook. "Let me see what Asimov wrote when we get to your place. Maybe we can talk it out."

A deer suddenly flashed onto the road ahead of us, showed tail, and bounded off through the wooded hillside. Only Cory and I in the front and Juanito in the back got a good look. Leigh caught just a glimpse, and Rob missed it entirely. I try to bring people by the scenic route, but they have to be prepared to look at things fast. Rob never bothers.

"Nice," said Leigh.

"We sat at sunset over on Geigel Hill Road the other week and watched a whole herd—twelve or more, and even more down in the draw—cross the road and stream up the long open hillside," I said. "And when our landlady's daughter was here for Easter from England, she said there was a herd in the woods on the State Park land just behind the farm."

"Just behind the farm?" Leigh said. "How far would it be?"

Cory said, "Not far. A ten-minute walk. We could go this afternoon and look."

Rob said, "Not me. I've been up for thirty hours. I need sack time."

"I'll go," said Juanito.

This Pennsylvania countryside offers you just about anything you want. We've been here the better part of a year and still discover surprises within five miles, and even within one, or within three hundred yards: wild onion, wild strawberries, poison ivy. In the space of a mile on a single road you can find high-speed intersection, three-hundred-year-old farmstead, random suburbia, crossroad community, and woodland, in any order and combination you like, strung across little valleys, hidden in hollows, up and over hills. There are even pockets of industry.

"What is that?" Juanito asked.

It's part of the scenery, but you have to be particularly quick to see it. If you could see more of it, perhaps it would have been closed down sooner.

I stopped our old Plymouth tank and backed up the hill to the curve. In early April, with the trees still bare or only barely budding, you can see it from one vantage on the road. Tinny prefab buildings and the half a dozen chemical lagoons perched overlooking the creek, with blue and yellow gullies staining the hillside.

"Every time it rains there's overflow," I said. "That's the Revere Chemicals dump. It was put in in 1965, and the State Health people said at the time that it was going to do this, and it took them five years to close it down. Now it just sits there and leaks. The manager is trying to start a new operation in the next township."

"I hope the deer doesn't drink from that stream," Leigh said.

"He has to take his chances the same as the rest of us," Rob said. Growing up in Springfield has left Rob with more than a little sourness.

When we got to the farm, I stopped the car at the head of the long gravel drive. "Somebody hop out and check the mailbox," I said.

Rob made no move. I said, "Rob, it's your side."

"I've been up for thirty hours," he said.

Juanito said, "I'll look."

He dropped the door on the big white mailbox with the blue and red hex sign matching the white hexes on the barn. I could see that it was empty—and the mail truck not in sight yet.

Juanito hesitated in order to let a semi pass, the wind by-blow whipping his hair and his serape, and then he came back to the car. He had a nonreturnable beer bottle in his hand, one of the little squat ones. It had been on the roadside long enough for the label to wash free, but then it has been a wet spring.

"What about this?" he said.

I was irritated. I had expected the mail to be there when we got back from the run to Frenchtown.

"Oh, throw it back!" I said. "Unless you mean to pick up all the trash along the frontage. Start with the chrome and the broken headlights up at the second phone pole."

The kid looked slightly bewildered at my vehemence. I was immediately sorry.

I switched the engine off, set the brake, and hopped out. "I'll tell you what," I said. "We'll strike a blow."

I walked to the back of the car and opened up the humpback trunk. Then I said, "Throw your bottle in there," and the kid did.

I stepped down into the front field and picked up the black and raddled truck-tire carcass I'd been meaning to police up ever since it was abandoned there. I lugged it up the grade and slung it into the trunk.

"There," I said.

The geese set up their automatic clank and clatter when we drove into the yard. Phoebe is the goose, Alexander the gander. Alexander is the main squawk of the barnyard, Phoebe just the harmony, but when they trudge around the farm, it is Phoebe who leads and Alexander who walks behind attempting to look impressive.

Fang skirted the geese and came skuttering past us, tail briefly raised in acknowledgment, a miniature panther in penguin clothes. We followed her into the house for lunch.

The house was once a carriage house. The original beams, marked with the holes and gouges of the gear used to raise and lower carriages, cross the twelve-foot ceiling of the living room, and a glass chandelier hangs from the lowest beam. The kitchen behind and the bedrooms upstairs in the original building, and the library and study in the addition, are cut to less heroic proportion. It's a tidy small house with an overwhelming living room. It has all the charms of Frank Lloyd Wright without the dim constricted little hallways Wright insisted on designing.

During lunch Cory took me aside and said, "We're going to need more bacon and a dozen eggs."

"I'll go to the Elephant this afternoon," I said.

"Get a couple of half-gallons of milk, too." Then she said, "Who is this boy, Alexei? He keeps looking around, but he doesn't say much."

I said, "He seems within the normal range of Rob's friends."

"Well, Rob's strange."

"True. I don't suppose I'd want to put this Juanito to a vote of the neighbors."

Then Cory said, "Alexei, what are we going to do about the taxes if the money doesn't come?"

I said, "We know it's coming. If worse comes to worst, I'll mail our check and we can deposit Henry's check as soon as it comes. Don't brood."

I don't worry about the money except when I absolutely have to. I juggle without thinking, and the money usually comes from somewhere when it has to be found. If I worried about money I'd be too busy to stare at my typewriter.

After lunch Rob said, "All right. Let me have a look at the Asimov idea before I collapse."

Cory and Leigh and Juanito went walking back toward the State Park land to look for the deer herd. Two lambs clowning in the plowed lands went ducking urgently under the wire fencing looking for mama at the passage of the people.

Rob and I went back inside the house and into the study. It's a small room. The people before us used it for a nursery. Now it holds our desks, two small armchairs, three small bookcases of reference books, including our prize, the eleventh-edition *Britannica* we bought for fifty dollars in Doylestown, and a catbox in the closet to keep us humble.

I scooped Wolf, our lesser cat, out of my easy chair. She's a tortoiseshell, pine needles and shadow, with an orange nose and a wide black greasepaint moustache. She keeps me company when I write. At five months she is still small enough to curl up to sleep in my typing-paper box like a mouse tucked up for winter inside a Swiss cheese. I sat down with her on my lap.

Rob said, "How's the collaboration with Cory coming?"

Cory and I have a contract for a fantasy novel in four books.

I said, "Cory has just been reading the novel I did at eighteen to give herself encouragement. She found it very encouraging."

"It's pretty bad?"

"I don't remember it too well, fortunately. Cory says it's about an incredibly narrow and suspicious young man whose only distinguishing feature is that he wants a way to leave."

"That's all?"

"That's all. I made the story up as I went along. I remember that much."

That wasn't all, but that's the way I talk to Rob. I remember there was a galactic empire in the story that did nasty things, and my hero wanted a way to leave it. If I were writing the story now, I suppose he'd try to change it.

"Hmm," said Rob. He wrote a novel at eighteen, too, making it up as he went along. The difference is that his was published and mine wasn't, so he has more to regret. "Let me see what Asimov has to say."

I searched through the clutter on the right-hand corner of my desk. While I was searching, Rob looked through the books on the opposite corner. He came up with *Personal Knowledge* by Michael Polanyi and began to thumb it.

"You weren't kidding about this?" It's a crabbed book in small type with heavy footnotes.

"I don't generally recommend it," I said. "It's epistemology. The nature and limits of knowledge."

"What have you gotten out of it?"

"The power of mind to shape the world. The need for responsible belief," I said. "Not that the idea is new. One of my ancestors . . ."

"I know. One of your ancestors founded Springfield." Rob isn't too sure whether I'm lying in whole or in part about William Pynchon. We do work at misleading each other. I like to tell the truth so that it comes out sounding like a lie for the pure artistic beauty of doing it, and I don't know how much to make of the stories Rob tells me.

"I was about to say, one of my ancestors was the brother of Hosea Ballou, who founded the Universalists. 'The Father of American Universalism.'"

"What's that?"

"They amalgamated with the Unitarians. They're all Unitarian Universalists now. And another ancestor was a cousin of Sam Adams. The point is, they were men of conscience."

"For whatever that means."

"For whatever that means." I handed him the Asimov proposal. "Here, read. This is the relevant part."

Rob read it several times. It said:

The Child as Young God. In this one we picture the society as possessing few children. If the average life expectancy has reached five hundred years, let us suppose, then the percentage of children should be, say, one-twentieth what it is now. In such a society biologic parenthood gives a person immense social prestige but no special rights in the child one has created. All children are children of society in general, with everyone anxious to share in the rights of mothering and fathering. The child is the Golden Boy/Girl of the neighborhood, and there is considerable distress if one of these children approaches adulthood without another child being born to take its place. This story can be poignant and young, for I see it told from the viewpoint of a child who is approaching adulthood and who doesn't want to lose the Goldenness of his position and is perhaps jealous of another child on the way: sibling rivalry on a grand scale.

I stroked Wolf while Rob read. Wolf was puffing but not lying quietly. She batted at my hand. I picked up a pipe cleaner and wrapped it into a coil around my little finger and dropped it on the floor. Wolf pushed off my lap, seized the little woolly spring in her jaws, growled fiercely, and ran out of the study. When she isn't batting them under the bookcases in the library and then fishing them out again, she loves to run from room to room with a pipe cleaner in her mouth, growling all the while. She's very fierce.

Rob finished reading, looked up, and said, "It's like something you've done, isn't it?"

"What's that?"

"*Rite of Passage.*"

Rite of Passage was my first novel. It's about a girl, a bright superchild on the verge of adulthood in a low-population future society. Otherwise it's not much the same.

"Hmm. I guess I see what you mean, but I don't think the similarity has to be close enough to be any problem. The thought of repeating myself is not what's hanging me up. What do you think of the proposal?"

"Well," said Rob, "when did you say the story is supposed to take place?"

I flipped to the front page of the proposal to check. "The next century. The only date mentioned is 2025. After 2025, I guess."

"Fifty years from now? Where do all the five-hundred-year-olds come from?"

I waved that aside. "I'm willing to make it one hundred or one hundred and fifty plus great expectations."

"These people would have to be alive now," Rob said.

"True," I said. "It's something to think about."

It was a good point, just the sort of thing I wanted Rob to come up with. It raised possibilities.

"Are there any restrictions on what you write?"

"Fifteen thousand words and no nasty language."

"What about nasty ideas?"

"Nothing said about that, but I don't suppose they are worried. Everybody knows I never had a nasty idea in my life."

"Oh, yes. Um-hmm," said Rob. "Look, I know this is a radical suggestion, but what's wrong with writing the idea as it stands? There is a story there."

"I know," I said. "I thought of writing it for a long time, but then when I tried, I just couldn't do it. That's where I got hung up. I like the opening phrase. I like it—'the child as young god.' That's provocative. It speaks to me. But what a distance to come for nothing. Sibling rivalry? Sibling rivalry? Why write it as science fiction? Why write it at all?"

"What's the matter, Alex?" Rob said. "Are you yearning for relevance again?"

It's a point of philosophical contention between us. Rob believes that all a story has to do is be entertaining.

I said, "Just read this." And I picked the *Whole Earth Catalog* off Cory's desk. I showed him their statement of purpose:

"We *are* as gods and might as well get good at it. So far, remotely done power and glory—as via government, big business, formal education, church—has succeeded to the point where gross defects obscure actual gains. In response to this dilemma and to these gains a realm of intimate personal power is developing—power of the individual to conduct his own education, find his own inspiration, shape his own environment, and share his adventure with whoever is interested. Tools that aid this process are sought and promoted by the *Whole Earth Catalog*."

"I'd like to speak to that," I said. "I don't have any final solutions. In fifteen thousand words I'm not going to lay out a viable and functioning and uncriticizable utopia, but for God's sake, Rob, shouldn't I at least try to say something relevant? As it is, I don't think the chances are overwhelming that any of us are going to be alive in twenty years, let alone live to five hundred."

"I know. You've said that before."

"Not in print. If the society has solved the problems Asimov says—and we're going to have to—that's what I ought to write about, isn't it? At the price of being relevant and not just entertaining. There is a story in the Asimov proposal that I want to write. Somewhere. And it isn't about a kid who doesn't want to grow up. I just have to find it."

Rob said, "How do you propose to do it?"

"Sit and stare at the typewriter until it comes to me, I guess. Or putter in the garden."

"Do you really have a garden?"

"Of course," I said. "Tom Disch tells me that a half hour in the garden every day keeps the soul pure." Tom's another writer. We tend to pass basic tips like this around our little circles. "I'm going to try it and see what good it does me."

"You do that," said Rob. "And good luck. But I've got to hit the sack now. I'm about to drop off."

I turned off my desk lamp. As I got up, I said, "By the way, just who is this kid, Juanito?"

Rob said, "He's no kid. He's your age."

I wouldn't have thought it. I'm pushing thirty. I said, "Who is he?"

"Who is he?" Rob grinned. He grins like that when he is about to say something that's more entertaining than relevant. "He's Juanito the Watcher. He's your test of relevance. He's watching and assessing. If you're okay, that's cool. But if you aren't right, he'll split without a word. Take your chances."

"Thanks a lot, friend," I said.

Rob went upstairs to flake out, and I walked down to the road to see if the mail had come. It had. My check hadn't. Junk mail.

93

I sorted the mail as I walked up the long gravel drive to the farm, and I stopped off at the main house to leave Mrs. S. her share of the bills and fliers. I collected ducklings and a spade and set to work on the garden.

I was unhappy about the check not coming, so I lit into the work with a vengeance, turning sod and earth. The ducklings, twice their Easter-morning size but still clothed in yellow down, went *reep-a-cheep* and *peep-a-deep* around my heels and gobbled happily when I turned up worms for their benefit. They knew there was someone looking out for their welfare. I was wishing I knew as much.

Spring this year was wet and late, and the only thing in bloom was the weeping willow in the back yard, with its trailing yellow catkins. The trees spread over the running hills to the next farm were still winter sticks. The day was cool enough for a light jacket in spite of the work, and the sky was partly overcast. Gardening was an act of faith that the seasons would change and warmth and flower come. Gardening is an act of faith. I'm a pessimist, but still I garden.

It's much like the times.

Our society is imperfect. That's what we say, and we shrug and let it go at that. Societies change in their own good time, and there isn't much that individuals can do to cause change or direct it. Most people don't try. They have a living to make, and whatever energies are left over they know how to put to good use. They leave politics to politicians.

But let's be honest. Our society is not just imperfect. Our society is an unhappy shambles. And leaving politics to politicians is proving to be as dangerous a business as leaving science to scientists, war to generals, and profits to profiteers.

I read. I watch. I listen. And I judge by my own experience.

The best of us are miserable. We all take drugs—alcohol, tobacco, and pills by the handful. We do work in order to live and live in order to work—an endless unsatisfying round. The jobs are no pleasure. Employers shunt us from one plastic paradise to another. One quarter of the country moves each year. No roots, no stability.

We live our lives in public, with less and less opportunity to know each other. To know anybody.

Farmers can't make a living farming. Small businessmen can't make a living anymore, either. Combines and monoliths take them over or push them out. And because nobody questions the ways of a monolith and stays or rises in one, the most ruthless monoliths survive, run by the narrowest and hungriest and most self-satisfied among us.

The results: rivers that stink of sewage, industrial waste, and dead fish. City air that's the equivalent of smoking two packs of cigarettes a day. Countryside turned to rubble. Chemical lagoons left to stain hillsides with their overflow. Fields of rusting auto bodies.

94

And all the while, the population is growing. Progress. New consumers. But when I was born, in 1940, there were 140 million people in this country, and now there are more than 200 million, half of them born since 1940. Our institutions are less and less able to cope with the growth. Not enough houses. Not enough schools. Not enough doctors or teachers or jobs. Not enough room at the beach. Not enough beaches.

Not enough food. The world is beginning to starve, and for all the talk of Green Revolutions, we no longer have surplus food. We are importing lamb from Australia and beef from Argentina now. How soon before we all start pulling our belts a notch tighter?

And our country acts like one more self-righteous monolith. Policing the world in the name of one ideal or another. In practice supporting dictators, suppressing people who want fresh air to breathe as much as any of us, with just as much right. In practice taking, taking, taking, with both hands. Our country has six percent of the world's population. We consume fifty percent of the world's production. How long will we be allowed to continue? Who will we kill to continue?

And as unhappiness rises, crime rises. Women march. Blacks burn their slums and arm themselves. Kids confront. And nobody is sure of his safety. I'm not sure of mine.

All of us are police, or demonstrators, or caught in between. And there is more of the same to come.

Our society may be worse than a shambles. Certainly, in spite of the inventions, the science, the progress, the magic at our command, our problems are not growing less. Each year is more chaotic than the one before. Marches. Demonstrations. Riots. Assassinations. Crime. Frustration. Malaise. General inability to cope.

We are in a hell of a mess. And nobody has any solutions.

Head-beatings and suppression are not solutions. Barricades are no solution. Bloody revolutions merely exchange one set of power brokers for another,

But the problems we have are real and immediate. Those who are hungry, unskilled, jobless, homeless, or simply chronically unhappy, cannot be told to shut up. The 100 million of us who are young cannot be told to go away. The 100 million of us who are old cannot be ignored. The 20 million of us who are black cannot be killed, deported, or subjugated longer at any cost short of our total ruin as human beings. And so far we have no solutions. Merely the same old knee-jerk reactions of confrontation and suppression.

There may in fact be no solutions.

We may be on the one-way trip to total destruction. These may be the last years of the human race, or the last bearable ones that any of us will know.

In times like these, gardening is an act of faith. That the seasons will change and warmth and flower come. But it is the best thing I know to do. We do garden.

95

So I worked and thought—and thought about my story. And how we might get from this now of ours to a brighter future. I'd like to believe in one.

And so I worked. As wet as the spring had been, the ground I was turning was muddy, and I was up to my knees in it. And down on my knees. And up to my elbows. Finding worms for the ducklings when I could. Some of the mud—or its cousin—appears on the fourth page of this manuscript. If our printer is worth his salt, I trust it will appear in true and faithful reproduction when you read this. When and wherever you read this, a touch of garden.

After a time Alexander the gander came waddling over to investigate us, me and the ducklings. There is truth to the adage "cross as a goose." There is also truth to the adage "loose as a goose," but that is of no moment. Alexander lowers his head, opens his beak, and hisses like an angry iguana. He and I have struck a truce. When he acts like an iguana, I act like an iguana back, and I am bigger than he is, so Alexander walks away.

The ducklings don't have my advantages, and Alexander began to run them around in circles. They peeped and ran, peeped and ran. Alexander was doing them no harm, but he was upsetting them mightily. They were too upset to eat worms, and that is upset.

After a few minutes of this I put down my spade and grabbed an armful of disgruntled goose. I held Alexander upside down and began to stroke his belly feathers. Stroke. Stroke. Stroke. After a moment he became less angry. He ceased to hiss. His eyes glazed and began to tick, every few seconds a wave passing through like the wake behind a canoe. At last I set him back on his feet and Alexander walked dazedly away. He seemed bewildered, not at all certain of what had happened to him. He shook his little head and then reared back and flapped his wings as though he were stretching for the morning. At last he found a place in the middle of the gravel drive and stood there like a sentinel, muttering to himself in goose talk.

It's what I call Upgraded Protective Reaction. I'd like to try it on our so-called leaders.

A sudden stampede of lambs back under the fence announced the return of Cory, Leigh, and Juanito from their walk to the State Park.

"Hello, love," I said. "Did you see anything?"

Cory smiled widely. "We set up the whole herd down by Three Mile Run. They bounded across the valley, and then one last one like an afterthought trying to catch up."

"Oh, fine," I said in appreciation.

Leigh nodded, smiling too. She doesn't talk a lot. She isn't verbal. I am, so we talk some, just as Rob and I talk. But when she and Rob talk, she gestures and he nods, and then he gestures and she nods. She found a worm in my well-turned mud and held it at a dangle for the smaller duckling, who gobbled it down.

Cory said, "We're going to have a look at Gemma's kittens."

"Good," I said. "I think I've put in my half-hour here. I'll come along."

"Have you gone to the Elephant yet?"

"Oh," I said. "It slipped my mind. I checked on the mail, though. The mail came."

"What?"

"Nothing good," I said. "Juanito, want to go to the Elephant with me?"

He really didn't look my age. But then I don't look my age either.

"All right," he said.

Cory and Leigh walked off toward the main house to have their look at the kittens. The ducklings hesitated and then went pell-melling after them wagging their beam ends faster than a boxer puppy.

"Now's our chance," I said.

But when Juanito and I got to the car, I remembered the truck tire.

"Just a minute," I said, and took it out of the truck. "Let me put this away while I think of it. Grab your bottle."

He fished the beer bottle from behind the spare tire where it had rolled. Then he followed me as I hefted the tire and carried it through the machine shop and into the tractor shed. I dumped the tire by the great heavy trash cans.

"Bottle there," I said, pointing to a can, and Juanito set it on top of the trash like a careful crown.

"What's going to happen to it?" he asked.

"When the ground dries, the farmer will take it all down and dump it in the woods." Out of sight, out of mind.

"Oh," he said.

We lumbered off to the Elephant in the old Plymouth. It was once a hotel, a wayside inn. Now it's a crossroads store and bar. We shop there when we need something in a hurry. It's a mile down the road. Everything else is five miles or more. Mostly more.

Juanito said, "Do you drive alone much?"

"Not much," I said. "Cory can't drive yet, so we go shopping together about twice a week." I'm conscious of the trips to Doylestown and Quakertown because they so often cut into my writing.

"Whereabouts you from, Juanito?" I asked.

"Nowhere in particular these days," he said. "I pretty much keep on the move. I stay for a while, and then I move on to the next place."

"Always an outside agitator?" I asked, maneuvering to avoid a dead possum in the road. Possums like to take evening walks down the center of the highway.

"Something like that, I guess," he said

"I couldn't do it," I said. "I hitched across the country when I was eighteen, but I couldn't take the uncertainty of always being on the move. I couldn't work without roots and routine."

On our right as we drove up the winding hill to the Elephant was a decaying set of grandstands.

"What is that?" asked Juanito.

"The Vargo Dragway," I said. "On a Sunday afternoon you could hear them winding up and gearing down all the way back at the farm. They finally got it shut down last year. It took five years. It always seems to take them five years."

I swung into the gravel parking lot beside the bar. They kept the bacon, eggs, and milk in the refrigerator behind the bar, so we went inside there rather than around to the store. There were two men drinking, but there was no one behind the bar, so we waited. Behind the bar are pictures and an old sign that says, "Elephant Hotel—1848," around the silhouette of an elephant.

One of the drinkers looked us over. A wrinkled pinchface in working clothes.

He said in a loud voice to no one in particular, "Hippies! I don't like 'em. Dirty hippies. Ruining the country. We don't want 'em moving in around here. Bums."

The man sitting at the other end of the bar seemed acutely uncomfortable and looked away from him. I leaned back against the pool table. This sort of thing doesn't happen to me often enough that I know what to do about it.

The drinker kept up the comments. At last I took two steps toward him and said something inane like, "Look, do you want everybody to dress and think like you?" It was inane because he and I were dressed much the same.

He threw his hands up in front of his face and said anxiously, "Get away from me! Get away from me!"

So I stopped and shut up and moved back to the pool table. And he returned to his comments to no one.

"Creeps! Making trouble."

From the doorway to the store Mrs. Lokay said, "Mr. Pinchen," and I turned, grateful for the interruption. She hasn't got my name straight and she knows nothing of William Pynchon or *The Meritorious Price of Our Redemption,* but at times, when I've come in for the Sunday *New York Times* and found no change in my jeans, they've put me down in the book on trust.

We followed her into the store. She said, "Don't mind him. He's mad about his stepson. He shouldn't talk to you that way. Thank you for not making trouble. We'll talk to him."

I shrugged and said, "That's all right," because I didn't know what else to say. I was calm, but I was upset.

Juanito and I waited in the store while Mrs. Lokay went back into the bar for our order. I carried the sack all the way around the building rather than walk back through and set him off again. I don't really like trouble much, and I'll go out of my way to avoid violence. I clutched the wheel tightly. Instead of driving directly home, I turned off into East Rockhill where the farm country plays out and the woods take over. I set my jaw and drove and thought about all the things I might have said.

I could have said, "That's all right, buddy. I've got a license to look like this. They call it the Constitution."

I could have said, "Have you seen Lyndon Johnson's hair hanging over his collar lately?"

I could have said, "What's the matter? Can't you tell a simple country boy when you see one?"

But I hadn't.

Juanito said, "What you ought to do is get a big plastic sack with a zipper and rig it up. You have two controls. One for warm saline solution, the other for your air line. Spend the night in that. It's very calming."

I said, "It sounds like what I've read about Barry Goldwater falling asleep on the bottom of his swimming pool. Never mind, I have something as good."

I stopped the car, pulling it off to the side of the road. On that side were woods. On the other were fountains, fieldstone walkways, planting, dogwoods, and two scaled-down pyramids, one six feet tall, the other twenty.

"What's this place?" Juanito asked.

"It's the Rosicrucian Meditation Garden," I said, and got out of the car.

The signs say it is open from eight-thirty every morning. I've never seen anyone else walking there, but no one has ever come out to ask me to prove that I was meditating.

After I walked around for a time and looked at the tadpoles swimming in the pool around the smaller pyramid—just like the Great Pyramid in Egypt—I got a grip on myself. Thank the Rosicrucians.

As we drove back to the farm, we passed the rock quarry.

"Rock quarry," I said in answer to Juanito's question. They don't call it East Rockhill for nothing.

"It won't always be that ugly," I said. "When they have the dam in, all this will be under water. Until the valley silts up, all we'll have to worry about is an invasion of speedboats."

They don't have lakes in this part of Pennsylvania, so they propose to make them.

"I know about that," Juanito said. "Cory mentioned it."

The lake will run through the State Park land. Where the deer herd is now. I don't relish the trade. Ah, but progress.

After dinner, after dark, we all gathered in the living room. Cory collected me from the study where I was taking ten minutes after dinner to stare at my typewriter.

"Are you getting anywhere?" she asked.

I shook my head. "Nothing written. Great and fleeting ideas only."

"Alexei, what are we going to do about the money?"

I said, "Henry said he mailed the check. We just have to trust it to come."

I opened my desk drawer and took out the checkbook with the undernourished balance. I wrote out a check to Internal Revenue for $371.92—more than we had to our name.

"Here," I said. "Put this in the envelope with the return. We'll mail it when the check comes from Henry, or on the fifteenth, whichever comes sooner."

Cory tucked the check under the flap of the envelope, but left it unsealed. She set it on top of the phonograph speaker by the front door.

When we came into the living room, Rob said, "Oh, hey. I almost forgot. I brought something for you."

He fished in his bag while I waited. I like presents, even if I don't lie awake on Christmas Eve in anticipation anymore. He came up with a paperback and handed it to me. It was *The Tales of Hoffman*, portions of the transcript of the Chicago Eight trial.

"Thank you," I said. "I'll read it tomorrow."

It was just the book for Rob to give me. His idea of the most pressing urgency in this country is court reform. Which is needed, as anybody who has been through the agonies of waiting in jails and courtrooms can attest. I'm more bothered by the debasement of thought and language—starting with calling the War Department the Department of Defense and proceeding down the line from there. One thumbing of the book told me Rob and I had a common meeting ground.

Rob said, "What about your story?"

I said, "I'll read the book in the bathtub."

"Are you going to spend the day in the bathtub?"

"If I have to."

We turned off the lights except for the chandelier, dim and yellow, and Cory brought out a candle and set it to pulsing in its wine-colored glass. Four of us sat on the floor around the candle, and Leigh sat in the easy chair. The light from the chandelier played off the dark veneer and outlined the carriage beams. The candlelight made the rug glow like autumn.

We talked of one thing and another, and I played records. Great Speckled Bird. Crosby, Stills, Nash and Young. The new Baez. Rob pulled out *Highway 61 Revisited,* and I got into it as I never had before.

Wolf and Fang went freaking in the candlelight, chasing each other round and round the room. I put on Quicksilver Messenger Service, the first album, and when "The Fool" reached its peak, Wolf went dashing in and out of the room, ending on the deep window ledge with the last bent note.

And sitting there into the night, we speculated.

Rob, sitting tailor-fashion, said, the conversation having carried him there in some drifting fashion, "Is there really a Mafia?"

"I don't know," I said. "You're closer to it than I am."

"I'm in daily contact with people who think there is," he said thoughtfully. "They think they belong. I could get myself killed. But what I'm asking is, is there *really* a Mafia? Or are there only a lot of people pretending?"

It's a good question. Is there really such a thing as the United States, or just a lot of people pretending?

I said, "Is there really a revolution?"

Last summer, just before Cory and I left Cambridge to move down here, in fact the day before we moved, I got a call from William James Stackman. Bill had been my roommate my senior year in prep school, and I hadn't heard from him since the day we graduated. He and I had never been friends and never seen much of interest in each other. But I told him, sure, come on over.

I was curious. In the spring, eleven years after we graduated, they'd gotten around to throwing a tenth reunion of my class. I'd had a book to finish and had to miss it, and been sorry. I'd been an outsider at Mount Hermon, and I was curious to know what had become of all the Golden People. I like to know the ending to stories, and eleven years later is a good place to put a period to high school. Bill hadn't been Golden People, either, but under the circumstances I was willing to let him serve as a substitute for the reunion.

Bill had changed. Fair enough—I've changed, too. His hair was starting to thin. He wore a mustache with droopy ends, sideburns, and a candy-stripe shirt.

We traded neutralities and ate chips and dip. He was in Cambridge to visit his former wife. He was studying theater at Cornell. He'd taken a course from Joanna Russ, a writer friend of mine, and mentioned that he had known me, and she had given him my address.

We spoke about relevance. He said that he wanted to do more than just entertain, too.

Then, in the hallway as he was leaving, he said suddenly and with more than a little pride, "I'm really a revolutionary. I'm working for the revolution."

"So am I," I said. As he disappeared around the curve in the hallway, I called, with a certain sense of joy, "So are we all."

Is there really a revolution, or are there just a lot of people pretending? What will happen when enough people pretend hard enough, long enough?

The five of us and the two cats gathered around our candle late on a spring night. If there really is a revolution, are we its leaders? What if we pretended to be long enough, hard enough?

And I wondered in how many other rooms people were gathered around a flame thinking the same things, dreaming the same dreams. There have to be new ways, there have to be better ways, and we all know it.

Later that night, when we were in bed, Cory said, "Did you find out anything about Juanito? I asked Leigh while you were gone and Rob was sleeping, but she didn't know anything. He was with Rob when Rob showed up."

I said, "All I got from Rob was a put-on." And I told her about it. We laughed and we fell asleep.

But when we got up in the morning, Juanito was gone.

Rob was still sleeping on the couch. Leigh was asleep in the second bedroom. And Juanito was gone.

I went outside to look for him. There was a full-grown ewe nibbling on the rosebush by the barn, and I waved my arms and stampeded her back under the wire, kneeling and humping to get through and leaving wool behind. But no Juanito.

There was a trash can by the front door that I hadn't left there. It was full of beer cans, soft-drink cans, rusty oil tins riddled by shot, beer bottles, plastic ice-cream dishes and spoons, cigarette butts, cigarette packs, a partly decayed magazine, and plastic, glass, and chrome from the last auto accident.

I hauled the trash can away, thinking. Cory was standing by the front door when I came back.

"I've got my story," I said. "I've got my story."

"At last," she said.

2

At the age of thirty Little John was still a child, with a child's impatience to be grown. More than anything—more than the long study and the slow ripening that his Guide assured him were the true road to his desires, as indeed they were, in part—he wished to be finished now, matured now, set free from the eternal lessons of the past now. He was a child, one of the chosen few, favored, petted, and loved just for living. On the one hand, he accepted it as his proper due; on the other, he found it a humiliation. It meant he was still only one of the Chosen, only a boy, and he wished to be a grown-up god like everyone else.

It was not that he lacked talent for it. People even more ordinary than he had made Someone of themselves. He simply hadn't yet gotten the idea. Chosen, but not yet called.

He conceived progress in his lessons to be his road to grace. It was what Samantha had taught him to believe, and believing it, he was impatient to gulp down one lesson and be on to the next. He had been led to believe that sheer accumulation was sufficient in itself, and he had closets full of notes. He had also been taught not to believe everything he was told and to think for himself, but this information was lost somewhere on note cards in one of his closets.

Impatient though he was, he tried to conceal his impatience from Samantha. He was awed by his Guide. He was awed by her age, by her reputation, by her impenetrability, and by the sheer living distance between the two of them, her and him. At the same time he accepted as right and proper that someone like her should be his Guide, for, after all, he was one of the Chosen.

Samantha encouraged his awe. Awe, like impatience, was a mark of his greenness, a measure of the distance he had to travel to reach the insight that lessons are to be applied, not merely amassed—that one thing in all the world that she could not tell him but could only leave him to discover for himself in his own time. Behind her impenetrable expression, however, she sighed at his awe, shook her head at his pride in advancement, and smiled at his wriggling impatience. And then tried his patience all the harder.

When he returned from his trip to 1381, she gave him a week to think about the experience before they began to discuss it.

"I could live in 1381 and be a god," Little John said. "It wouldn't be easy, but I saw enough. It takes endurance. That's the chief thing."

They talked about it for a month, day after day. The problems of being a peasant in those times, and still a god, relating as a god should to his fellow men. The problems of overcoming ignorance. And all the while, Little John visibly eager to be done and on the next trip.

At last she sent him on one. She sent him back to 1381 for another look from a new perspective. It is, after all, one problem to be a powerless peasant courting godhood, and quite another, as Buddha knew, to be a noble aiming for the same end. Little John didn't really see that. All he recognized was 1381 come 'round again when he felt he ought to be off to a new time and new problems of godhood. As though godliness could be measured in trips and not in what was made of them.

So he said again, "I could live in 1381 and be a god. Endurance. That's the main thing. Isn't it?"

She told him to think it over. So they talked about it for another month. And in time he finally said something about the psychological difficulty of shedding power when power is held to be a birthright.

He said, "You could give your money and property to the church. That's a way."

"Is it a godly way?"

"Well, it could be," he said. "They thought it could."

"Do you think so?"

"I met a very decent Franciscan."

"Organized godliness?"

So they talked further about the times and how it might have been possible to live well in them when your fellow wolves were ready to stay wolves until they died and ready to die to stay wolves. And Little John saw that it was indeed a very different problem than being the godly victim of wolves.

He felt that the last juice had been squeezed from the trip and was ready for the next long before Samantha was ready to send him. And when that trip was back to 1381 again for a stay in a monastery, he felt—well, not cheated, but distinctly disappointed. And he took nothing away from the experience, except for the usual stack of notes.

And after a week of discussion his impatience finally got the better of him.

He said, "Keats died at twenty-five. Masaccio died at twenty-seven, and so did Henry Gwyn-Jeffreys Moseley." He had memorized a long series of people like that, from Emily Brontë to Mikhail Yurievich Lermontov. "I'm nearly thirty. I want to do what I have to do and be done, and be out in the world."

He didn't understand the point. If you are going to do, you do. Those who wait for freedom are never free.

And Samantha, who had a reputation for tartness, said, "Yes, and Christopher Marlowe died at twenty-nine and still wrote all of Shakespeare. Do you think forty or fifty years are too many to spend in preparation for a life as long as you have ahead of you?"

"Oh, no," he said. "Oh, no." But in his heart he did. "It's just that I'm tired of 1381. It's easy to be a god then. It's too easy. I want something harder. Send me to 1970. I'm ready. Really I am."

The year 1970 had a reputation. If you could be a god then, you could be a god anytime. Little John looked on it as a final examination of sorts, and he wanted nothing more than to go.

"Do you believe you're ready to handle 1970?" Samantha asked.

"Oh, yes," he said. "Please."

He was sitting cross-legged before her. They were on the hilltop circle standing high above the community buildings and the flowering fields. The outdoor theater was here, and convocation when decisions had to be made. It was a good place to watch sunset and moonrise. His walks with Samantha often brought them here.

He was more than a little apprehensive at making his request, and he watched Samantha's face closely as she considered, anxious for the least sign of the nature of her answer, impatient for the first clue. And, as usual, her face was composed and gave him no hint.

Little John waited so long and her face was so still that he was half afraid she would fall asleep. He tried to make a still center of himself no less than three times before she spoke, and each time fell victim to wonder and lost the thread. He managed silence and reasonable stillness, and that was all.

At last she said, "This is not a matter for haste. I think we've spoken enough for today. Walk, meditate, consider your lessons."

"And then?"

"Why, come tomorrow to my chambers at the regular time." And she gave him the sign of dismissal.

So he rose, and gathered his notes, and went down the hill, leaving Samantha still sitting. He turned for a look where the stony path made a corner, and she was still sitting, looking over the valley.

Shelley Anne Fenstermacher, the other Chosen, who was ten years old and half his size and used him as a signpost as he had used Hope Saltonstall when he was younger, was waiting for him. She emptied her bucket of garbage into the hog trough, climbed down from the fence, and came, running.

"Did you ask? Did you ask? What did she say?"

"She said I was to walk and meditate," said Little John.

"What do you think it means?"

"I don't know."

He went into his room and got his latest notes from the closet. He didn't know what Samantha had in mind, but if it made the slightest difference, he meant to follow her advice. He always followed her advice to the best of his understanding.

"Can I come?" Shelley asked when he came outside. "Not today," he said. "Today I'd better walk alone."

"Oh," she said.

"I'm sorry."

So he walked in the woods and meditated and read his note cards, anxious to stuff the least and last of it into his head. If it made a difference, if she quizzed him, he meant to be ready. He had every word she had said to him down on paper. Ask him anything, he'd show he was ready.

And the next day when he and Samantha met, he was ready, that is, ready for anything except what he received, which was nothing. Samantha acted as though he had never spoken. She took up the discussion where he had broken it the day before, and they walked and they talked as usual and she never said a word about his request.

And Little John, afraid to speak, said never a word, either. He did wriggle a lot, though.

At the end of the two hours, however, she said, "A fruitful session, was it not?"

And dumbly he nodded. And then he said. "Please ma'am, have you made a decision?"

"Yes," she said. "I brought you something." She reached into her pants pocket and brought out an embroidered pouch. "It's a present. Take this grass up on Roundtop tonight, and when the moon is two full hands above the horizon, smoke it and meditate."

That night he sat up on Roundtop on his favorite log. He watched the sun set and he watched the moon rise. And he measured with his hands. When the moon was two full hands above the horizon, he filled his pipe and smoked. And he thought, and his thoughts filled the night to its conclusion. They were good thoughts, but they were all of 1970 and of graduation to godhood. It was good grass.

In gratitude he brought Samantha the best apple he could pick. He searched the whole orchard before he made a choice.

His teacher was pleased with the apple. "Thank you, Little John," she said. She ate it as they walked and wrapped up the core for the pigs.

"What conclusions did you come to last night?" she asked.

His thoughts had been ineffable, so what he said was, "Novalis died at twenty-eight."

"So he did," Samantha said.

They walked on in silence. They walked in silence for two hours. For someone her age Samantha was a brisk and sturdy walker. They circled Roundtop. The day was heavy and hot. There was a skyhawk wheeling high overhead, drifting on the current, and Little John envied it. He wanted to fly free, too.

When they reached home, walking up the lane between the ripe fields, Samantha finally spoke. "Spend the night in Mother," she said. "Then see me tomorrow."

"Without Tempus?" he asked.

"Yes, without Tempus."

"But I've never done that."

She said, "We had Mother before we had Tempus. Try it and see."

"Yes, ma'am," he said.

He had kept Shelley Anne apprised of his progress. When she sought him out after dinner, sitting on the porch in the warm and quiet of the evening, he told her what Samantha wished him to do.

"Really?" she said. "I never heard of that. Does she expect you to change your mind?"

"I don't know," he said. "But I have to do it if she wants me to."

While they were talking, Lenny came out on the porch. "Hi, children," he said. "Are you going to the convo tonight?"

Shelley Anne said she was. Little John said he was busy and had other plans. When Lenny left, Shelley Anne went with him, and Little John was left alone in the evening. He could see the fire up on Roundtop and hear the voices.

At last he went inside and set up Mother, just as though he were going on a trip, but without the drug. He checked the air line. He checked the solution line. And he set the alarm to rouse himself.

He undressed himself and kicked his clothes into the corner. It was something he'd been known to do since he had decided that it wasn't necessarily ungodlike. He picked them up himself sometime and as long as he did that eventually he figured it was all right.

Then he unzipped Mother and climbed inside. It was overcool on his bare skin until he got used to it, like settling down on a cold toilet seat. He fitted the mouthpiece of the air line into place. He didn't close the bag until he was breathing comfortably.

As the warm saline solution rose in the bag, he cleared his mind. He basked and floated. He had never used Mother except on official trips and had never thought to wonder why it was called Mother. Now he leaned back, drifted and dreamed in Mother's warm arms, and she was very good to him.

Strange undirected dreams flitted through his mind. Pleasant dreams. He saw Shelley Anne Fenstermacher as an old woman, and she nodded, smiled, and said, "Hi," just as she always did. He saw Samantha as a ten-year-old with a doll in her arms. He saw his old friends in the monastery in 1381, making their cordials and happily sampling them. And he wheeled through the blue skies along with his friend the skyhawk, coasting on the summer breeze high above the temperate world.

And then he passed beyond dreams.

In the morning, the cool, calm morning, he sat in the slanting sunlight listening to the song of a mockingbird shift and vary, and tried to pick it out with his eye in the leaf-cloaked branches of a walnut tree. At last Samantha came out to join him. He thought he could see the ten-year-old in her, even without the doll.

She said, "How did the night pass?"

Though his skin was prunish, he didn't think to mention it. "Well," he said. "I never spent a night like that before." But already he planned to again. "It was very soothing."

"Ah, was it?" And then, without further preamble, she said, "Do you still want to travel to 1970?"

"Yes, ma'am," he said. "I'm ready for it. I'll show you I am. What else do you want me to do first?"

"Nothing. If you still want to go, if you're still determined to go, I'll send you."

Little John nearly jumped up and gave her a hug, but awe restrained him. If Samantha had been asked, perhaps she would have had him retain that much awe.

So Little John got his trip to 1970, his chance to graduate. Mother was readied again, not for general wandering, but for a directed dream. Samantha calculated the mix of Tempus herself.

She said, "This won't be like any other time you've been."

"Oh, I know that," he said.

"Do you? I almost remember it myself, and it wasn't like now."

"I can handle it."

"Let us hope," she said. "I'm going to see that you are in good hands. Nothing too serious should happen to you."

"Please," he said. "Don't make it too easy."

"Say that again after you've returned. I'm going to give you a mnemonic. If you want to abort the trip and come back before the full period, then concentrate on the mnemonic. Do you understand?"

"I understand," he said.

She checked him out on all points, once, twice, and then again before she was satisfied. Then, at last, he climbed inside Mother and drank the draft she handed him.

"Have a good trip." she said.

"Oh, I will, ma'am. Don't worry about that," Little John said as the sack filled and he drifted away from her, back in time, back in his mind. "I expect to have a *good* time."

That's what he said. Nothing hard about being a god in 1970. They had had all the materials, and by now he had had experience in godhood. He was ready.

But he came back early. And he didn't have a *good* time.

In fact, he was heartsick, subdued, drained. He wouldn't speak to Shelley Anne Fenstermacher. And without prompting by Samantha or anyone he disappeared into the woods to be by himself, and he didn't come back for two days.

He spent the whole time thinking, trying to make sense of what he had seen, and he wasn't able to do it. He missed two whole sessions with Samantha. And when he did turn up at last, he didn't apologize for being missing.

"You were right," he said simply. "I wasn't ready. Send me back to 1381 again. Please."

"Perhaps," Samantha said.

"I don't understand. I don't understand. I knew things weren't right then, but I didn't think they would be like that. Taxes was what they cared about. They didn't even see what was going on. Not really. And it was just before the revolution. Are things always that bad before they change?"

"Yes," she said. "Always. The only difference this time is the way things changed. And you didn't see the worst of it. Not by half, Little John."

"I didn't?" he said in surprise. "I thought it must be."

She was too kind to laugh. "No."

"But it was so awful. So ruthless. So destructive."

Samantha said, "Those people weren't so bad. As it happens, they were my parents."

"Oh I'm sorry, ma'am," he said.

"And your grandparents weren't so different. And they did learn better. That's the important thing to remember. If you take away nothing else, remember that. If they hadn't changed, none of us would be here now."

He cried out, "But they had so much power. They all had the power of gods, and they used it so badly."

Little John may have been stupid, abysmally stupid, he may have been green, and he may have had more years ahead of him than little Shelley Anne Fenstermacher before he was fit to be let out in the world, but there were some things he was able to recognize. Some things are writ plain.

3

Endings of stories come easy. It is the beginnings, when anything is still possible, that come hard.

Start now.

Sky Blue

Sky Blue waits for Landlord Thing. He holds the most powerful gun Groombridge Colony can hand him. He sits on a small unnaturally comfortable rock in space.

Overhead the heavens wheel. Beneath him the brown planet whirls. Like a midge on a grain of wheat, he passes between millstones.

✦

A fat spaceship blipping on business like a slickery black watermelon seed went astray one day between Someplace Important and Someplace Important and wound up lost on the great black floor of the galaxy. It was the pilot's fault, if you want to blame someone. He was stargazing at the wrong moment, misapplied his math, and then fritzed the drive in a fruitless attempt to recoup.

The ship came to drift without power in a place where the stars glittered nervously and all the skies were strange. It was weird there, and after one look the curtains were hastily drawn. Nobody wanted to look outside except one boy named Harold who held the curtains in his hands and peeked.

The pilot killed himself in another fit of overcompensation, but nobody noticed. They were all dead men in their dark powerless ship in that strange icicle corner of the universe, but nobody would say so. They huddled together in various parts of the ship and talked of usual matters.

Now, this wasn't just any old ship. This was a big-deal colony ship on its way to settle Groombridge 1618/2, a planet foredoomed for importance. It was so juicy a place that you had to pay high for a slice of the pie.

The passengers on this ship had all paid. They were men of moxie. They knew the answers. Here's a topper: Triphammer and Puddleduck, who had more answers than anybody, were aboard, too. They were along for the dedication ceremonies and a quick return home. They moved in high circles.

Being lost so suddenly was as painful and frustrating to Triphammer and Puddleduck as an interrupted fuck. Suddenly their answers were of no use to them. Oh, it hurt.

Triphammer, Puddleduck, and Mount Rushmore were the highest huddle of all. They gathered by a candle in one room. Triphammer paced frantically, Puddleduck nodded at appropriate moments, and Mount Rushmore loomed. Harold looked out through the curtains into the universe.

Triphammer said, "Oh, losings. Screamie! The action, pop-a-dop." Her face could not contain her regret.

Puddleduck nodded. "Misery," he said.

"Misery," said Mount Rushmore.

Harold said, "There's somebody walking by outside."

He was the son of Triphammer and Puddleduck. They hadn't given him a proper name yet, and he wasn't sure they meant to keep him. He needed them, so until he discovered their intention he was playing quiet.

"Out of mind," said Puddleduck, beating his brow. "Replebed and forgot."

Triphammer held a sudden hand before her mouth. "Oh, speak not."

"Misery," said Mount Rushmore.

Harold waved. "Hey, he sees me." He waved again.

Triphammer and Puddleduck didn't hear what Harold said. It was his fault. He didn't speak up. They had told him that it was his fault if he wasn't heard.

Great Mount Rushmore pounded himself on the chest. "Gelt gone blubbles. Misery. Misery."

Puddleduck said, "Misery."

"Miz," said Triphammer.

There was a tug at her sleeve and she looked down. It was Harold waiting for her attention.

"Again?"

Harold put on his best face and straightened to the full extent of his undergreat height, which was what he had been taught to do when he asked for things.

"Can I go out and play, Mama? Please?" he asked, waving at the window.

Triphammer's expression made it clear that any request at this moment was a fart in church, and that the gods were displeased with the odor.

"What what? Bird twitter while empires fall? Shame and a half, Harold, you nameless twirp. (Forbearing, but not much.) Forbidding."

"I'm really extremely sorry I asked," Harold said.

There was sudden consternation in the room. Out of nowhere—certainly not through the door—had come a being altogether strange. And here it was, making five now around the candle. It had pseudopods and big brown eyes.

"Wowsers, a creature!" said Mount Rushmore. He backed away. "Bling it."

The creature looked at Harold and said, "Are you coming or not?"

Triphammer had a tender stomach. She tried without success to stifle a retch.

"Faa," she said. "Bling it."

Harold said, "I'm not allowed. I asked already."

Puddleduck looked around and around the room, nodding furiously and muttering constant instructions to himself lest he forget, but there was nothing ready at hand to bling the creature with. Puddleduck waved his arms like frustrated semaphores.

"But of course you are allowed," the creature said. "If you want to come with me, you may. I don't forbid anyone."

It broke off abruptly and looked around at Mount Rushmore, Triphammer and Puddleduck as they recoiled.

"Is something the matter?" it asked, flexing its polyps in wonderment.

Triphammer looked at it with a glance like a pointing finger and vomited reproachfully.

"I beg your pardon," the creature said.

It gathered itself together, contracting its pseudopods into the main mess of its body. Its brown eyes bulged hugely and then blinked. And, speedy quick as a hungry duck, its appearance was altered. Where there had formerly been an—ugh—amorphous monster, now there stood a dark sweet old man with a short brushy mustache and a nose like a spearhead, as definite as geometry. He was dressed in a khaki shirt and shorts to the knee and sturdy walking shoes.

"Is that better?"

"Oh, scruples!" said Triphammer.

And it was better. Triphammer and Puddleduck knew how to deal with people. Creatures were another matter. They brightened to see him, for the old man looked like a mark, and they desperately needed someone to take advantage of.

The sweet old fud looked around that dim room there in the dead and silent spaceship as though it were a very strange place.

"Pardon me if I'm being overcritical of your favored pastimes, but is this really what you like to do? It seems limited. You could be outside on a day like this," he said.

Mount Rushmore shook his head like a rag mop. "Not happy, not happy," he said. "Oh, not. Gelt gone blubbles, you know."

"Lost and out of it," Triphammer explained. "Unjuiced, weenied and paddleless."

"Screamie-a-deamie!" said Puddleduck. "Massive frust! In the name of our importance, unpickle us."

"I had the feeling things weren't just right," the old man said. "Don't ask me how I knew. I have an instinct for these things. Well, I'll help you as much as I can. Come along with me."

He turned and walked abruptly through the wall of the ship. Gone. And no one followed him.

He stuck his head back into the room, looking like a well-seasoned wall trophy.

"Well, come along," he said reasonably.

Harold, smiling brightly, took a happy step forward. Then he noticed that Triphammer and Puddleduck were standing stock still. Above all else, he desired to please them and be kept. He couldn't help himself. He stopped and wiped his smile away, and then he didn't move, he didn't breathe. He did check to see what his parents did, eyes flicking left, eyes flicking right, under their eyelash awning,

"Aren't you coming?" the old man asked. "I am willing to help you."

Mount Rushmore boggled at him. Triphammer and Puddleduck, with infinitely greater presence of mind, shook their heads silently.

"What's the matter?"

"Nary a feather to fly with," they said. "We told you that, pooper. We're stuck, that's what."

The dear old goat stepped back into the ship and nibbled his mustache.

"Are you sure you can't follow me?" he asked.

"Can't."

"You could if you wanted."

"Can't."

"Why don't you just give it a try?"

"Can't, and that's that."

"Well, what are we to do, then?" the old man asked. "It seems we are at an impasse."

He thought. They all thought, except Harold. He watched. He witnessed.

Then the old man said, "I have it. I knew I'd think of something. Mechanical means."

And hardly were the words out of his mouth when the lights came on in the room, at first flickering as dim as the candle, then coming up strong and smiling.

The phone rang. Puddleduck answered.

"Quack?"

"Kiss us," the excited face in the visor said. "We've made the auxiliaries putt. We can limp to haven."

"Grats," said Puddleduck. "But can't we blif for home?"

"No way. The mains will have to be made anew."

"Oh," said Puddleduck, and rang off.

"Can you come along now?" asked the old man.

The ship limped where he directed, and in time they came to a planet, green as Eden. It wasn't half bad, except that it wasn't near anything. They went into orbit around it, keeping close company with a small pitted whizzer of a satellite.

"That's my seat, that rock," said the old man. "That's where I sit to oversee when I visit. This is one of my planets. It's small, but it's a good home. If you will love it well, nurture and tend it, and take good care of it, I'll lend it to you. How about that?"

"Done," they said.

"Done it is, then," said the old man. "Well, I must be about my business. I'll check back shortly to see how you are getting on. If you need me, sit on my rock and give me a call. I'll show up in no time. Now, if you will excuse me."

"Wait, wait," they said. "Before you tippy along, we must know—who are you, freaky old pooper?"

"You may call me Landlord Thing," the old man said. He turned to Harold. "Are you coming?"

Harold looked at his parents with one quick sweep of his eyes and then he shook his head as fast as a suckling lamb can shake its tail. "No," he said. "Thank you."

Landlord Thing took a hitch on his shorts and stepped lightly through the wall into space. Then, just as they were opening their mouths to speak of him, he stuck his head back through the wall one last time.

He said, "Mind you, take good care of my world."

And then like a guru skipping barefoot through Himalayan icefields he was gone.

✦

Sky Blue waits for Landlord Thing. He has a heavy gun in his hands and he means to bling the Thing good and proper. That's what he is there for, sitting on that dinky rock in space.

His mind wheels with the high heavens above. His mind whirls with the bare brown planet below. His mind is ground to flour between great stones.

He thinks, "Come. Come. Come and be killed."

✦

They called the planet Here or East Overshoe or This Dump. They didn't love it. They didn't take care of it. They didn't nurture and tend it, or any of the other stuff they promised. They didn't plan to stay, so why should they?

They called themselves Groombridge Colony. As soon as they fixed the drive, they meant to tippy along. They meant to blif. They meant to go. Onward to Groombridge 1618/2 and the way things were supposed to be. After all, they had paid good money.

Since Triphammer and Puddleduck wanted to get back into the galactic big time worse than anybody—quack, yes!—they were in charge. Like proper leaders, they exhorted everyone to do his utmost.

Recall: to fix the drive, the mains had to be made anew. To do the job, they needed some of This, some of That, and some of the Third Thing.

They didn't wait a moment after they set down. They dug shafts like moles. They built towers like ants. They hammered and smoked and smelted and forged. They electrolyzed and transmuted. They ripped and raped and turned the planet upside down in the search for what they needed. They turned the green planet brown, these Groombrugians. They really made a mess of things.

Here's the hard part. This is rare in the universe. They came by it in no time. That you can't just buy at any corner store. They found twice as much as they needed. But the Third Thing, which everywhere else is common as dirt, was elusive as the wild butterfly of love. After years and years they had barely accumulated a single pood of the stuff, and that wasn't nearly enough.

When they were planning to leave East Overshoe come morning, the Groombridge gang cared naught a tiddle what they did to the planet. When it sank in finally that they weren't leaving all that soon, there were some who began to worry what Landlord Thing might make of their handiwork.

It wasn't anything you could sweep under the carpet and smile about. It was more obvious than that. Well, yes.

It was Triphammer who began to fuss about it first. And Puddleduck caught it from her. But it was Puddleduck who thought of the answer, and Triphammer who found it worthy. It often worked out that way. They were a team.

Their answer was to set Sky Blue on that whirling rock to slay their monster for them. Within their terms, it was a perfect solution. Puddleduck remembered that Landlord Thing had said he would come instanter than powdered breakfast if he were called from that rock. Ha! at their beck, when they were ready for him, and then, bling! Then they would have all the time and peace they needed to rip the planet to the heart. And Sky Blue was the man.

They shook hands on it, and set out to look for Sky Blue. That was what they called Harold now. They called him Sky Blue because he was so out to lunch. But they had need of him now. He could shoot.

Yes, he could shoot. It was one of the things he did that no one else would think of doing. Sky Blue had grown up eccentric.

The heart of it was that he took responsibility seriously. He had been there when the agreement with Landlord Thing was made and he had said, "I promise," in his heart. And like the loser he was, he wasted his time trying to live by his word.

Where things were brown, he did his best to green them again. Futile. Where the Groombridge gang pared and cored the planet, he repaired and corrected. Outnumbered. Where they ripped and raped, he nurtured and tended. That is, he tried. Every day he fell further behind.

Where it was necessary for balance, he shot things. He would think, "Come. Come and be killed." And because all of Landlord Thing's planet knew he had their best interests at heart, they would come, and he would kill them with love and sorrow.

If Triphammer and Puddleduck were not consummate politicians, hence tolerant, and if they hadn't enjoyed the fresh meat he brought home from time to time, they would have disowned him. They probably should have anyway. As it was, they named him Sky Blue and allowed him his amusement.

And because Triphammer and Puddleduck were Triphammer and Puddle-duck, Groombridge Colony went along.

As Mount Rushmore said, speaking for the community, "Pretties need dippies for contrast, nay say?"

When Triphammer and Puddleduck found Sky Blue, their boy was up to his ears in dirt, beavering away making a large hole smaller. In the time it would take him to fill it, three more would be dug in search of the Third Thing, but he was not one to complain. He knew his obligation, even if no one else did, and he lived by it.

"Hey there, dull thud, child of ours," they said. "Muckle that shovel for the mo and hie thee hither. Busyness beckons."

Sky Blue did as they directed. He stuck his shovel in the sand and hur-ried over to them. He still yearned for their good opinion whenever it was compatible with what he thought was right. Oh, tell the truth—he might even strike a compromise with right for the sake of their good opinion. They had him hooked.

"Yes, yes," he said. "Progen lovies, put my knucks to your purpose."

"Oh best bubby, trumpets for your eagerness," they said. They produced the gun, Groombridge Colony's most powerful splat-blinger, and placed it in his hands. "Elim Landlord Thing for Mum and Dad, that's a good dumb-dumb son."

"Bling Landlord Thing? Where? Why? Oh, say not!" And Sky Blue tried to return the gun to Triphammer and Puddleduck, but they would have none of it.

"Yours," said Puddleduck.

"Yours," said Triphammer.

"Nay, nay, not I," said Sky Blue.

Triphammer said. "Do you treacle-drip for This Dump, nurdy son of mine?"

"Certain sure, I do."

"One boot, two boot, when the rent is due, and out go you. You lose."

"Misery mort," said Sky Blue. "Me, too? But no—holes ubiquate. I'll screege from view."

"Ho, ho, Hermit Harold, all by his onesome," said Puddleduck. "You lose."

"Unhappies," said Sky Blue. And he looked at the equalizer in his hands. "What what? Oh, double what what?"

Triphammer drew close and whispered sweet in his ear: "Bling him to frags, and lovings and keepings."

How's that for a promise?

◆

So Sky Blue waits for Landlord Thing. Above above. Below below. He sits on that rock, the call gone forth, and waits.

And there Landlord Thing is! The old man wades through space toward the rock where Sky Blue sits.

Trembling, barely able to control himself, Sky Blue raises the gun in his hands—butt coming up to his shoulder, muzzle swinging down to point. The gun is aimed, centered on his brushy mustache. And Sky Blue pulls the trigger.

A beam lances and there is a blinding flash. The face piece of Sky Blue's spacesuit polarizes at the glare.

He casts the rifle from him into space, sobbing. His eyes clot with tears, He cries harder than he can remember, as though he has lost forever his last infinitely precious hope.

But as he sits there desolate, a pseudopod wraps comfortingly about his shoulders, and a warm voice says, "How have things been? Tell me about them."

Sky Blue turns his head and opens his eyes. There, sitting beside him on that unnaturally comfortable rock, is Landlord Thing as first he saw him through the tight-pinched curtains so long before. Warm brown eyes and pseudopods.

"Nothing is right," says Sky Blue. "Look down there at your planet. It's been turned to brown. Nobody likes it there on your world but me. Everyone else wants to get away and no matter how I try, I can't clean it up."

"That isn't the worst thing in the world," says Landlord Thing. "We'll see what can be done. Follow me."

He shifts around to the other side of the rock and Sky Blue follows.

"This is the top side," says Landlord Thing. "Now look."

Sky Blue looks up at Here. It fills the sky above him. He is overflooded with a great warm wave of mystery and awe. It is momentarily too much for him and he must close his eyes and look away before he can look back again.

"I never realized," he says.

Landlord Thing says, "You can heal the world. You can make it green again."

"Me?" says Sky Blue. "No, I can't."

"Oh, but you can," says Landlord Thing. "I have faith in you, Sky Blue."

Sky Blue looks at him in astonishment. He hasn't told Landlord Thing his new name.

"How can I do it?" asks Sky Blue. "I don't know how."

"You must take yourself out of yourself and put it in the planet. Nurture and tend the planet. Make it well again. Concentrate very very hard. Look at the planet and spread yourself so thin that you disappear."

Sky Blue is unsure. Sky Blue does not believe. But Sky Blue is determined.

He looks up at Here, dominating the sky like a great mandala. It is a wave—he drowns. It is a wind—he dissipates. It is a web—but he is the spinner, spinning thin, spinning fine, losing himself in the gossamer. He handles the world tenderly.

Landlord Thing watches. Landlord Thing witnesses. And above them in the sky, the world turns green.

When Sky Blue reassembles, he is not the same. He looks once at Landlord Thing and smiles, and then they sit there in silence. They have called. They wait for their call to be answered. And after a time a ship lifts from the planet and comes to the rock.

It is Triphammer and Puddleduck. They wave to Sky Blue as though he were alone. He and Landlord Thing go aboard the ship. Triphammer and Puddleduck act as though they are blind to Landlord Thing's presence. Sky Blue removes his spacesuit.

Triphammer and Puddleduck say, "Gasp, splutter, quack! No, no, no! The frust just must bust—screamie-a-deamie!"

Sky Blue is bewildered. He turns to Landlord Thing and says, "I don't understand a word of it."

Landlord Thing waves a sympathetic polyp. "It can be that way at first. Listen to them very closely. Concentrate on every word and some of it will come clear."

So Sky Blue cranes an ear to the words of Triphammer and Puddleduck and concentrates harder than when he healed the planet. And, just barely, meaning filters through. They are nattering about the sudden return of the planet to its original condition. In the process, it seems, their castles have all been thrown down. Their mines are theirs no longer. Their stockpiles of This, That, and the Third Thing have disappeared in a lash flicker. They quabble about what has happened and what they should do.

Sky Blue listens to them until they run dry. Then he shakes his head in wonder.

"Offense. Unfair. Disrespect," says Triphammer.

Puddleduck nods. "*Wanh* for our importance," he says. "All toobies."

Landlord Thing nods. "All toobies, indeed," he says. "Tell them they are being given a second chance. Their only hope is if they take good advantage of it."

Sky Blue relays the message. "Return to Here," he says, "and learn to live there. It's your life. Use it well."

Triphammer and Puddleduck are astounded at these words. Their jaws drop like a gallows trap. Their nurdy son has never spoken to them like this before.

Landlord Thing says, "Come along, Sky Blue. I have some people to introduce you to. I think you'll like them."

He passes through the wall as though it were nothing to him. Sky Blue looks at his parents one last time, and then he follows. He steps through the wall of the ship and into space.

"I'm coming," he says to Landlord Thing, striding the stars before him.

Sky Blue has held the curtains clutched tight in his hands this long time. Now he throws them open wide and peaks.

When the Vertical World Becomes Horizontal

The rain is coming closer, sending the heat running before it. I can see the rain, hanging like twists of smoke over the roofs. The city will be scrubbed clean.

This is an acute moment. The wind is raising gooseflesh on my arms. I can feel the thunder as electricity and the electricity as thunder. Down in the street I hear voices calling around the corner. I think I even hear the music.

This is the moment. I know it's here.

I've been waiting so long. I'll savor this last bit of waiting. The dark is so dark, so close-wrapped. The electricity is white. The streets are going to steam.

There has never been a better moment since the world began. This is it! It's here.

It's never happened since the last time, and it's going to happen now. The beginning of the world was a better moment. It was exalting. As nearly as I can tell, there have been two good moments since. I missed them both.

I'm going to be here for this one.

So are you.

I know the sun is baking the sidewalks now. The heat is on now. But listen with your skin. Rain is in the air.

It's going to be good. When you see the rain and steam and sun and people all mixed together in the afternoon, you'll know their tune is the one that's been in your head all along. Close your eyes. Feel the wind rising.

I'll tell you how good it's going to be. I'll tell you what it was like for someone who knew even less than you do about what is happening:

◆

Woody Asenion was raised in the largest closet of an apartment at 206 W. 104th St. in Manhattan. Once there had been four—Papa, Granny, Mama, and him—but now there were only two. There was room now for Woody to stretch out, but at night he still slept at Papa's feet, just like always, for the comfort of just like always.

Woody had never been out of the closet without permission. Well, once. When he was very small, he had slipped out into the apartment one night and wandered the aisles alone until the blinking and bubbling became too frightening to bear and the robot found him, shook a finger at him and led him back home. He had never done it again.

That was before they moved to 206 W. 104th St., back when they lived in the old closet. The new closet was about the same size. Its shape was different. That had taken growing used to.

The closet was the same size, but the apartment outside was larger. He wouldn't dare go out there at night.

But on this day the vertical world was turning horizontal. People were no longer cringing and bullying. They were starting to think of other things.

It was already this close: When Woody's father, who was very vertical, flung the door of the closet open while in the grip of an intense excitement, Woody had his hand on the knob and the knob half-turned. That was a quarter-turn more than he usually dared when he toyed with strange thoughts of an afternoon.

Mr. Asenion broke Woody's grip on the knob with an automatic gesture. "You promised your papa," he said and rapped the knuckles with a demodulator he happened to have in his hand. But the moment was quickly forgotten in his excitement.

"I had it all backward! I had it all backward! It's the particular that represents the general."

That was part of the vertical world turning horizontal, too. Since he had left Columbia University in 1928, Mr. Asenion had been working on a Dimensional Redistributor. He had been seeking to open gateways to the many strange dimensions that exist around us. He had never been successful.

He had never been successful in the vertical world, either. He had fallen out of the bottom. He told himself that he did not fit because he hadn't yet found his place. He was very vertical. He knew the power that would be his if he ever invented the Dimensional Redistributor, and so labored all the harder through the many years of failure. It was his key to entry at the top of the pyramid.

But suddenly, on this day when the vertical world was turning horizontal—enough people being ready for that to happen—he had been struck with a crucial insight as he was standing with a demodulator in his hand. He suddenly saw that you could turn things around. The answer was *not* many gateways to many strange dimensions. It was *one* gateway. One gateway into this world.

He knew how to build it, too.

"I'll need a 28K-916 Hersh.," he said. That was a vacuum tube with special rhodomagnetic properties that had been out of stock for forty-two years.

There was only one place in New York, perhaps in all the world, where such a tube might be found—Stewart's Out-of-Stock Supply. Stewart's has *everything* that is out of stock. Mr. Asenion had seen a 28K-916 Hersh. there in 1934. However, he had no need of it then.

Stewart's has everything out of stock that an out-of-date inventor might need, but they may not sell it to you if they disapprove of you. Mr. Asenion had not been welcome in Stewart's since the fall of 1937 when he had incautiously announced his intentions under stern cross-questioning.

"Woodrow," Mr. Asenion said, "you must go to Stewart's in Brooklyn. They will have a 28K-916 Hersh. It's all I need to finish my machine. Then I will rule the world."

"Brooklyn?" said Woody. "I've never been to Brooklyn, Papa."

He had heard of Brooklyn from the lips of his dead mother. She said she had been to Brooklyn once.

Sometimes he had thought of Brooklyn as of some strange wonderland when his father was out experimenting in the apartment and he was alone in the closet.

He had seen the Heights of Brooklyn once, the great towering wall of rock that conceals all but the spires of the land beyond. Or he believed that he had. Sometimes he thought that he must have imagined it when he was small. He would know if he should ever see it again.

But to go to Brooklyn? "It's farther than I've ever been. Why don't *you* go, Papa?"

"There are reasons," said Mr. Asenion with dignity. "You wouldn't understand. At this special moment I must stay with my machine. Further inspiration may come to me at any moment. I must be ready."

He had a point. Lack of success in the vertical world is no index of lack of skill in invention. He had something in the Dimensional Redistributor. What's more, his insight on this day when the vertical world was turning horizontal was valid: With the particular representing the general, one reversed (and modified) gateway, and a 28K-916 Hersh., his Dimensional Redistributor would work. And there are even alternatives to the 28K-916 Hersh., if you want to know, which inspiration could reveal and ingenuity confirm.

Woody shook his head in fear and excitement. "I can't do it."

Mr. Asenion heard only the fear and reacted to that. "There's no need to be afraid, just because it's Brooklyn. I'll write out the way, just as I always do. And I'll send the robot along to keep you company. You will be safe as long as you stick to the path and carry your umbrella."

The robot nodded dumbly from behind Mr. Asenion. When Woody ran errands in the neighborhood, the robot always kept him silent company.

"I don't want to," said Woody.

"I command you to go. You owe it to me, your father, for all the many years I've fed you and kept a roof over your head and let you sleep at my feet."

He was right if you look at things vertically.

"All right," said Woody. "I'll go."

Mr. Asenion patted Woody on the head. "Good boy," he said.

When the Dimensional Redistributor was in operation, he meant to pat the whole world on the head, when it did what he said. "Good boy," he would say.

As soon as Mr. Asenion turned away, Woody kicked the robot. It could not complain, but it did look reproachful.

So there you have Woody Asenion—raised in a closet, lower than the lowest in the vertical world, somebody who knows even less than you do about what is going on. He is even more limited than you know. Last birthday, Woody was thirty-seven years old.

Woody gave the robot one of his hands and held his map and directions tight in the other so as not to lose his way, said good-bye to his father, who turned away to putter with his machine, and with one deep breath cleared the first three thresholds—the door of the closet, the door of the apartment, and the door of the building at 206 W. 104th St. in Manhattan—and stood blinking in the sun, heat, and sidewalk traffic. There were threats, noise, and distraction all about him. Cars clawed and roared at each other, seeking advantage. Signs in bright colors loomed at Woody yelling, "Number *1* in Quantity" and "Do As You're Told, Son" and "Step Backward." It was confusing to Woody, but he knew that if he did not panic, if he followed his instructions and stayed on the path and did not lose his umbrella, he could pass through the danger unscathed.

He let his breath out. The air in the street was wet and sticky. The sunlight was oppressive. He seized the robot's hand all the tighter, and they set off down the street. It was the robot who carried the rolled umbrella.

The people they threaded through were these:

Three white men—one in a business suit, one old, one a bum.

Two black men—one grateful, one not.

A student.

Three old women.

Five Puerto Ricans of both sexes and various ages.

Two young women—one bitter, one not.

A Minister of the Church of God.

A group of snazzy black buccaneers talking bad.

And a little girl who also lived at 206 W. 104th St. in Manhattan.

"Hi, Woody," she said. "Hi, It."

Five of these twenty-five saw Woody Asenion walking along the street with his hand in the hand of a tall skinny cuproberyl robot that carried an umbrella, and knew him instantly to be their inferior. All the others weren't sure, or else they didn't care about things like that anymore.

That's how close the vertical world was to turning horizontal. But it hadn't happened yet.

The map led Woody directly to the subway station. There was a hooded green pit, an orange railing, and stairs leading down.

In the old closet, when Woody was small, he could feel the force of the subway train. When it prowled, the building would shudder. His mother had told him not to be afraid.

Sitting on a stool in the booth was a blue extraterrestrial being. It looked something like a hound, something like Fred MacMurray. It was dressed in a blue Friends of the New York Subway System uniform.

Woody looked at his directions. They advised him to ask for tokens.

"Four toll tokens," he said to the alien in the tollbooth. "Please."

The alien said, "Are you Woody Asenion?"

Woody ducked behind the robot in surprise. "How do you know my name?"

The alien waved it away, and turned for the telephone. "Just forget I asked. It really isn't important, Woody. Forget the whole thing."

He dialed a number. While he waited for the ring, he said, "I'd only buy two toll tokens, if I were you. You'll only need two. Oh, hello, Clishnor. Listen—'It's about to rain.' Right."

Woody looked at his directions. They said to buy four toll tokens. He set his jaw.

"Four toll tokens, please," he said bravely. "And how did you know me?"

"I was set here to ask," said the blue alien in the blue Friends of the New York Subway System uniform. "I ask everybody if they're you. We're here for the rain, and we wanted to have warning."

"Rain?" said Woody.

"The weather forecast says that when Woody Asenion goes to Brooklyn, it's going to rain." The alien passed four tokens under the grill of the booth. "Now, you just see if it doesn't."

"Oh, is that how it is," said Woody, who wasn't sure how weather forecasts were made. He hadn't thought he was that important, though of course he was. Well, he was safe. The robot had the umbrella.

Woody and the robot turned away. There was a white electric sign on the other side of the booth. It had a black arrow and black letters that blinked and said: "To the Subway."

They followed the arrow. Behind them the tollbooth quietly closed and the yellow light went off.

The directions and map mentioned the black arrow and the sign. They walked through the darkness between the metal pillars until they came to another stair. An automatic machine guarded the top of the stair. It held out a hand until Woody gave it two toll tokens, and then it let them pass.

There was light at the bottom of the stairs and the stairs were very tall. Down they walked, down and down, until Woody was not at all sure that he wanted to go to Brooklyn at all, even to buy his father a 28K-916 Hersh. so that he could finish his Dimensional Redistributor and control the world.

The station was a great vaulted catacomb. The walls were covered with grime-coated mosaics celebrating the muses of Science and Industry. Woody and the robot were all alone on the echoing platform.

Then suddenly a wind blew through the station, fluttering the map and directions in Woody's hand. A chill wind. Following the wind, the squealing, clashing, and roaring of the great behemoth. Following the noise, the subway train itself. It hurtled into the station under the tight command of the pilot, whom Woody could see seated in the front window, and came to a stop with a tortured screech of metal. A voice more commanding than Mr. Asenion's said, "Passengers will stand clear of the moving platform as trains enter and leave the station!" A shelf of metal moved silently out to the train as a pair of doors opened in front of them. Woody squeezed the robot's hand hard.

The robot nodded reassuringly and led Woody onto the metal shelf and then aboard the train. One last look. The shelf began to withdraw and the doors closed like a trap, and Woody was committed.

Woody was afraid, as you can well imagine. He sat, uneasy as a cricket, on the seat next to the robot. Blackness hurtled by the window behind his head. There was great constantly modulating noise. All the passengers stared straight ahead and pretended they were alone.

But this was no ordinary subway train, even though it now ran on an obscure local line. There was a plaque on the wall across from Woody. It said, "This train, the *Lyman R. Long*, was dedicated at the New York World's Fair, July 7, 1939, as the Subway Train of the Future."

Then, in no time at all, they were in the great gleaming Central Station of the New York Subway System. They left the Subway Train of the Future and ventured out into the echoing bustle of the bright high-ceilinged underground world. The walls were alive with texture and color. High overhead, dominating Central Station, was a great stained-glass window lit like a neon sign. It, too, celebrated the muses of Science and Industry, but it was much grander.

Woody took no notice of the wonder around him. He ignored the people. He ignored the color. He ignored the light. He ignored the shops that filled the caverns of the Central Station. He held tight to the robot's hand and looked resolutely straight ahead. All this around him was distraction. He was going to Brooklyn to buy his father a 28K-916 Hersh. so that he could finish his Dimensional Redistributor and control the world. If he were distracted and left the path, he would not dare to guess his fate.

His directions said . . . but there it was, directly before him, the sign that said, "To Brooklyn." Under it sat a new modern plasteel train, doors open wide, waiting patiently. The *Lyman R. Long* was 1939's vision of the future, now relegated to a local line. This was the future made present. This was tomorrow now.

It was far more frightening somehow as it sat, quietly waiting. This open door was the last threshold. If Woody passed beyond it, he would be swallowed whole and carried to Brooklyn. He would not be able to help himself.

But he had no choice. He could not help himself now. He must stay on the path, and the path led to Brooklyn. Stepping aboard the train had the same disconcerting finality as the bursting of a soap bubble.

There were but two seats left together in the car, and Woody and his robot companion sat down. As soon as they sat, as though on signal, the doors of the car slid shut automatically and silently, and automatically and silently the subway train slid out of the Central Station of the New York Subway System, bound for Brooklyn. It plunged immediately into the cold dark earth tunnel under the East River, and down down it went without consideration of what it might discover. Down. Noiselessly down. Relentlessly down.

One instant they were in the station. One instant there was still connection to the familiar world. One instant they were still in Manhattan. The next moment they were hurtling into an unknown nether world. It was all too sudden. Woody was paralyzed with fear.

It felt to him as though a hand were wringing his brain, and another hand was squeezing his throat, and another hand was tickling his heart, toying with his life and certainty. And the only hand that was really there was the strong cuproberyl hand of the robot Woody Asenion's father had made to keep Woody in the closet and safe from other harm. Woody held that familiar hand tight. He looked at the map and directions that he held. That was his talisman. He had not left the path. As long as he did not leave the path, he would be safe.

The train bumped a bottom bump and the lights in the car dimmed and then came up. The door between cars at Woody's left slammed open, allowing a brief snatch of the whirring whine of the rubberite wheels on the tracks, and three young people burst threateningly in. They were very dangerous because no one in the subway car had ever seen anything like them. They were not apprentices. They were not secretaries. They were not management trainees. They were neither soldiers nor students. They were not hip, but then neither were they straight.

One was a boy, narrow, tall, ugly and graceful as a hatchet. He wore an extravagant white suit, dandy and neat, and carried a yellow chrysanthemum to play with. The other boy was short, dark, curly, and cute. He wore a casual brown doublet over an orange shirt. He bounced and bubbled. The girl wore cheerfully vulgar purple to her ankle with a slit to the thigh. She was pale and her black hair was severe and dramatic.

The girl was the first into the car. She swung around and around the pole in front of Woody, laughing. The bouncy boy galloped in after her, swung with her around the pole, and then stopped her with a sudden kiss, even though Amy Vanderbilt in an ad overhead suggested that public emotion is not good manners. The ugly one strolled in gracefully, shut the door to the car, and blessed the two with his yellow mum, tapping them each on the head, saying nothing.

Then he turned and waved his flower menacingly at the rest of the car. He danced. This was too much for one still-vertical soul, who leaped to his feet and said authoritatively: "We are all good citizens here on our way to Brooklyn. What do you mean by this intrusion?"

"Don't you feel it?" the bouncy one asked. "The world has changed. The Great Common Dream is changing, and so is the world. We're going to Brooklyn to dance in the rain and celebrate. Come on along."

The girl looked directly at the questioning man. "Listen with your skin," she said. "Don't you feel it? Don't you want to be dancing?"

The man looked puzzled. But he listened with his skin and he knew they were right, even if they were a little early. He was horizontal in his heart, which is why he was so quick to seem vertical. He still thought it might be noticed if he wasn't.

But now he said, with joy in his voice, "I do feel it! I do feel it! You're right. You're right!" He howled a joyous howl of celebration.

And he began to dance in the aisles.

"I feel it too!" someone else yelled. "I do."

Who? It might have been any of the first six people to join him in the aisles.

Now that's how close the vertical world was to turning horizontal. All that was necessary was the suggestion. People were ready to go multiform as soon as they knew it was time. Woody tugged at the sleeve of the tall boy in the extravagant white suit.

"Yes, sir, may I be of practical assistance?" said he, and winked.

"Is it raining now?" asked Woody. It seemed important that he should ask, since the strange blue toll-token seller had suggested that it was going to rain and he wanted to be prepared. The robot carried Woody's umbrella in his capable cuproberyl hand. Woody would be all right. If it did rain, Woody would stay dry.

"Raining," said the ugly one. "Raining? How would I know if it's raining? We're in a subway train under the East River."

"Oh, hey now, it's Woody," said the girl. "Go easy on Woody. It's going to rain, Woody. Don't you want to come along with us and dance in the rain?"

But she was too insistent for poor Woody. He didn't know enough of the world to be sure what it was that she intended, but he suspected the world too much to want to learn. She was a distraction. The whole car was a distraction, dancing, gadding, and larking. He stared fixedly up at the subway ad for Amy Vanderbilt's new etiquette book. "Know Your Place in the Space Age," the ad whispered to him when it knew it had his full attention. And that was another distraction.

"Hey, dance with us, Woody," said the curly one in orange. "You can do any step you like. You can do a step no one else has ever done."

Woody explained: "I have this map and these directions." He pointed to them. "I'm very busy now. I'm running an errand for my father. I'm going to buy a 28K-916 Hersh. so that he can finish his Dimensional Redistributor and control the world."

The tall narrow boy said, "Why doesn't your father run his own errands? He's all grown up now." He said it gracefully because that's the way he was.

Woody stared straight ahead with all the best deafness he could muster. It was the deafness he did when he sat in the corner of the closet with his back to the world and wouldn't hear. He could shut out lots and lots.

The other boy and the girl said, "Come on, Woody. The vertical world is turning horizontal. Come with us, Woody. We're in Brooklyn now. This is New Lots. This is our stop. This is our place. Take a chance, Woody. Dare. Dance. Dance in the rain."

And everybody in the car said, "Come one, come all, Woody. There's room for you. There's room for everyone."

But Woody stared straight ahead, which made everything on either side blurry, and wouldn't hear. It was as good as shutting his eyes. He held onto his map and his directions with both hands so that he would not become lost.

Woody felt the subway come to a smooth stop. He wouldn't admit it, but he heard the doors slide gently open. He wouldn't admit it, but after a long moment he heard the doors slide gently shut again. He only unblunked his eyes when he felt the train begin to move again.

He was alone in the car. There was no one else there. The girl in that purple dress down to her ankle and up to her thigh was gone. The boy in the white suit was gone. The boy in the brown doublet and orange shirt was gone. All the people in the car were gone. Even the robot was gone, and the umbrella with him. You can imagine how that made Woody feel.

No hand to hold. No umbrella to keep him dry and safe.

But still he had his map and directions. He wasn't completely lost.

He was driven to walk the length of the train. Every car was empty. Every car was as empty as his car when everyone had gone. He was alone. He walked from one end of the train to the other and he saw no one. When he got to the head of the train he looked in the window at the driver. But there was no pilot.

And still the train hurtled on. Woody was afraid.

He went back to his own seat. He sat there alone studying his map and directions. They said to get off at Rockaway Parkway.

And then the train came to a halt. An automatic voice said automatically, "Rockaway Parkway. End of the line." And the door slid open. Woody bolted through it and up the stairs.

There was an orange railing here, too. The stairs ended between two great boulders with white lamps that said, "Subway." Woody was standing in a great rock garden. And this was Brooklyn.

It was not raining. The air was hot, damp, and heavy in Brooklyn, like a warm smothering washcloth. Woody wished he had his umbrella.

He looked at his directions. They said, "Follow the path to Stewart's."

So he followed the path, and in a few minutes he came to the edge of the hill. He could see the flatlands below and on across the damp sand flats even to the palm-lined shores of Jamaica Bay itself. He could see the palms swaying sullenly under a threatening sky. He followed the path further, never straying, and when he reached Flatlands Avenue, he could suddenly see the great porcelain height of his landmark, white, but marked by stains of rust. That was the Paerdegat Basin—and close by the Paerdegat Basin was Stewart's.

It was an easy walk. Woody had time to study his instructions. They were frightening, for they asked him to lie. He wasn't good at that. When he lied, his father always caught him out.

And then, almost before he knew, his feet had followed a true path to Stewart's Out-of-Stock Supply. It was a small block building. He hesitated and then he entered.

The small building was filled with amazing machines, some of them a bit dusty, displayed to show the successes of the shop. All of them had been made of parts supplied by Stewart's. There was a four-dimensional roller-press, a positronic calculator, an in-gravity parachute—which seemed to be a metal harness with pads to protect the body—and a mobile can opener.

At the back of the building was a sharp-featured, crew-cut old man with a positive manner. He looked as though he had his mind made up about everything.

"Don't tell me. Don't tell me. I've got my theory," the old man said. He looked at Woody, measuring him with his eye. Then he punched authoritatively at a button console on the counter in front of him. The wall behind him dissolved as though it had forgotten to remember itself, and there were immense aisles with racks and bins and shelves filled with out-of-stock supplies. A sign overhead said, "1947-1957." And another sign said, "At Last. 4 Amazing *New* Scientific Discoveries Help to Make You Feel Like a *New Person* and *More Alive!*"

The old man put on a golf cap and said, "There. I'm right so far, aren't I? Now, let me see. The rest of it should be easy. Yes, you're really quite simple, young man. I see to the bottom of you."

He punched a series of buttons. A little robot rolled by, made a right turn down an aisle and then a left turn out of sight. The old man stood waiting with a surefooted expression on his face. In a moment the robot rolled back. It placed a flat plate in the old man's hand, and he placed the plate on the counter. Then he patted the robot on the head and it rolled away.

"There, you see. You're the right age. You're obviously a broad-headed Alpine. The half-life of strontium-90 is twenty-eight years. So you're here to replace the tactile plate on your Erasmus Bean machine. Am I right?"

Woody shook his head.

"But of course I'm right. I'm always right."

Woody shook his head.

"Then what are you here for?" the old man asked in a disgruntled tone.

Woody said, "I want a 28K-916 Hersh. It was discontinued in 1932."

The old man hung his golf cap on a peg. "Don't tell me my business. It's strange. You don't look like a 1932."

He punched again at his console of buttons, and the configuration of aisles flickered and restabilized. The overhead sign now said, "1926-1935." And another sign said, "Are You Caught Behind the Bars of a 'Small-Time' Job? Learn Electricity! Earn $3,000 a Year!" The old man slapped a straw skimmer on his head.

"We did have a 28K-916 Hersh.," he said. "Once. We don't have much call for one of these. I recollect seeing it along about 1934."

The little robot rolled out once again, made a right turn down an aisle and then a left turn out of sight.

The old man turned suddenly to Woody and said, "This tube isn't for your own invention, is it? You're not a 1932 at all. Who are you here for? Murray? Stanton? Hyatt?"

Woody lowered his eyes. He shook his head.

The robot rolled suddenly back into view. It placed an orange-and-black box, as shiny and new as though this were 1932 and it was fresh from the Hersh. factory, in the hand of the sharp-featured old man.

"This is a rare tube with special rhodomagnetic properties," the old man said. "Just how do you propose to put it to use?"

Woody looked down again. Below the counter top he looked at his instructions and he read his lie.

In a thoroughly unconvincing manner he read, "I am a collector. I mean to collect one of every vacuum tube in the world. When I own a 28K-916 Hersh., my collection will be complete."

But the old man looked over the counter and caught Woody reading and his suspicions were aroused. He seized the map and directions from Woody's hands, and discovered their meaning with a single glance.

"Woodrow Asenion!" he said. "I barred your father from this store in 1937! You know what that man intends. He means to make a Dimensional Redistributor and control the world. Well, not with help from Stewart's. Power is to be used responsibly."

He threw the map and instructions behind him, seized Woody, and hustled him through the showroom, past the four-dimensional roller-press, the positronic calculator, the in-gravity parachute, the mobile can opener, and all the many others. He threw Woody onto the sand under the palm tree in front of the building.

"And never come back," he said. He straightened his skimmer. Then he looked up.

Very slowly he said, "Why, I do believe it's going to rain."

The old man slammed the door and pulled down a curtain that said, "Closed on Account of Rain."

Woody looked around desperately. He looked at the sky. It was going to rain and he had no umbrella. He had not bought the vacuum tube. He had no map and directions. He was almost lost. He beat desperately on the door, but it would not open. While he pounded, all the lights within went out. The building was silent. Then thunder rumbled overhead.

In panic Woody retreated along Flatlands Avenue. The sky was crackling and snarling. It was flaring and fleering. Woody wished desperately that he were safe at home in the comfort of his own familiar closet. He felt very vulnerable. He felt naked and alone in a strange country. He was hungry, too. What was he to do? What was he to do? He was bewildered.

Woody thought that if he could only find the subway station in the rock park again, the green stairs with the orange railing under the lamps that said, "Subway," he might find his way home to 206 W. 104th St. in Manhattan. Desperately he began to run across the sand.

And then, suddenly, there they all were. There was the boy in the white suit. There was the boy in the brown doublet. There was the girl in the long purple dress. And behind them was a pied piper's gathering of people—dancing, larking, and gadding. And that was just anticipation, for the moment of shift when the old vertical world was forgotten and the new guiding dream was dreamed had not yet come. It had not yet begun to rain.

"Hi, Woody," said the boy in brown. "Are you ready to join us?"

"Hi, Woody," said the girl in purple. "Are you ready to dance in the rain?"

That was too frightening. Woody said to the tall ugly boy in white: "Where is my robot? It has my umbrella."

"He," said that one, and tapped Woody on the forehead with his yellow chrysanthemum. "He. And he isn't yours. And I have my doubts about the umbrella, too."

"Ha," everybody said. "Get wet."

"Ho," everybody said. "It will hardly hurt."

That was terrifying. Now, Woody knew who he was. He was the one at the bottom. It was a certain place. If he left the path and joined this many, who would he be? He would be lost. He would not know himself.

"Who?" he asked. "Who?"

"You," they said. "You."

They laughed. And they were singing, some of them. And doing other things. Celebrating beneath this final black threatening sky, this roiling heaven.

Woody could not bear it. "I have to find a 28K-916 Hersh.," he said. "How else can I go home? I can't stay. I have to go."

"Good-bye. Good-bye," they called as he hurried away. He looked back from the hillside, and they were looking up at the sky and waiting. Waiting for the clouds to open and the rain to pour down. Woody feared the rain. He ran.

No map. No directions. No map. No instructions. No umbrella. But he still had two toll tokens.

Down the path he ran into the rock park. Along the path. Still on the true path. And there before him were the twin boulders. Before him was the green stair with the orange railing. Before him was haven.

But there was a chain across the top of the stair. There was a locked gate across the bottom of the stair. And the lamps at the entrance were not lit. All said, "Closed." All said, "Try Other Entrance."

The other entrance. The other entrance. Where was the other entrance? There it was! It was visible on the other side of the rock park, marked by another pair of lamps set atop another pair of boulders.

Woody left the path and struck toward them. He ran in all his hope of home. He ran in all his fear of the rain. His understanding was not profound, but he knew that if he were rained upon, nothing would be as it was.

He did not notice that in leaving the path his father had marked for him before Woody had ventured out of the closet, he had lost his last protection. First the robot, sturdy and comforting. Then the umbrella to shield him. Then he had lost his map and instructions. And finally he had left the true path.

Woody reached the other entrance. There was a chain across the top of the stairs. There was a gate across the bottom of the stairs. There were signs, and the signs said, "Closed" and "Try Other Entrance."

The other entrance. The other entrance. Where was the other entrance? There it was! It was visible on the other side of the rock park.

Woody hurried toward it. But then halfway between the two he stopped. That was where he had already been. He looked confused. He began to spin. Around and around on his toe he went. He did not know what to do. Overhead the skies impended. Poor Woody. He really needed someone in charge to tell him what to do next.

Around and around he went. Suddenly an imposing figure flashed into being before him. It glowed lemon yellow and it was very tall.

"Halt. Cease that," it said. It was a stranger foreign creature than the blue alien in the Friends of the New York Subway System uniform. "Woody Asenion?"

Woody nodded. "Yes, sir."

"I know all about you. You're late. You're very late. It's time for the rain to start. It should have started by now."

"Is it going to rain?" Woody asked. "Is it truly going to rain?"

"Yes, it is."

"But I don't want it to rain," Woody said. "I want to be home safe in my own closet. Is it because I left the path?"

"Of course," the strange creature said. "And now you must get wet."

"No," said Woody. "I won't. I'll run between the raindrops. I won't get wet."

And he started to run in fear and in trembling. The lightning lightened, to see him run. Thunder clapped the stale air between its hands. The forefinger of the rain prodded at Woody.

Rain fell at Woody, but he dodged and ducked. He ran down Grapefruit Street, and it missed him. He ran up Joralemon and it spattered around him and never touched him. He ran past the infamous Red Hook of Brooklyn, sharp and deadly. He ran through the marketplaces and bazaars of the Arab Quarter. He ran through a quiet sleeping town of little brown houses, all like beehives, full of little brown people. He ran through all the places of Brooklyn and the rain pursued him everywhere.

He would not be touched. This was Woody Asenion, who was raised in a closet and who didn't dare to open the door by himself. Who would have thought he would be so daring. Who would have thought he would be so nimble. Fear took him to heights he had never dreamed of. Fear made him magnificent.

Watching people paused and cheered as he passed. They had to admire him. Pigeons fled before him. Lightning circled his head. Thunder thundered. The skies rolled and tumbled blackly, but not a drop of rain could touch Woody Asenion.

Then at last as he ran up the long slow slope to Prospect Park, he began to tire. His breath was sharp in his throat. His steps grew labored. His dodges grew less canny. And of a sudden lightning struck all around him. It struck before him. It struck behind him. It struck on his either hand. All at once. Woody was engulfed in thunder, drowned in thunder, rolled and tossed by thunder. He was washed to the ground. He was beached. He was helpless.

And as he lay there, unable to help himself, it rained on Woody. A single giant drop of water. It surrounded him and gently drenched him from head to toe, and after that Woody was not the same.

That was a very strange drop of rain.

And now Woody was all wet. He stood and looked down at himself. He held his arms out and watched them drip. Then he laughed. He shook himself and laughed. He was really changed.

All the other multiforms, all the other people, came running up to Woody and surrounded him.

They were all wet, too.

"Here," said the boy in the doublet. "Look what we found for you."

It was an orange-and-black box, factory new. It was a 28K-916 Hersh. It said so on the box. He gave it to Woody.

The girl said, "Woody. You made it, Woody." She kissed him and Woody could only smile and laugh some more. He was happy.

The boy in the white suit handed Woody his chrysanthemum. "We waited for you," he said. "We didn't get wet until you did."

It was such a great secret to be included in. It didn't matter to Woody that he was the last to know. He was the first to get wet. How lucky he was.

Woody began to dance then. If fear had made him an inspired dodger, the promise of the new horizontal world made him an intoxicated dancer. His dance was brilliant. His dance was so brilliant that everybody danced Woody's dance for a time. But nobody danced it as well as he did.

Woody danced, and with him danced all the no-longer-verticals. With him danced three alien beings—two blue, one lemon yellow. With him danced the two boys and the girl. With him danced all the people from the subway train. With him danced all the people from his neighborhood, including the little girl who also lived at 206 W. 104th St. in Manhattan. She danced between two robots, one small, one tall and skinny.

Then Woody saw his father. His father was dancing Woody's dance, too! There were three other men of his age dancing with him.

Woody danced over to his father and everybody danced after him. Mr. Asenion said, "These are my good friends, Murray, Stanton, and Hyatt. We are going to invent together."

Woody said, "I have your 28K-916 Hersh."

"No need," his father said, waving it away, never ceasing to dance. "No need, indeed. I made do without it. As you can see." And everybody cheered for Woody's father.

Then the step changed and everybody danced his own way again. Woody was happy. Woody celebrated, too.

And the horizontal world began.

Lady Sunshine and the Magoon of Beatus

1

This is a true story. Some stories are lies, or half-truths. This is a true story of those desperate days when men still confined themselves to the ninety planets of the Dispersion, in the nodding afternoon hours before Nashua summoned the nerve to declare herself an Empire.

This is the story of young Jen, who was as beautiful as you may dream and who was known as Lady Sunshine, and of how she became the partner of the Magoon of Beatus. Lady Sunshine was her own chosen name, but at the time of her meeting with the Magoon it was a true description only of her exterior. She did not radiate. She did not illuminate. She was not fit to be the partner of anyone.

The times were bad for mankind, as bad as any the race has ever known, and Lady Sunshine was a product of the times. Mankind lived on the Ninety Worlds of the Dispersion and did as they thought all the generations of men before them had done. They ruined each other in the name of business, politics, fashion, and fame.

But mankind was sick and horizonless. There was not a man alive who did not know that Earth, the source, the wellspring of man, was dead, ruined by man. Mankind lacked all commonality and purpose. Men whirled in the closed circle of the Ninety Worlds, seeking advantage wherever they could, grasping and seizing.

The universe was limited and life was short.

Lady Sunshine was taught this last lesson by her grandmother, who was Madame O'Severe. Yes, her. Lady Sunshine was the heir of Madame O'Severe and was taught by her to be cynical and treacherous, to deliver more blows than she took, to use power for advantage, and to stand alone.

Madame O'Severe taught Lady Sunshine so well that the day came when Lady Sunshine realized the limitations of their alliance. Whatever Madame O'Severe might say, Madame O'Severe stood alone—a unity sufficient unto herself. And what was Lady Sunshine's place in that unity? She was being ripened to be eaten alive.

Lady Sunshine must flee from that to preserve her own unity. She laid a long plot of escape. She trained and prepared herself. She made herself a spaceship pilot. She used Madame O'Severe's absorption in the busyness of real life to make her own secret plans.

As delicate and precious as she appeared, Lady Sunshine was strong and determined in pursuit of her own purposes. She fought Madame O'Severe, and never admitted that she fought her. She merely said that she was unfond of the planet of her birth, that O'Severe had bent her, and that she wished to travel to some one of the other worlds of men in her spaceship. And she fought so long and well that at last, in order to save her other interests, Madame O'Severe was forced to loose her grip.

Madame O'Severe said, "You disguise your rebellions against me as criticism of this planet."

"But I am the very type of O'Severe," said Lady Sunshine. "It has made me thin and fragile. I wish to see what I would be like elsewhere."

"It is I who made you," said Madame O'Severe, "not this planet. If I had raised you elsewhere than here, you would still be the same."

"I wish to discover this for myself."

"You will shortly enough. Your proper place is here with me, doing as I train you to do. It is only by following my direction that you will ever be a fit instrument to inherit my powers and position. But I am far too occupied at the moment to coerce you properly. So I will indulge you in your whim. You may go. I grant you permission to find out just where it is that your best interests lie. I guarantee that you will learn that they are with me and with O'Severe. Now thank me and go."

"Thank you, good Madame O'Severe," said Lady Sunshine.

"One last thing before you go," said Madame O'Severe, halting her escape. "Remember well all the lessons I have taught you. You will find that you have need of them."

Lady Sunshine ran in her trim white spacecraft to Amabile, which was one of the playground worlds of men. She had in mind to leave her planet and Madame O'Severe far behind her.

There was freedom and gaiety on Amabile, which there never was on O'Severe, and Lady Sunshine tumbled headlong into it. It looked like fun, sporting with rich and handsome men and lovely, carefree women. She threw herself into the whirl and let it do with her as it would.

She was stripped clean by Amabile. She was demeaned and debased by it. She played at pleasure, ever harder and harder, trying to find an end and never finding it. Instead she found that she had good use for every lesson she had ever learned from Madame O'Severe. She did many pointless and destructive things that you would not enjoy hearing about.

She discovered that the people of Amabile and the people who came to Amabile were as bent as the people of O'Severe. Was Madame O'Severe right? Was this life? Was this the entirety of life?

Lady Sunshine woke one day on Amabile. She was alone and she hated herself and what she had become. In desperation, she fled.

She ran again in her spaceship, desperately lunging from world to world in search of a planet that was not as monstrous as Amabile or O'Severe. She was strong in pursuit of her purposes, and it became her purpose to find somewhere among the Ninety Worlds of the Dispersion one world where she would not be bent.

But she did not find it.

She came to Beatus from the planet of Cromartie, which was her sixty-first planet. She was tired and hopeless. She had had small hope of Cromartie. It was for her not a place of search, but a place of retirement.

She had stayed at the home of Lord Brain, who was her grandmother's Vassal on Cromartie. It was unnecessary for Lady Sunshine to encounter anything more of Cromartie than Lord and Lady Brain for her to know that this was not the planet she sought. It was more of the same.

Lord Brain had persisted in trying to amuse her with his minute knowledge of fashion that was new to him but that was irrelevant, not to mention old, to her. His manner was unctuous subservience, which made his matter all the more difficult to endure.

For her part, Lady Brain preferred to meditate aloud on her few well-savored moments of interaction with people of importance. ("My people.") She spent much time in calculation of various stratagems by which the miracle might be repeated, and presented these to Lady Sunshine in hope of approval of the arithmetic

They inflicted a house party upon her, when all she sought was a moment of peace in which to reorder her own priorities. And they pressed at her a ninny who styled himself the Count de Pagan. He was a pale shadow of the men of Amabile, but by the testimony of Lord and Lady Brain he was the best that Cromartie had to offer. He pursued her everywhere urging her to allow him the privilege of harvesting her grapes ere winter's deadly finger touched her vines with frost.

He did not know what she was. He did not know what she had been. He did not know how much his proposals sickened her, and he did not know what she truly sought. None of them knew.

They said to her:

"You are such an inspiration, my lady. It is enough to know there is one like you, a lovely butterfly, flitting from world to world, to give us hope."

Or, "*I* have never traveled through space, and I have no intention of ever doing so. Cromartie is quite good enough. Whatever you may think of me, I do not care. I am quite satisfied with myself. So there."

Or, "Forget your fantasies of escape, my sweet Jen. You have no need of other worlds. Reality is *here*. Find the world here in my arms."

She said, "Jen is not a name for your use, Count. To you, I am Lady Sunshine." And turned away.

At last, in desperation, she allowed herself to shock and bewilder them with a brief and partial glimpse of what she really was. In her ship she raced a pilot hired in a pool organized by the Count de Pagan. The pilot's reputation was considerable on Cromartie. She scandalized the party by carelessly distributing the whole sum of the wagers she had won, and had insisted on collecting, to their various servants and mechanicals.

And even so, they did not understand that there had been no risk to her in the race. Even less did they understand that her demonstration of power was no pleasure to her, since it furthered her purposes in no regard. At best, it furthered the purposes of Madame O'Severe, who was pleased to see the power and repute of O'Severe spread farther abroad. To Lady Sunshine, it was a surrender to her own weakness.

She announced her intent to leave immediately for the planet of Beatus. That was a convenient name for her escape, snatched out of fleeting house party conversation.

Beatus, someone had said, was a place where for morale the people wore buttons that said "Beatus is not as bad as Beatans say it is."

Everyone nearby but Lady Sunshine laughed familiarly. The man added, "Only it is. Who ever heard a Beatan speak ill of Beatus?" And everyone laughed again.

Lady Sunshine had heard of Beatus. It was one of the Ninety Worlds of the Dispersion, and it was not far from Cromartie. But she had never heard anything of Beatus to make her think it was the planet she sought where she would not be bent, and she had had no plans to visit the place. For Cromartie, however, Beatus was more than a miserable place. It was the local wellspring of humor.

"What is the difference between Old Earth and Beatus?"

That caught her attention. Lady Sunshine had an interest in Old Earth, the source of the varieties of man.

Several unacceptable answers were tried, to general amusement, before the proper answer was given:

"Nothing. Both are unfit for human habitation."

She asked about Beatus.

Beatans, the jokesters said, were squat and unhealthy men who lived in a deadly blue murk and made machines that did not perform properly. They were guaranteed to operate only on Beatus or in the hands of Beatans, but Beatans did not travel well through the transitions of hyperspace and no one else would willingly live on Beatus.

"What is the difference between a fool and an idiot?"

"A fool is a man with a machine from Beatus. An idiot is a man who travels there."

"Oh. You've heard it before."

Lady Sunshine said: "But the men of Beatus are professional machinists?"

"Of necessity. It is only by virtue of their machines that men live on Beatus at all."

It was small wonder that Lord and Lady Brain were frank enough to ask how they might have offended her, and the means by which they might repair their error. For Lady Sunshine proposed to ruin their house party entirely. Her distribution of the money she had won had shocked Lord Brain, but he had accepted it. He had placed his own wagers on her because that was where he thought his advantage lay whether she won or not, and he had been amazed and pleased by the result. But now this—desertion in mid-party for Beatus, of all places.

Lady Sunshine was politic. She did not inform Lord and Lady Brain that she preferred the blue fog of Beatus to the pleasures of their hospitality. No, she chose instead to tell them that she traveled to Beatus on the chance that it might supply her with a machine, a remote planetary analyzer, that she needed for her purpose.

"You travel to Beatus in search of a machine?"

"Yes, Lord Brain."

"For a machine."

"Yes, Lord Brain." Lady Sunshine had nothing left to her but her purpose. She had no better place left than Beatus to search for a planetary analyzer.

"But what shall we tell your grandmother when she inquires?"

"If my grandmother should inquire after me," said Lady Sunshine, "tell her that I have gone to Beatus."

But she did not think that her grandmother would inquire. Madame O'Severe had given Lady Sunshine permission to find out where her best interests lay, and she did not interfere with her now. She was too busy otherwise to do that.

It was in discouragement that Lady Sunshine came to Beatus. Her purposes were come to nothing, and she feared that O'Severe and Madame O'Severe, waiting patiently for her, were the sum of greatest possibility that yet existed. She hated the thought. Even the transitions of hyperspace, usually a tonic bath, a stimulation of every nerve, were no answer for her discouragement and her lack of hope. The fight against hyperspace left her drained and weary.

When she was given leave to land on Beatus, and was brought down through the murk to a safe landing on a planetary grid, she discovered that the worst that Cromartie had to say of the place was understatement. The men of Beatus seemed hardly human. They were lumpish and hairy creatures, and they did wear buttons that said "Hang on, Beatans!" and "If you think it is bad here, you should see where the Munglies live."

But Lady Sunshine had seen where the Munglies live, and Beatus was worse. It was the most unfortunate and minimal home of man that Lady Sunshine had ever visited.

The machines of Beatus pounded away eternally to keep the men of Beatus alive in their holes and warrens. The cold blue fog of Beatus penetrated even through the protective equipment that she wore. It was corrosive. It made her eyes sore and watery, her throat raw, her lungs painful. It confused her mind and upset her balances. Every moment she spent here demanded double the time elsewhere for recuperation.

But yet, she had come here for the sake of her search. The men of Beatus, whatever else might be said of them and their planet, were technicians and machinists. So down she went into their warrens, doing her best to ignore the seeping blue fog and the pulsing throb of the great machines. She made her usual inquiries and offered her usual inducements:

"I seek a machine by which I may inspect a planet such as Beatus from orbit without the necessity of landing on a grid. A remote planetary analyzer. I am prepared to bear whatever expense is involved."

But all that she received was the usual response:

"My lady, why inspect Beatus remotely? We have a landing grid firmly in place. And, after all, here you are."

"I mean to inspect planets that have no landing grids."

"Pardon my laughter, my lady, but what reason could there be to inspect a planet that lacks a landing grid? If it was worth landing on at all, it would already have a grid so that ships might land there."

And other familiar responses:

"How about another novelty just as good, my lady, but different?"

And, "It is not possible. Begging your pardon, but even to contain such a machine would require a naval vessel of unprecedented size. It is beyond your resources, whatever your willingness or ability to pay."

And, slyly, "How much money might be advanced for preliminary researches into the matter?"

One answer was not usual. It came from a belligerent, lumpish little man who wore not one, but three buttons boosting Beatus:

"What do you suggest? As all Beatus knows, at the Dispersion men were settled on the best existing planets. If a better world than Beatus existed, we would be living within it today. Since we are not, it is hardly in my best interests to build a planetary analyzer, now is it? I am not the fool you take me for!"

But then one day, a man who was lumpish and hairy like other Beatans, but who had more seeming confidence than most Beatans since he wore no buttons, came to her and said, "Please follow me. The Envied One wishes to see you in his hole."

"Who is the Envied One?"

The man was taken aback. "Why, Himself. The Magoon. The mirror in which Beatus sees its hopes reflected."

Ah, the Magoon of Beatus. Lady Sunshine recalled him now by this title. The Magoon was not the mirror for all Beatans, but there were many on Beatus who surrendered the care of their hopes to him. He was a very mysterious figure, reputed to live in deeply dug seclusion.

"Why does he wish to see me?" she asked.

"I don't know," said the man. "I am but a messenger."

There was no hope left in Beatus for Lady Sunshine, but no greater hope elsewhere, so she followed the messenger. She was passed from one pair of confident hands to another, deeper and deeper, until at last she was ushered into a room where the cold blue fog penetrated only in faint nauseating wisps, and there she met the Magoon himself.

The Magoon of Beatus was not beautiful. He was almost as queer and humorous as his title. Like less important men of Beatus, he had been bent by his planet and made squat, lumpish and hairy. He was short and brown. His hands and feet and nose were large. His eyes were sad. He was as ugly as a man may be and still be reckoned human. Lady Sunshine pitied and feared him in his awfulness.

Above the penetrating humble-mumble of great engines, the Magoon said to Lady Sunshine: "I understand that you seek a machine that would sense the nature of a planet at a distance."

"That is true, Magoon," she said, casually mangling his title to demonstrate their true relativity.

"Why do you have need of such a machine, Lady Sunshine? Why don't you use a landing grid like everyone else? If a planet is inhabited, it does not need your analysis. If a planet is not inhabited, it hardly merits analysis. Do you mean to be some sort of spy whirling about our heads and peering down at us?"

"No," she said.

"Then state your purposes."

After a moment she said, "I mean to go to unsettled planets, planets unknown to men, and analyze their fitness for human habitation."

"To what point?" he asked. "Are ninety planets not enough?"

"No," she said. "Some planets are more desirable than others. I seek to find new planets and to distinguish between the more and the less desirable among them. I feel that somewhere there must be a planet more desirable than ... say, this one."

"But common sense says that if there were some planet beyond the worlds of the Dispersion that was preferable to any world among the Ninety, we would be living there now. Ergo, this planet is more desirable than the next best alternative."

Lady Sunshine stared directly at the Magoon, even though it was impolite to gaze fixedly at what was so deformed.

"Will you not agree that in the haste of the Dispersion, somewhere a planet might have been overlooked that was preferable to Beatus?"

"I cannot believe so," he said. "It would be disloyal."

"Then contemplate this possibility. An error was made five hundred years ago. An agonizing, foolish error. Earth was about to breathe its last, and desperate men—poor clerks—overlooked some better place and condemned their fellows to endure the hell of the Mungly Planet forever."

The Magoon contemplated the possibility. At last he said, "And for this search you need a planetary analyzer so that you may evaluate worlds without landing on them?"

"Yes," she said. "It is essential, if I am to find a world better than the Mungly planet."

"But isn't this properly the job of some planetary navy? A major vessel on an extended expedition of exploration and survey?"

"Properly, it is," she said, "but no navy cares. Not even the great Navy of Nashua. The interests of Nashua are commerce and power, not search for a hypothetical planet better than that of the Munglies. It is, however, my chosen work. My computer spends all its available time mulling the probabilities of various candidates for my inspection."

"I have asked my advisers," the Magoon said, "and one and all they seriously doubt whether a ship smaller than a major naval vessel could adequately contain a planetary analyzer that meets your specifications."

"Is this idle speculation, or could you build such a machine?"

"It is not idle speculation. I command the best resources of Beatus—the best advisers and the best technicians—and they give me good reason to believe that your desires are impossible. Unless you have a major naval vessel at your command?"

"No," said Lady Sunshine. "Only a modified Podbjelski Model Seven."

And she sighed.

The Magoon said, "However, other possibilities have occurred to me. If you will come—"

Lady Sunshine inhaled in wonder at the phrase "other possibilities," but then coughed and choked on a wisp of blue. Still, she followed the Magoon as he led the way through the intricacies of his warren. As they passed great pulsing machines, Lady Sunshine held her ears against the noise. But the Magoon had been so bent by his planet that he did not even seem to notice the hulking black monsters.

At last they came to a deep interior room at the very heart of the warren, a child's room with many toys and lathes, workbenches and small machines. It was equipped with an airlock. It was a strong room against the blue fog of Beatus, and none penetrated here. Lady Sunshine liked the room on that account.

The Magoon said, "When I was young, I lived my life here. My health did not permit me to leave this room, not even to play in the corridors of the warren. The machines you see about us were my only given playthings. This was my particular favorite. In fact, I have continued to use it until this day."

He patted a metal bowl, polished and featureless, that hung suspended in the air. There was a seat beneath it. The Magoon sat, pulled the bowl over his head like a bucket, placed his hands in gloves, and positioned his feet in stirrups.

"I fail to understand," Lady Sunshine said.

But the sad hillock of a man was wandering in his toy. He did not seem to hear her.

"I do not understand what you mean by this," Lady Sunshine repeated.

There was a sudden rap at the door. Lady Sunshine looked again to the Magoon, but he was lost to the sound.

She answered the door herself. It slid back to reveal a subtle spidery little mechanical about one and a half feet high, crouching there in the airlock on its universal motivator.

It spoke.

"Lady Sunshine," it said thinly, "it is I, the Magoon."

"No," she said. "Is it possible?"

"Indeed," the queer little thing said. "I present you with an alternative to your planetary analyzer."

"This?" she said, looking down at it.

The mechanical hoisted an eye on an extensor until it was on an equal height with her own eyes, and stared directly back. The lens of the extended eye flickered and altered.

"There is green in your eyes as well as brown," the small mechanical said. "How very strange."

Lady Sunshine looked from the small mechanical to the Magoon, lost in the parent machine, and back again. The mechanical rolled into the room on its motivator and demonstrated its agilities before her.

It said, "I am suggesting that you send a small drone down to the worlds you propose to examine. Onboard the drone will be a mechanical such as this one. Then, just as I have experienced the surface of my planet of Beatus through my mechanicals, so may you experience the surfaces of these unsettled planets."

"But what is it like?" Lady Sunshine asked of the mechanical circling about her. "What is it like? Permit me to test your system for myself."

The Magoon withdrew his hands from the gloves and raised the large featureless helmet. Consciousness had fled from the mechanical, and it balanced lifelessly on its motivator, a mass of inert metals and plastics.

The Magoon said, "I constructed large parts of the original system myself, and made all of the later modifications, of which there have been many."

"Very clever, Magoon," she said, and was glad somehow that she was taller than he, and that he lacked the extensors of his little mechanical to make himself equal to her.

With his assistance, she put the cumbersome helmet over her head and put her hands in the gloves. In spite of the fact that both were large enough to fit the Magoon comfortably, it seemed to her that her head was held in a vise and her hands in pinions. She felt loomed about. And she thought that it smelled bad there in the helmet.

But at the same time, she could hear with the little robot's ears. She could see with its eyes.

She looked across the room and saw the Magoon standing over Lady Sunshine in the probe machine, placing her feet in proper position. And yes, she could feel her legs being moved. It was very strange and dissociating to be in two places at once.

But then, suddenly, she could feel the floor move beneath her motivator. She pressed with her right foot and swung right. She pressed with her left foot and wheeled.

"Ha, ha!" she cried, and heard her thin voice with her robot ears. "Wow!"

She tapped at a wall with an experimental extensor as she spun crazily by on her motivator. She felt the shock. She heard the sound, almost as though it were immediate.

"Magoon," she said. "This is very shrewd. What is the price of your machine?"

Its possibilities were incalculable. It was everything the Magoon had said. It was a viable alternative. With this machine she might circle a planet in her trim white spacecraft and see and hear and feel and manipulate it at a distance. That was more than she asked.

The Magoon stepped in front of the progress of the mechanical. Lady Sunshine pulled up short.

"Do you propose to buy me?" he asked. "The wealth of O'Severe means nothing to me. I have wealth enough of my own."

"Do you make me a gift of the machine?" she asked.

"No."

Lady Sunshine moved backward on her motivator. Then she stopped again. She pulled her hands abruptly from the gloves with their fingertip controls. She freed her head and looked at the Magoon, his back to her, standing before the little mechanical.

"So there is a price," she said. "What must I do to earn the use of your machine?"

He turned to face her. Lady Sunshine was amazed to see tears in his eyes.

He said, "I share your ends. I have the hope that there are other worlds where men may live in harmony, rather than in disharmony as here on Beatus. I do not believe that these worlds exist, but I dream that they might. Since I am the mirror of the hopes of Beatus, there are many who share this secret dream of mine. I have never been allowed to chance travel to other worlds. I do not know whether my dream is true.

"You may use my machine, Lady Sunshine, if you will find with it a world to exchange for Beatus. Not the Mungly Planet. Beatus first. The agony of my people must end."

"I will," she said. "You have my word, Magoon. You may have your choice of the worlds I find."

But then she said, "There is one small problem that still concerns me. Your machines have a poor reputation on other worlds. How may I be certain that nothing will go awry at a crucial moment?"

The Magoon waved the criticism aside without rancor.

"There will be no problem," he said. "I guarantee it. I will see the system installed in duplicate, and you have my word that it will work for you in crucial moments."

"We will see," she said. "We will test it on Beatus."

"Agreed," he answered. "Now satisfy my curiosity. You must have given considerable thought to the problem of search. What is your method?"

"I follow the best advice of my ship's computer," Lady Sunshine said.

"I understand," he said. "But on what basis are your computer's choices predicated?"

"Statistical inference," she said.

"Ah, yes. There are interesting possibilities in statistical inference. But what about intuitional methods? Have they no part in your search?"

"No. Intuition plays no part in my search."

"How did you come to land on Beatus?" the Magoon asked. "Was that recommended by your computer?"

"No," she said. "It was an accident."

But it was not an accident. In this universe, those things that are alike find each other out. Affinities gather, and computers be damned. What do computers know of true affinity? Only what they are told.

Computers are also weak in intuition. They cannot jump to wild conclusions and be justified.

2

It took time to install the double system of planetary probe machines in Lady Sunshine's white spaceship, and more time to make the necessary mechanicals and drone landing crafts. All the Magoon's great resources were turned to the problem and he himself oversaw the installation of the probe machines in her ship.

Lady Sunshine meanwhile practiced operation of the mechanical until she was adept at manipulating it on its motivator and directing its various extensors. It was subtle to operate and she wished to be in control when the time came to actually explore another world.

She also asked her computer to devote its spare time to selection of a choice short list of near places of search for the new world she hoped to find. She was interrupted in this by the need of the Magoon to coordinate the probes with the computer. Computer rectification of imperfect data from the distant mechanicals was absolutely necessary.

No matter how directly and immediately one seemed to be in habitation of the mechanical now, the ship's computer was an essential bridging link in exploration from space. Otherwise, what gaps in reality might appear? What blurring?

But there proved to be continuing problems of coordination.

"I don't understand it," said the Magoon.

He found it necessary to adjust the probes again and again, until at last they were in agreement with the computer. It was a long, slow and tedious process. But finally it became time to test the probe machine on Beatus from the spacecraft in orbit.

The Magoon participated in the test. It was only his second opportunity to see his sickly fog-enshrouded world from space. He had never been allowed to travel when he was young, and his sense of responsibility and best advice had kept him confined to Beatus now that he was older and Himself. He was excited. Lady Sunshine beheld him calmly and did not comment on his antics. He was a queer and ugly hairy brown creature, Magoon was.

From orbit they sent a drone vehicle down to the surface of Beatus. All went well, to the Magoon's great delight. When the safe landing of the drone was indicated, Lady Sunshine nodded to the Magoon and donned the probe helmet.

But all was not as it should be. It was not as it had been in all her occasions of practice.

The helmet did not work. The fingertip controls did not respond.

Lady Sunshine became overwhelmed by panic. She smothered. She drowned. She could not breathe in the close confines of the helmet. She could not escape from its grip. At last, she fought free of the probe machine.

She breathed deeply. She had found it frightening. It was all that she feared that was inert and dead.

Then she said, "This machine does not operate properly, Magoon. Will your duplicate machine serve any better, or have I wasted all this great time on Beatus, where the machines are untrustworthy?"

"Perhaps it is a matter of some small adjustment," the Magoon said.

He assumed her place. He put his head in the helmet, his lumpish paws in the gloves, his feet in the stirrups. He was gone for a moment while Lady Sunshine waited, peering at his engulfed body.

But then he raised the helmet and said, "It operates quite satisfactorily for me. Try entering the other probe machine, Lady Sunshine."

She took the other seat and after another deep breath donned the helmet. She found herself in the drone vehicle on the surface of Beatus. She rolled forward on her motivator out of the drone.

It was Beatus beyond question. It was horrid where she found herself. The ground beneath her motivators was spongy and uncertain. It was dotted with viscous purple pools that were vile and of unknown depth. They seethed.

Virulent deep blue roils of fog billowed about her. Lady Sunshine rolled forward tentatively on her motivator and found herself almost immediately surrounded by the pools of oily putrid purpleness, unable to proceed. She paused in the poisoned air and poisoned earth, unable to see, uncertain of her direction. She heard nothing but howling. For the first time in her experience of Beatus, there were no great throbbing machines to show where men made their truces with this awful place. Where to go? She poked a cautious extensor out to test the nearest pool, but paused again in fear that the vileness would dissolve her appendage.

Suddenly a great animal of a Beatan, a large misery, came running out of the fog at her. His protective devices were old and inadequate. He was eaten by sores and his hairiness was untended. He splashed through the purple pools and loomed large before her. She saw that he wore a great plate button.

It said, "I do not understand Beatus, but I accept it."

He cast himself down in the putrid purple slosh. He abased himself before her, coughing and choking and retching in the thick corrosive liquid. He rose and fell in it, thrashing and gasping, but always returning to it.

He cried, "Your pardon, O great Magoon! I have not been among your followers. Forgive me! I never thought to see you here in this solitary corner of mine. You are my one hope! Alter my life! Favor me with your blessing and I will be your faithful follower forever. I have never had a hope before!"

This pathetic creature attempted to paw at her. She rolled backward on her motivator to avoid the contact. With one eye she watched him; with the other she looked to her safe footing so that she would not join him by accident in the vile slop in which he wallowed.

"I am not the Magoon," she said.

To her great relief, she saw the second mechanical then.

"I am the Magoon," it said. It passed her by and rolled up to the Beatan, even into the slop, where it rode gently on the surface of the seething pool. "That is Lady Sunshine. It was a natural error. Now allow me to bless you."

The mechanical soothed and comforted the man, who rose dripping from the rottenness into the poison roils of fog. The Beatan reached vainly toward her.

"Bless me, too, Lady Sunshine! Please bless me! My condition must alter!"

The Magoon looked at her. At last she rolled forward a little distance, reached an extensor out to the man, and touched him with it, as a rock might be prodded with a thin stick.

"Bless you," she said.

The man stood and shook himself with happiness, like a wet dog.

"Oh, grace! Grace unforeseen! I do not deserve, but I will be worthy!"

He ripped off the poor remains of his protective devices and cast them away. He hurled his button into a purple puddle and ran into the fog, shouting and crying his joy.

Lady Sunshine said to the other spidery little mechanical: "Does this happen to you often?"

"Yes," said the other mechanical that was the Magoon. "Often. Their hopes are my chief burden. Their condition must surely alter."

When they faced each other again in Lady Sunshine's orbiting spaceship, Lady Sunshine said, "After that initial difficulty, your machine did all that I could ask. I'm more than satisfied, but I must know—what went wrong?"

The Magoon shook his head. "All that went wrong was that you operated the machine alone. That is all. The machines of Beatus need Beatans to direct them. Otherwise they are uncertain."

Lady Sunshine said, "Then you cannot guarantee the success of the probe when I put it to my own purpose?"

"I guaranteed that the probe would work for you," the Magoon said. "And it will work if I am present. Therefore I propose to accompany you in your search."

"Did you have this in mind from the beginning? Is that why you installed two probe machines?"

"Yes," said the Magoon.

"You were not frank with me."

"No."

"Do you dare to make this journey of exploration?" she asked. "The best advice you have been given has been not to travel."

"Do you dare to travel?" asked the Magoon of her in return. "Who has advised you to make these explorations?"

"No one," Lady Sunshine said. "All have advised against it, but it is my chosen work. And I do not stand the dangers from hyperspace that you Beatans do."

"Who knows what dangers I stand?" the Magoon asked. "I have never traveled through hyperspace. For that matter, who knows what strange and terrible things you may encounter in the course of your exploration? The unknown may be more frightening and dangerous than you can imagine. And yet you persist."

"I have my reasons for persistence," Lady Sunshine said, smiling.

"And I have mine," said the Magoon.

She shook her head. "You may die," she said.

It seemed to her that the Magoon was a frail being for all his gross bulk, and that any great shock might disinhabit this heapish ugly man as firmly and finally as the inert mechanicals they had just abandoned to the various poisons of Beatus.

"I may die tomorrow here at home, and what purpose will my death have served then? Better death in search, even fruitless search, than death in stagnation. I must alter the lives of my people, even though I die in the attempt. For good or for ill, I must cast the hopes of Beatus into the wind of the unknown. And no one may do this thing for me. No one may do this but me.

"So I ask: May I go with you on your journey of exploration?"

Lady Sunshine could not say no. She, too, would rather die in the search for an alternative to all that she had ever known than return to O'Severe to die and become her grandmother.

Moreover, if she were to persist at all, it was quite clear that she needed the Magoon to operate the probe machine.

"Yes," she said, because she could not say no. But she did not like saying yes. It took away from her something that had been hers alone.

The Magoon smiled in great relief, and then he said, "Before we leave, I must alter your computer. It is your ship's computer that has been at fault through all these days of adjustment and readjustment, and not my probe machines. Beatus as we just experienced it is no Beatus that I have ever known before. I have never seen it that blue and vile."

Lady Sunshine asked, "Do you remember that you were not frank with me?"

"Yes."

"I have not been frank with you."

"What do you mean?"

"I have not told you my true purpose. I have not told you all."

"Do you mean to say that your purpose is not to find somewhere a planet more hospitable to man than . . . the Mungly Planet?"

"No," she said. "Though I am sure that I will find such a place in the course of my search."

"Then what is your true purpose?"

Lady Sunshine had confessed her full intent to no one. Who understood her progression from one planet of the Dispersion to another in her own spacecraft? Few. Very few. They called her a butterfly, admired and dismissed her. Who understood her desire to find new worlds outside the tight bounds of the Ninety Worlds? Only the Magoon, this singular foreign creature.

Who would understand her true intent?

She said, "My purpose is to find True Earth, and that is why you may not change the computer. It holds singular precious data."

"I do not understand you, Lady Sunshine," the Magoon said. "Earth was destroyed long ago. There is no Earth anymore. There are only the planets of the Dispersion. Or do you speak of New Earth? That is a fine world, I am told."

"I have been there," Lady Sunshine said. "And it is not the place for which I search. It is not True Earth. Let me tell you my heart. I believe that in the Dispersion men were not taken to the best planets that exist, but were scattered carelessly on first-found worlds. I have been on sixty-two planets, and I know what worlds are like. I have never found a straight one. They have bent us, everyone, every one. They have made us strange and separate. They have made us scrambled and aimless. They have made us hateful. I know. I have been everywhere, and it has been like that everywhere that I have been."

"If New Earth is not True Earth, then for what do you search?" asked the Magoon.

"I search for the one planet where mankind will not be bent, but will grow straight and true. It will not be Beatus. It will not be O'Severe. It will not be New Earth, which is but a pale shadow with a name it does not deserve to bear. Until we find True Earth, we will never know what mankind really is. And I know what True Earth will be like. It will have the mountains of Aurora. It will have the forests of New Dalmatia. It will be made of Amabile, and O'Severe, and New Earth, and even Beatus. It will be all the best and more of sixty-two worlds. That is the standard by which my computer reckons.

"If Beatus was bluer and viler to your eyes than ever before, that is because for the first time in your life you saw Beatus truly, and not as it has bent you to see it."

The Magoon said: "Truer eyes do not improve Beatus."

"No, I suppose they would not," said Lady Sunshine. "But you must realize that by the standard of True Earth, every place looks the less. As the men of True Earth will outmatch the bent men of Nashua, or of anywhere else."

"Your model of True Earth is composed of all the planets that you have visited?" the Magoon asked.

"Yes."

"What of Beatus was added to the standard by which True Earth is to be known?"

"All that which is not blue and vile and lumpish, Magoon," Lady Sunshine said. "Now, if you promise not to alter my computer but accept the truth, then you may still accompany me. You may still venture your adventure and by the way we will discover many worlds that are better than Beatus."

"Your dream of True Earth seems a fancy to me," said the Magoon. "I do not dare to dream your dream. I hardly dare to dream my own dream. But I agree. Let us travel together in search of our dreams, and discover what we may."

The Magoon's departure was opposed by his advisors and his dependents, but he would not be gainsaid. He dared to risk all for his dream, and he prevailed over men who did not. He addressed his people as a whole and named to them the purpose for which he meant to travel. And, as his hope was their hope, they responded as one, and his advisers must then change their advice.

So is it always, when all is risked for a dream.

And so the two set off together in search of a better world than Beatus.

But though they traveled together, Lady Sunshine and the Magoon of Beatus were not yet partners. Lady Sunshine traveled in search of her own purpose, not the Magoon's. She searched for True Earth, the world where her unity would not be bent as it was bent and twisted on other planets.

The presence of the Magoon aboard her ship was no more than a means to this end.

3

Lady Sunshine and the Magoon traveled through hyperspace to the nearest place of those selected for search by the computer. Hyperspace was a stimulation and a joy to Lady Sunshine, a welcome antidote to the debilitations of Beatus. For the Magoon, hyperspace was a shock that left his sad eyes even sadder. But that was an expected reaction. He seemed to survive it ably enough. Lady Sunshine asked if he were all right, and he said that he was.

They emerged from hyperspace near a sun that was living green fire. Lady Sunshine pursued the directions indicated by her ship's computer, and found a planet! An unknown world! A candidate for True Earth.

She settled the ship into orbit around the planet and with the advice of the computer launched a drone. The Magoon looked down at the mystery that waited below them.

"This is more than I ever expected," he said. "And so soon. At this moment, I can almost believe in your True Earth. But I will be more than satisfied if this world is the superior of the Mungly Planet."

But what they discovered was not equal to the Mungly Planet. Not as a place of human habitation. It was not even to be preferred to Beatus.

The two mechanicals rolled forth from the dome. There was nothing to be seen in the somber green light of the distant sun that was not rock or shadow. The shadows were ripe violet in color and strangely cast. There were no clouds in the sky. No wind breathed. All was silence.

Lady Sunshine wheeled slowly on her motivator, looking all about them. The Magoon stood still, but slowly rotated an eye.

The rock that surrounded them was brown, and green, and red-black and gray. In some places these colors were separate. In others they were streaked and intermixed.

The texture of the rock also varied, independently of color. In some places it was delicately roughened, like the hide of a beast. In other places it was as smooth as though it had been finished. And yet, as they looked about them, each in his own separate way, they saw that in still other places it was slick and polished, like a natural glass in which they might see themselves reflected.

There were no straight lines anywhere. All was curves and undulations. The rock was rippled in places like the surface of a pond, and otherwhere it was waved like the surface of an ocean. It was molded in many ways.

In the absence of other life, rock had grown here after its own ways, unmodified. It had slowly fashioned itself. It had made itself into fairy spires, into private abstractions and unknown plastic shapes. Or it brooded through time, considering what it would become.

It was many, but it was all one, for there was nothing in this world but rock, and the shadow of rock. It was natural, but its nature was strange to them. As they were strange to this place.

As they looked about them, they saw that the drone had landed on top of a great singular rock formation, so that they looked at the world about them from a height among heights. They were very near the brink of a smooth and graceful swoop to destruction.

They did not speak to each other, these two mechanicals. How much time passed as they looked about them they did not know, for they did not reckon time.

If this world was strange, it was all the stranger for being judged by the standard of True Earth. That standard was not applicable here. No computer could rectify what the mechanicals perceived, but only make their perceptions more singular and unique. Nothing here could be judged by any human standard. It had its own reasons for being.

At last, Lady Sunshine said, "This is not the world I seek."

She struck at the rock with an edged extensor. The rock gave forth a light hollow sound as though it were brittle. Then it chipped. Now there was a great visible mar in the perfect surface of the planet.

"Nor is it the world I seek, either," said the Magoon. His voice rang thinly, overwhelmed by the towering rock about them.

"And yet," he said, "to think that we stand here where no other sentient observers have ever stood before. Could there be a lonelier place than this? What we see now has never been seen before. When we leave, it will remain unchanged through the eons, never to be seen again."

But the planet gave counterevidence. Where it had been chipped, the rock healed itself. Where it was marred, it slowly grew smooth again. Where fragments lay, they were absorbed by the mother rock.

And then something most strange and awesome happened. The rock face shrugged beneath them. A great blind ripple passed through the surface of the rock as the hide of an elephant might involuntarily shudder to dislodge a fly.

Lady Sunshine was nearer the edge of the formation, close to the long shattering swoop to the lower rock. The surface beneath her motivator was slick and she could not gain traction. The rock undulated again, and she was skidded against her will toward the great hurtling slope. She was helpless to stop her progress. She spun her motivator futilely.

The Magoon did not move to aid her. He watched her silently. And then as another wave passed, he fell over. She wondered why he made no effort to rise.

He was far away. She was helplessly sliding, falling, and destruction had her. It was like a slow and silent dream.

Then the helmet of the probe was lifted and she was free and safe. The Magoon, that brown and hairy creature with great large nose and deep sad eyes, looked down at Lady Sunshine. She was disoriented.

"I think the mechanicals were best abandoned," he said. "That world is no place for us."

"Yes," she said, still falling. "Yes."

And they did not discuss the world of rock further then. It was too strange a place to be lightly spoken of and their experiences were too much with them.

They put that world far behind them. They went immediately from there to the second place of search indicated by the computer. This was the solar system of a flawless and brilliant white sun.

But search as they might, they found no planet there in the place predicted by the computer. They paused while the computer reintegrated its data. And during that pause, they took silent thought. It was only when they were to leave that they finally were able to speak to each other about Eterna, the rock world.

In the meantime, it occurred to Lady Sunshine that her ship's computer had failed in its first two attempts to find True Earth, or even a world preferable to Beatus. These failures were of course discountable. She had asked the computer for its nearest and best choices, and these had merely been nearest.

Nevertheless, the Magoon might have criticized the computer for its double failure, and had not. She liked him for that. And she liked him for not making an unnecessary fuss over the pains of hyperspace, which she suspected that he suffered and hid. She found that she thought of him as specifically ugly less often now than before.

At last the computer suggested rather abruptly that they had spent altogether too much time in this wasteland solar system where no hospitable planet was likely to be found. So they prepared to leave this sterile emptiness around the white sun.

"We have our release now," Lady Sunshine said. "Let us strike out to see what better place we may find waiting for us at our third rendezvous."

"There is no need to feel disappointment," the Magoon said. "We have had a good beginning. One planet in two attempts is a good beginning. It is more than I expected."

"And that planet was worthy of a visit," said Lady Sunshine. "It was like a cathedral of some forgotten religion. It was awesome and majestic, but also incomprehensible and inhuman."

"Did you think so?" asked the Magoon. "I felt the same, but I thought it must have been a disappointment to you, since it was so clearly not True Earth."

"No," said Lady Sunshine. "That visit was not one I would repeat, but I would not surrender it. The slow power of that place overwhelmed me. I think it has followed another road than ours, one far slower and less headlong, one less improvised, one more well-considered. Even before life arose on Old Earth, I believe that planet was making itself. It has never considered an alternative to being rock. If impetuous man and that which impetuous man becomes are not the true way of the universe, then the rock of that world may slowly demonstrate its own truth. It is an alternative to us. We may not criticize it, but only leave it abide."

"I am sobered by such patience," said the Magoon. "I wonder on what day we will communicate with that world?"

"And on what terms?" said Lady Sunshine.

"And to what ends?"

The third hyperspace transition was longer and more oblique than the first two they had made. Lady Sunshine had always accepted oblique and acute hyperspace transitions as much the same. Now, for the first time, she realized that there were qualitative differences between the two.

The sun of this new place was pink.

Lady Sunshine called the Magoon to view it. And he rose from his bunk once again when they were settled in orbit and she announced another new world in place beneath them.

"A new world! A new enigma!" exclaimed the Magoon. "It looks promising. I wonder what it will reveal to us."

"It is an enigma better resolved with your probe than with the planetary analyzer I never found, Magoon," Lady Sunshine said. "I would not like a remote and bloodless examination half so well as this direct engagement. With a mere analyzer, we would have known no more of the rock world than its unsuitability for human habitation."

"But are you certain you wish to explore so soon after travel? We may rest if you like. I feel a responsibility to your people for you."

"You have no responsibility for me," said the Magoon. "My fate is not in your hands, except now-and-then, and by-the-way. You are not one of my advisers, Lady Sunshine, but there are times when you sound like them."

"I apologize," said Lady Sunshine.

"And rightly so," he said.

"Let us explore now, then."

But as soon as Lady Sunshine saw the planet, she knew it was not True Earth, whatever else it might be. True Earth would have no room for a place as dull as this.

The drone had landed on a featureless gray plain. The sky above was a lighter shade of gray. Plain and sky met at a distant seamless horizon. A tired wind lifted a handful of dust and then let it settle in dribbles. As they silently looked about them at the new world they had found, a great furry-winged flying creature came flying ponderously near, and then was eventually gone, lost to sight in the grayness.

In great excitement, the Magoon said: "Why, this is fantastic! Look at the gauges! Perceive how habitable this world is! Why, it is my dream!"

Was this place better than Beatus? Lady Sunshine inspected her meters and then double-checked them against the Magoon's readings. All readings were startlingly normal, as though this grayness were somehow a boring and temperate average, a mediocre mean. Indeed, seemingly this dusty flat would make a suitable location on which to place row on row of long houses.

Lady Sunshine said, "I wonder if your people of Beatus would be happy here. It seems monotonous after the varieties of your planet."

The Magoon raised an eye on an extensor a great distance in the air and looked all about them. He fixed finally on the direction that the flying creature had flown. "I see a grove of green in the distance," said the Magoon. "Since you seek variety, let us go investigate it. As we travel, let us propose names for this world we have found."

"Perhaps later, when we know it better," said Lady Sunshine.

They rolled on their universal motivators over the dusty plain in the direction that the Magoon had indicated. The ground was so hard that they left no visible marks of their passage.

Lady Sunshine said: "Does this place delight your heart, Magoon?"

"Indeed it does," he said. "It is living proof of my dreams! I can hardly believe in a world as habitable as this. If I were not within this mechanical and unable, I would hug myself."

A strange reaction! Unless, of course, one had never known any world but Beatus.

"Do you not wonder why I have been so discouraging?"

"Have you been discouraging?" asked the Magoon. "I have not noticed that you have been."

"Perhaps it is a failure in the perceptions of your mechanical," said Lady Sunshine. "For I have been being discouraging. This planet may be better than Beatus, but it is not much of a planet. You would stop here, and rest content."

"You would not?"

"Of course not! I have traveled more than you, Magoon, and I have never seen a planet more lacking in grace! It may be habitable, but it would bend you worse than Beatus has bent you. You would be very strange then, your bentness compounded. We have been here only briefly and distantly, and I feel oppressively bent already."

The Magoon said anxiously, "But perhaps we have already been more than fortunate in finding two planets. How many more than this will we find?"

"Many. In the course of my search for True Earth, many. Worlds so almost perfect they will make you weep and your teeth ache. Take your people of Beatus there.

"Or take them here, if you still prefer. We will remember where this nameless temperate flat was. I will not forget, at any rate."

"But what of this world's groves of green?" asked the Magoon.

Lady Sunshine raised her own eye on its extensor. This gave her the peculiar experience of seeing both near and far simultaneously. With her lower eye, she looked at the Magoon. With her extended eye, she looked in their direction of travel across the gray plain.

She asked, "If there are other groves of green on this planet, are they also giant cabbages?"

"Giant cabbages, Lady Sunshine?" asked the Magoon. "I cannot believe that my grove is giant cabbages!"

"It is not," Lady Sunshine said. "It is one single solitary giant cabbage. That is your grove entire. Do you wish to look for yourself?"

Slowly, in his piping voice, the mechanical that was the Magoon said, "I think you are testing my devotion to this world. I have always found cabbages peculiar."

He rolled forward.

"Pull your eye in," he said. "Let us continue. We will discover soon enough if you are testing me."

Lady Sunshine looked at him with her extended eye, changing the magnification until she saw him whole and clear. He looked quite strange from this angle.

"Very well," she said. "But I, for one, propose that we name this place Cabbage Flat."

The ground under their motivators was now less hard. It was damper and darker. When the green grove was clearly visible to them, even at their proper minor height, the ground had turned to black mud, which tried to enmire them. But their universal motivators were more than equal to mud. Instead of rolling, they now slid smoothly over the top of the bog.

When they came closer, it became apparent that Lady Sunshine had not been testing the Magoon. The grove of green was indeed a single huge plant bearing a distant similarity to a gigantic cabbage.

It was the center of the local dampness. Indeed, close about it the mud was thick liquid, a sloppy black muck.

Though the great enfolding leaves of the massive vegetable were apparent to them at a distance, the Magoon did not admit its nature until they were close upon the enormous green-and-purple bulk. He stopped in the muck and studied his grove.

"You are right," he said at last. "It is very like a giant cabbage."

"Do you wish to examine it more closely?" asked Lady Sunshine.

"Or does it wish to examine us more closely?" asked the Magoon. "Does it seek to eat us?"

The black muck around the cabbage begun to swirl slowly. As they rested on the slop, they were being pulled around in a spiral toward the cabbage. Around and around, and closer and closer they were brought to the plant. It looked much the same on all sides—a few leaves spread high and wide, the rest folded together in a central bolus.

They were closer than Lady Sunshine liked when the Magoon finally said: "I have seen as much of this peculiar vegetable as I care to see. Let us retreat a distance."

The swirl on which they were carried seemed so inexorable that Lady Sunshine wondered if they could retreat, or whether they must again abandon their exploratory vehicles. But, in fact their motivators propelled them easily across the spiraling tide of muck. They settled at a more comfortable distance.

The pull of the swirling current increased, but they resisted it, floating easily in place. It increased yet again, but never becoming more than a frantically stolid movement. They held their place against it lightly.

"Again you see the advantage of your probe to my analyzer," said Lady Sunshine. "An analyzer would have given us a very different picture of this world. It would have reported that this place was temperate, but not that it was Cabbage Flat."

The Magoon said, "If the planetary analyzer were properly made—and if you had a battleship to contain it—it would take such things as cabbages and flatness into consideration."

Suddenly the mud around them ceased its churning. In moments, the face of the bog was still again, the last ripples fading away.

"Observe your meters," said Lady Sunshine. "This planet is less habitable now than formerly. Its disharmony now exceeds that of Beatus."

And, indeed, their gauges did show that the atmosphere around them had become radically altered. There was now an over-concentration of several potent chemicals.

"I suspect the source is the cabbage," said Magoon.

"Does it seek to attract us, to overcome us, or to repel us?" asked Lady Sunshine.

"How can one tell with a cabbage? Perhaps it is attempting to communicate with us."

The bog began to swirl again, but this time in the opposite direction. Instead of the cabbage drawing them in, it was now doing its best to push them away from itself.

They resisted the movement of sludge and continued to hold their places to see what would happen next.

Then, without warning, the great central bolus of the cabbage fell apart. The overlapping leaves flapped back with the sound of ship's canvas filling. They spread wide, opening the plant but still hiding its interior from their view.

A large furry-winged flying creature, perhaps the same that they had seen earlier, leaped into the air with a raw-voiced cry. It flew to them and seized the little mechanical that was the Magoon of Beatus. It carried him up into the air away from the cabbage with great effortful wing beats, and flew away into the grayness.

Lady Sunshine looked at the unfolded vegetable. She was too small to see over the great spread leaves into the mystery of its interior.

She looked with her other eye at the moving thing in the sky, now only a single undefined spot. She magnified the spot until she saw it clearly again as flying-creature-carrying-mechanical. She did not know what to do.

Lady Sunshine abruptly pulled her hands from the gloves and raised the featureless metal helmet. It was quiet there in the ship in orbit. She might as well have been all alone.

She looked at the Magoon. She rose and went to him.

Should she rescue him from the machine, as he had rescued her? He was more experienced in its use than she. He might not be as lost as she had been. Would he not abandon the mechanical if he were dropped from a height?

She observed him until she was certain that the Magoon was still in voluntary control of his mechanical's faculties. She saw his feet work his motivator with smooth and knowing precision, and she knew that he was well.

Lady Sunshine left him then and ran back to her probe machine. She had left her curiosity unsatisfied. She hurriedly resumed her place. She pulled the helmet back over her head.

The cabbage had managed to push the mechanical she inhabited to the very edge of the muck while she was gone. But she wished to penetrate its towering bulk. She wished to see from where the flying creature had come.

But the resources of her mechanical exploratory vehicle were insufficient. Lady Sunshine raised her extensible eye to its limit, but the green-and-purple plant would not let her see its unknown interior. It denied her. It lifted its leaves in a tremendous effort that cracked the air loudly, and folded itself together again.

Lady Sunshine looked all around her again. In the distant sky she saw the flying creature returning. She magnified her vision and saw that it was empty-handed. It was returning for her, but she would not let it have her.

She withdrew from the probe machine to save herself. She saw the Magoon rising and standing free of the other machine.

"Are you all right, Lady Sunshine?" he asked.

"Yes," she said. "What happened to you, Magoon?"

"It was quite strange. The flying creature carried me back to the drone and set me down with another raucous cry. Then it flew off without looking back, returning again to the vegetable. What happened to you?"

"Nothing," she said, as though she did not realize the limitations of the mechanical that had just been demonstrated to her. As though she had not been afraid.

Then she said, "While you were being carried, did you think of a better name for this planet than Cabbage Flat?"

"No," said the Magoon. "Cabbage Flat it will be. This is not the planet to replace Beatus. I see now that your dream is a better dream than mine. Mine will produce nothing but Cabbage Flats. But in looking for your dream, perhaps we will find the world better than Beatus for which I and my people hope.

"Let us look on. What is the next place on your computer's list?"

4

The sun that Lady Sunshine saw before her when they emerged from hyperspace was radiant gold of a lustrous richness more orange than yellow. It glowed like her hair, or like a treasure house.

But the Magoon did not rise from his bunk to witness it, though it was lovely. He was not yet recovered from the hyperspace transition.

"Seek our new world, True Earth," he said. "Don't fix your attention on these pains of mine, which will pass."

"You are a dear creature, Magoon," said Lady Sunshine, and turned again to her piloting.

She followed the statistical inferences of her computer and found a planet not too very far from where one was predicted to be. She settled into orbit around it and allowed the computer to calculate the most probably optimal destination for the drone.

But when all was ready, the Magoon was still in pain.

He said, with great effort: "I have not been candid with you, Lady Sunshine. I have been more affected by hyperspace than I have allowed you to know."

"You should have told me so that I might have returned you to Beatus," she said.

"No. What is important is your dream of True Earth, and the fruits of that dream."

"But are you sure that you can survive another transition?"

"No. But that does not matter. You need me, and now I have failed you."

The Magoon ceased to speak then. He did not respond to Lady Sunshine. He was very sick, and she did not know what to do.

She found that he had armed himself with medicine, and that he had used it all. She spoke to him, but he did not answer. She touched him. She washed his face. She felt ashamed.

The Magoon's motives and behavior had been so much nobler than her own. She had selfishly insisted on pursuit of her private goal at all costs. But what had been her true goal? To demonstrate to Madame O'Severe all that Madame O'Severe denied. To show her that there was a world somewhere in which Lady Sunshine could be someone else and not the creature that Madame O'Severe had made.

For this petty end, she had used the Magoon willfully, taking no notice of his pain. Discounting it. Ignoring it. She had not cared what he needed or suffered because she had required his services.

What were her choices in this moment of the Magoon's collapse? She could take him to Beatus. She could take him by the easiest acute hyperspace transition to one of the Ninety Worlds.

But any hyperspace transition might kill him.

Then there was this new enigma, this unknown planet below them that might be more living rock, or more cabbages and flying creatures. This planet might be anything.

If, with all her great skill, she brought her trim white spacecraft down to the planet in the absence of a landing grid, then in spite of her great skill, they would never be able to leave this world again. They would be bound to it forever.

Lady Sunshine was lost in the twists of a great paradoxical knot. She had brought the Magoon to this place to operate the probe machine. Because she could not. Now, however, the Magoon could not operate the probe machine. Because she had brought him here through hyperspace to operate the probe machine. It was for the Magoon's sake that the probe machine was necessary now, to explore the world below them. But without his ability to operate it, the probe machine was useless. Because Lady Sunshine had brought the Magoon through hyperspace to operate the machine. Because she could not.

It was a horrible knot. It made no sense.

She could not land on this planet. Neither could she fly elsewhere through hyperspace. Neither could she do nothing.

She cried in agony. She was alone, more alone than ever before in her life. She was a unity, a singularity, and it was not enough to be that.

She had but one temporization available to her. If she sent the drone down to the planet, the Magoon might recover sufficiently to activate the probe so that they might determine whether or not to land themselves on the secret world below, the unknown planet of the golden star.

She pressed the button to launch the drone. But when it had landed safely, the Magoon had not recovered.

The squat brown creature, ugly and dear, continued to lie unconscious in his bunk. While she looked, he suddenly cried and thrashed behind the glass. Then he became still.

Terror-stricken, she pulled the ship's emergency unit from its private closet. The Magoon was still alive, but he was much worse. She strapped him in and attached the emergency unit. The computer monitored his functions. She could keep him alive in this fashion, but for how long?

For the first time her self-sufficiency failed her. Even in her worst moments on Amabile or in her most discouraging moments of search, she had not been this helpless. She had never needed aid before.

Aid? That was not the way of Madame O'Severe. That was not the way of mankind.

Each for himself. Above all, each for himself, until one stood alone atop the pyramid, master of all. Above all. One.

It suddenly occurred to Lady Sunshine that she had operated the mechanical on Cabbage Flat after the Magoon had quitted the system. He had been standing apart from the machine when she had raised her helmet. Was it possible for her to operate the probe without him?

"Poor Magoon," she said, and touched him. He did not respond, but lay inert in the grip of the emergency unit.

She closed the glass. She checked the automatic functions of the ship.

"Mind your business well," she said to the computer.

Then she went to the probe. She sat down, placed her feet in the stirrups, pulled the helmet over her head and put her hands into the gloves. And immediately it seemed to her like the first time she had tried to operate the machine around Beatus. She was aware of rigidity. Her head was gripped closely. Her hands were imprisoned. Her legs were dead.

But what did that matter? The machine operated!

She could see. She could hear. It was as though she were on the unknown world and not lost in a computer-rectified machine somewhere in orbit above it.

Lady Sunshine looked at the other mechanical beside her, still and silent. She looked out of the drone into the world that awaited her beyond.

It was amazing. It was seeming Arcadia. It was Eden.

It was trees and grass and brilliant golden sunshine. It was a jolly little brook and an alternation of perfect hills stretching to the horizon.

"Can this be True Earth?" she asked, but the other mechanical gave her no answer.

She would have to discover for herself. Amabile had been attractive at first appearance, and also other planets, before they revealed their bentness.

She labored her mechanical body out of the drone. It was an annoyance to labor, but somehow she was unable to work the mechanical smoothly. Her fingers had forgotten themselves. Her feet were asleep.

Was the difference the missing Magoon? Or was it somehow this planet?

Then suddenly she careened forth, ran in a desperate curve, spun helplessly on her motivator, and fell over. A wise little bluebird twittered mockingly at her. It watched her flail to rise and jeered again.

She watched it take to flight as she lay. It disappeared in midair, leaving nothing but a swimming mote of emptiness in her vision. She could not believe what she saw. Had she imagined that she saw the bird? Had she imagined that she saw it disappear?

She finally managed to lever herself upright. Her mechanical body seemed heavy and out-of-balance. Her control was uncertain. At any moment she feared that the mechanical would have a lurching fit, or suddenly refuse to answer her intended direction. She could only move at angles, not in direct forward progression, so she tacked one way and then another in order to proceed.

Was this True Earth? Lady Sunshine wondered why she did not love its golden perfection better.

But then she looked more closely. This was difficult because her mechanical eyes would not focus. But she saw that the world had a plasticene quality. It was overripe. It melted into itself in a way she did not like. Trees intertwined themselves blindly, groping at each other with long tendrils. There were strange distant animals in this pastoral land, moving together. As she watched, a doggish creature—not a dog, more than a dog—rubbed itself intimately against a tree and then urinated on it.

Not knowing why, she was again reminded of Amabile. But why?

She watched a creature that was like a golden-furred rabbit hopping idly on the hillside. It disappeared like the bird, and then appeared again.

There were strange spots of blankness in her vision. The colors of this world drooped and threatened to run together, to spill and mix and whirl. There were flickers at the edges of her eyes. She spun her eye around to catch them, but though she rotated it madly, they always managed to elude her.

She did not like this place. It made her uneasy. And yet to appearance it was perfect and golden like some California or Huy Brasil. Was the fault in the machine? Or was it this place?

She moved forward, tripped over something she didn't see, skated wildly, fell, bounced fortuitously, and came to rest upright. It was so strange. She could not move properly. She could not see clearly.

Lady Sunshine felt the need of the Magoon. There were spaces in her expectations, and she was deeply disturbed.

She began to watch one particular area of blankness in her vision, a swimmingness that moved this way and then that, and could not be pinned down. She was determined to see through it.

She raised an eye on an extensor to see it from a height. She did this with all due carefulness lest she fall over, which she felt that she might do. She watched the mote with separate eyes and it did not go away.

She became certain then that it was not the computer that was at fault. It was not the mechanical. It was not herself. The source of strangeness lay in the planet.

She heard a piercing squeal which unnerved her. Then suddenly the blankness—that blankness—was no longer there. Instead, she saw a black rabbit-creature mounted on the golden rabbit she had seen before. It turned its face to her as it thrust and pumped, and she saw that it had long sharp unrabbitlike teeth. Then it fell off and lay panting, its little pink penis extended from its furry sheath.

The golden doe tried vainly to hop away, but the black buck leaped up again. It seized the golden doe by the neck and bit down savagely. The doe squealed again and then its neck was broken.

It thrashed helplessly, exposing its underbelly. And then Lady Sunshine saw that it was not a doe at all, but another buck, and that it had an erection of its own in the throes of death. Even before it stopped moving, the black rabbit-creature fell to feeding on its warm body.

Lady Sunshine retracted her extended eye. She feared she could not move without falling with her vision radically split.

She moved forward carefully. She was successful except for one inadvertent reckless lurch.

The rabbit-thing continued to feed greedily on its fellow until she was close. Then it lifted its head, gave her a knowing look, hastily licked the blood from its black-furred mouth with a delicate pink tongue, and hopped away into an anomaly. It was gone into a swimming blur, disappeared again.

The look it gave Lady Sunshine remained with her. It had included her somehow in its crimes with that look, and the knowledge frightened her. She wanted to separate herself, but the golden corpse remained, bloody and mangled, lying on the hillside, as though it were hers. Her property.

Abruptly, a loud moan began, starting low, rising, breaking into howls. What was that? It was painful and intimidating. It unnerved her to hear. It came from nowhere and from everywhere. It surrounded her and filled her ears, filled her world. It was as though the whole uncertain planet were shrieking its pain at her.

Lady Sunshine wished that it would stop. When it became too much, she cried for it to stop.

It stopped.

Then two people suddenly appeared. They seemed to walk out of a bush with brown and crumbling leaves. One was a woman with long black hair and sharp foxy features. She led a man who was covered with overlapping triangular scales. Both were naked. Her muff hair was as golden as the dead rabbit-creature.

His penis was slippery and wet, and dripped mucilaginous strings of gleet.

Lady Sunshine was amazed to see people here. This planet was not one of the Ninety Worlds of the Dispersion from Old Earth.

Naked people.

The woman saw Lady Sunshine first. She put one hand to her muff and the other to her mouth, sucking her fingers in a parody of concern. She prodded the man with an elbow and made a suggestive twaddle to Lady Sunshine with the fingers from her crotch.

Then the woman and the man walked through each other and were a place of emptiness. They were not visible. Gone, impossibly gone.

Lady Sunshine tried to calm her distress by placing the worlds of origin of the two naked people. They seemed definite types, as definite as the Magoon from Beatus. As definite as a lace-veil butterfly from O'Severe. These people were formed, malformed, bent into special shapes.

But Lady Sunshine could not remember any place where the people looked so vulpine. Or any place where men had evolved scales like a pineapple. And that was even more distressing.

In the emptiness about her head, there were suddenly tears, screams and silence. Silence. Then more screams.

She looked wildly about her. Nothing, nothing, nothing but golden sunshine and a sky as blue as the benighting fog of Beatus.

The planet uttered a final explosive raw-voiced agony, which turned to laughter and trailed away.

"There are those who need time to get used to it here," someone said in an exquisite throaty voice.

The voice came out of nowhere.

"And then there are those who take to it right away."

The voice seemed to come from above, out of a tree. A mass of creepers, tendrils and black writhing vines lowered itself. There was a flickering within the web, at times flashes of paleness, at other moments only writhing blackness. The squirming nest reached the ground and broke open. But there was nothing within the tentacles but unfocused shimmer, an anomaly.

Then a dryad stepped forth, out of the nothingness. She was fat, middle-aged, coy and horrid. She was naked and flabby and white as rice. She looked like an evil pig. A great festering wound, a gumma, had eaten away most of her nose and turned it into an open snout. A few of the black creepers broke away from the main mass and remained with her, winding and twining intimately about her body like snakes. Where they touched her they left welts on the whiteness like intense broken red veinlets.

The creature of the tree, this dryad, reached out to Lady Sunshine, who started back from her, nearly toppling.

"May I touch you?" the dryad asked pleasantly. "I want very much to touch you. May I? I like to be the first to touch new people. It is almost my only vice."

The gumma seemed to shift on her face. Her nose was now there, where it had not been before. It was a red blobby thing. But now part of her forehead was eaten to the bone, which showed whitely through the open wound. And a lip was lifted high to reveal skeleton teeth smiling at Lady Sunshine.

"No!" said Lady Sunshine. She did not want to be touched. Above all, she did not want to be touched.

The dryad said, "I just thought that I would ask while it occurred to me. You mustn't think I was insisting, just because it occurred to me."

She walked in a circle around Lady Sunshine, while Lady Sunshine watched her with a wary rotating eye, ready to lurch if the dryad attempted to move in her direction. Then, suddenly, the dryad sat down beside her. She stroked and petted her various creeping companions, and moved a favored thick black tendril into her crotch where it curled itself around her leg and snuggled intimately.

The dryad licked her lips obscenely, tongue running over white teeth where she had no lip, and leaned toward Lady Sunshine. Lady Sunshine inched away.

"From what planet do you come, my dear?" she inquired.

"O'Severe," Lady Sunshine said. "Originally."

"O'Severe. That's nice! That is such a distance to have come. Your need for us must have been very great. Why, that means that sooner or later I will see more of you, doesn't it? But it would be so nice to be first. You are so sweet and fragile. I do like that in a girl."

The dryad, that fat fountain of unknown delight, suddenly stood again.

"You must excuse me, really," she said. "I have tarried too long with you. For here is someone new that has been sent to me. And I must not be selfish, must I?"

She turned and galloped off to intercept one of the distant animals that Lady Sunshine had seen, which now approached them. Or was it a man? Or a boy? Or was it a creature part human and part something other than human?

Lady Sunshine could not say. His genitals made him male. But he had the narrow-hipped, smooth-muscled body of an adolescent boy. His skin was mottled green and yellow, and seemed of different textures, smooth where it was yellow, pebbled like a turtle or lizard where it was green, everywhere hairless. His tiny head was bald and chinless and bobbed atop a neck fully two feet long as though it had a life of its own separate from its body.

This strange and improbable creature took no notice of the maiden of the tree come tripping to intercept him. He detached a bit of yellow from his green leathery body, tossed the gobbet into the air, and snapped it down with a lunge of his long neck.

Lady Sunshine realized then that the yellow patches on his skin were fleshy moving things like creeping leeches. He plopped another with great relish into his lipless mouth, and bulged his eyes hugely.

"Match for unity," the dryad challenged him. She seized him by his limp dangling member, and her black-creeper familiars bound him to her otherwise.

He nodded and picked a yellow blob off his body. He squeezed it until it popped and ran like dripping custard. He smeared it on her face, and she gagged and sputtered.

"One for me," he said, laughing. "Unity."

They began to contend, to wrestle, to twine like the trees of this planet. The doggish creature that Lady Sunshine had seen earlier came trotting over as they swayed for advantage. It sniffed them closely, snapped at their genitals, and was slapped smartly by the thick tendril that the dryad wore as guardian of her privacy. The doggish one whined, and then deliberately urinated on them.

"Unity," it said audibly, and trotted briskly away. Lady Sunshine was amazed to hear it speak.

The gross dryad never let go of the green boy's penis. She ripped at it with her nails. She gnawed at it with her skeleton teeth. She rubbed and snorted it in her decayed nose. Lady Sunshine could hardly bear to watch.

The turtle boy whimpered and chittered at her attack, but in spite of all her painful work, he did not yield to her. He had weapons of his own. He bashed, nudged and butted her blindly with his small bald head on its long neck. He struck her again and again with great blows. With soft, nailless fingers he strove to pry away the thick black tentacle that protected her.

He suddenly broke away with a triumphant cry, holding the tendril. His neck grew stiff. His tiny head grew dark and engorged. He struck the dryad with her tendril and she screamed and loosed her grip on his penis.

The green boy-creature made the dryad bend and present her rear to him. He whipped her with the tendril and she screamed with each blow. Her body was a mass of red welts. He cried, "Louder! Louder!" and whipped her ever harder.

Then he penetrated her with his bald head on its long neck. He plunged into the dryad again and again, and she filled the world with the sound of her pleasure and agony. The tendrils that clung to her stood out from her body and writhed blindly.

And then, at the climactic moment when the green leather-skinned creature was about to expend himself within her, somehow the black tendril he used as a whip wrapped itself tightly around his neck. He was blocked, prevented. The tendril squeezed tighter and tighter, and the rising tide within him had no outlet.

He withdrew his lipless, chinless head. He was under stress. He was in dire straits. He pointed to his neck desperately. With his other hand he pried vainly at the thick tentacle. His green skin was almost black.

The dryad snapped his neck with sharp impertinent fingers. She slapped his cheeks. She prodded him in the gut. At last, she recovered her black companion and stood aside.

The boy rang the world with his howl. Then he vomited gouts of delayed yellow matter that had been blocked from ejaculation.

"One for me," the dryad said. "Unity."

"Unity," everyone cried, and applauded her. They knew a winner when they saw one.

The poor sick boy looked at the great crowd that had gathered. He retched and cried. He flickered madly, and then disappeared.

The dryad showed her teeth in her most hideous smile, and then yawned elaborately. She passed her black familiar between her legs. It wrapped itself around her right leg and nestled into its home again.

Lady Sunshine looked at the many beings gathered around her. It was impossible to say how many there were because they became and they unbecame.

All of this awful world threatened to come unpinned about her now. There was more flicker than stability.

All the strange and naked people she saw standing around her in the dark rainbow drip and swirl were diseased. Or they were deformed. Or they were inhuman.

There was one being that looked like a baboon with immensely swollen genitals. It had the face of a lovely woman. It sat on the ground and played with crawling spiders.

A woman with skin like rough tree bark fondled a balloon-headed dwarf. A creature with the body of a man and the head of an elephant groped them both with its trunk. The woman seemed to be unaware of where she was, of what she did, and of what was done to her. The dwarf smirked.

Another woman with twin lines of dugs that stretched from chest to groin lay on her side on the ground while an assorted brood of squirming things fought each other for her tits. Two fought to the death. Their wet nurse picked up the parts of their bodies and tossed them to the sharp-toothed rabbit-thing, which savaged them.

Lady Sunshine whirled on her motivator, but everywhere she looked, it was the same. She felt dizzy. This place was not an accident. It was intentional. It was directed at her. It was a trap for her.

She had a vision of this planet: plants, animals, humans, and creatures in between, all intertwined in one great rapacious, battling, steaming, creaming, moaning, sucking, fucking, slavering, groping, dying, crying, pyramidal unity.

The creatures whirled in a sickening flux around her and sang to her:

"Earth is dead."

"Nothing matters."

"Sufferance."

"Desolation."

"Pleasure."

"Unity."

"Forever and ever, amen."

Lady Sunshine was bewildered and beset.

"Who shall initiate her into the mysteries?" the creatures asked.

The dryad stepped forward. She wriggled her wet and gaping snout.

"I saw her first," she said. "I should have first turn."

"You've had your first turns, darling," said a filthy grandmother with a neck that hung in wattles like a turkey, and empty withered breasts. She gnawed on the leg bone of a child. "But I have experience, and experience counts."

"Match experience," said the dryad. "Match your unity against mine."

"Very well," said the grandmother. "Have a nibble," she said, and handed her bone to the dryad.

"And you," said the dryad, handing her black companion to the ancient.

The fat dryad munched at the leg bone. The filthy old woman tried to bite the wriggling creeper she held, but it evaded her and struck at her wrinkled neck.

The old woman snapped like a mongoose and the tendril was caught and bitten in two. It fell limp. The dryad shuddered and ululated. Then she flickered and was gone.

"One for me," said the old one. "Unity."

The crowd shuddered and cried, "One for you."

"As you see, it is experience that counts. Oh, what I will teach this sweet child."

But then a man stepped forward, naked except for black socks. In this company he was unusual, because he looked fully human. He did not flicker at all unless you watched him very closely, and his dark hair was neatly combed.

He said, "You forget me."

"I did forget you, Dr. Wrongsong," said the grandmother, "but only for the merest moment. Let us step aside and match ourselves one against one."

Dr. Wrongsong smiled sincerely. "One against one," he said.

"Unity," said everyone. "Unity above all."

They all disappeared, the man, the grandmother, and all the various creatures. The world around Lady Sunshine shattered, sharded, pinwheeled, blurred, spilled, swirled and ran. There was only one stability in all the chaos. That was the doggish creature.

It came sniffing up to Lady Sunshine. She tried to back away from it, but could not move.

"Try to leave," said the doggish creature. "Just try to leave us. You will find that you cannot. We are yours, and you are ours. I will be last. I'm always last. But in the end, there will be one for me."

To her horror, it lifted its leg and urinated all over her, and she could not prevent being marked.

"Unity," it said. Then it disappeared, too.

Lady Sunshine was helpless and alone, lost in lovelessness. She tried vainly to move, but her head was vise-gripped. Her hands were cuffed. He fingers were paralyzed. She could not move her motivator. She could not extend her extensible eye. She could not rotate her rotatable eye.

She could not leave the mechanical. She could not retire from this place. She could not take her ship through hyperspace and escape as she wanted. She could not move at all.

She knew now why this place reminded her of Amabile. But it was far more terrible than Amabile had ever been.

She realized that Madame O'Severe was right.

She had hoped to remain aloof from corruption. She had longed to remain untouched. But now she was lost, eternally damned.

This was the entire universe, forever and ever. And it was the same everywhere:

Disease . . .

Decay . . .

Death . . .

Devolution . . .

O'Severe = Amabile = Beatus

As counterpoint to her thoughts, this planet played for her its single eternal song of ecstatic revulsion, of solitary abandonment and humiliation. It filled Lady Sunshine's head and heart as the one real thing.

But no! There was a realer thing. There was one hope.

There was True Earth. Somewhere there was True Earth.

No matter what else, there was True Earth.

The awful keening stopped as abruptly as it had begun. There was silence. Long, empty silence.

Then the sincere man stepped into being through the swirling colorful dissolve. He was alone.

Dr. Wrongsong's hair was still perfectly in place, but he was now missing a sock. Lady Sunshine saw that his bare foot was not human, but was other.

"Here I am at last," he said, licking his lips and teeth clean of blood. "Have I kept you long?"

Lady Sunshine looked blindly at him and tried to hold onto her dream of True Earth.

"You think you understand now," Dr. Wrongsong said, "but of course you don't. You must be dominated. Experience is the only true teacher."

She protested. "I don't understand! I won't understand!"

"No false innocence. You say you don't understand, but of course you do. Deep in your heart, you do. You did not come here by accident. You sought us out. This is the place for which you have longed."

"What do you mean?" she cried.

"This is True Earth."

No! If this was True Earth, then there was no hope.

"And now you must be touched," Dr. Wrongsong said. He reached out, and she could not prevent him. She could not resist. She could not help herself. There was no escape.

Escape? To what? To where?

He touched her. He spun her ruthlessly on her motivator, and around and around she went. She spun in her mind. Helplessly.

Hopelessly she cried cried cried to be saved.

And then, all around Lady Sunshine, the dissolving spinning world split apart and there was light. The helmet of the probe machine was lifted from her head and she lay open to the radiance of a new universe.

"Magoon," she said. "It's you."

5

He had come somehow. Out of his coma. Out of the grip of the emergency unit. From behind his closed doors.

The Magoon was naked and hairy. He dripped tubes, wires, and broken needles, but he took no notice of them. His eyes were for her, otherwise unseeing.

He said, "I heard you call for me, and I came."

She hugged and kissed him desperately.

"Bless you, Magoon," she said. "This is an awful place and we must get away from it."

The Magoon looked at Lady Sunshine.

"This is the place," he said. "I know it. There is no other."

And he collapsed.

She cried, and laughed, and gasped because he was hurt and he was her love. She plucked the thorns and darts from him. With impossible strength, she carried him in her arms to her bed.

She had not yet thought of him when she said they must leave, but now she did think of him. She thought of him above herself.

The Magoon could not go elsewhere than this planet. And she must take him there, for his sake.

If this was True Earth, it did not matter. One place was like another. The one thing she was sure of was the Magoon, and if they were together, it did not matter where they traveled. The Magoon transformed the universe.

She kissed him and tenderly stroked his hairiness.

Then she turned to her piloting. With the aid of the computer and her own skill, she brought her white spaceship safely to land not far from the drone on this planet without landing grids, this awful world she had just quitted. And felt relief.

Not so far distant, Lady Sunshine could see her former mechanical body. It stood alone. Abandoned. Inert.

But something was strange. She felt as she had never felt before in all her life, and she did not know what it meant. She glowed within herself. Her heart was lifted.

What did it mean?

This was not the way it had been when she inhabited the mechanical. That was remote and queer. And this might almost be a different world. Or was the difference in her?

This world was changed. It was not the same. She saw it differently.

She threw open the doors of the spaceship and stared about her in wonderment. The planet was lit from within itself. Colors were everywhere pure and luminescent. They glowed and streamed with inner life like the slowly pulsing breath of a stained glass dove.

The planet was filled with notes that hummed and fluttered and chimed. Occasional notes that came and went, or stayed, or changed. Rare harmonies. And the colors interplayed and shifted with the notes of the song the planet sang. All in goldenness and sunshine.

The Magoon joined her, risen from her bed, and she turned to him. He was well. He was healed. His eyes were no longer sad. He was beautiful.

He was beautiful, but at the same time no less the Magoon that had been. He was not altered. He was transfigured. And he smiled at her.

Lady Sunshine looked at him, and in him she saw enhanced all that was good in herself and all that was glorious in this strange planet. She loved him, not as ultimate truth, but for the ultimate truth that she saw within him.

And if he was made well, so was she. She, who had not even realized that she was sick.

A great oppression that had been with her always was now lifted. And it was only with its passing that she realized its existence.

She, who had been bent, was no longer bent.

"I love you, my dear Magoon," she said. "In you, I see more than I can ever say."

"And I love you," he said.

It was then that they became partners. They were no longer solitary self-ish unities, but were joined together in a Oneness that was more than either of them, that was more than their sum.

They exchanged names. Hers was Jennet. His was Lester, which means "lustrous."

She had never told her true name to anyone before.

They turned to the planet again and went out into the world together, hand in hand. Lady Sunshine cast her white clothing from her and let herself be touched by the winds of color. They played on her body and she laughed in surprise. She was lifted into the air on a chiming note and became part of the dance of color and the song of songs. She was ecstatic. Her bare body sailed in the iridescent streaming rainbow swirl.

It was all so strange and wonderful. It was the same world that she had encountered before, but it was seen with transformed eyes.

As they played, knowledge came to them. It surrounded them. Knowledge was this world, and in their play they became knowledge. They knew truth.

There was no more bentness.

They saw the computer's standard of "True Earth" as the poor, partial composite that it was. This planet could not be recognized by any sum of ad-dition. It was of another order.

They saw the probe mechanicals in all their inadequacy. How could truth be perceived as truth by means of this fractional version of human percep-tion? It could not.

And they saw themselves for what they had been: distorted, half-human creatures.

And they knew other things. Together Lady Sunshine and the Magoon laughed and shouted, rolling through the singing shafts of luminous color. They were together with each other and with this world. They were locked together in Oneness.

Love was experienced. Love was known to them.

This world was love, and love was knowledge. Knowledge, love, and knowledge this world.

And then suddenly the sounds and colors around them were altered to new orders of complexity, far beyond their range. They looked and found themselves in the presence of three people—a boy, a mature woman, and an old man, all clothed in reclarified light.

"Welcome," they said. "Welcome. The celebration of your homecoming is in progress, and we have been sent to bring you. Array yourselves and come."

Homecoming!

Lady Sunshine said, "Is this True Earth?"

They laughed.

The woman said, "No. True Earth is every human world."

And Lady Sunshine suddenly perceived

O'Severe = True Earth = Beatus

The Magoon—Lester, the Lustrous One—said, "Yes! Yes! And now I know how to make the Ninety Worlds True Earth."

"Of course," the boy said. "That is what you came to learn."

Lady Sunshine said, "But if this is not True Earth, what place is it?"

"This is Livermore," the old man said. "This is the world where everything is possible to those who can perceive."

6

When it was fully time for Lady Sunshine and the Magoon to leave Livermore, there was another celebration. Then the others made a grid in their minds to hurl the white spaceship into space.

They went first to O'Severe by long passage. Hyperspace was no trial now to the Magoon, for he knew better.

Madame O'Severe said, "So you are returned at last. You took long enough about it."

"You gave me permission to find out where my best interests lie," Lady Sunshine said.

"And here you are. I should not have thought it would take you this long. Who is this grotesque that accompanies you?"

Lady Sunshine said, "This is the Magoon of Beatus. He is my love and partner."

"You have never had good judgment," said Madame O'Severe. "You have never known what was important and what was not. My patience with you is nearly at an end. You must rid yourself of this monster if you would be my instrument."

"I will not be your instrument," said Lady Sunshine. "I know now where it is that my best interests lie, and they do not lie with you."

"I disown you," said Madame O'Severe. "You are not a serious person."

Lady Sunshine and her partner, the Magoon, traveled to Beatus. There they turned the mighty machines of the planet to new purpose. They changed the blue fog into dissipating mist, and performed other wonders.

Lady Magoon and the Sunshine of Beatus.

And that was not the last of what they did. They healed many worlds, among them O'Severe.

Farewell to Yesterday's Tomorrow

All our lives we have assumed that the near future would hold one of two likely possibilities. One possibility was atomic war between us and the Commies. We used to practice huddling under our desks in school and guarding our eyes against the bomb flash, but in our hearts we knew that our chances of survival were slim and that those who survived would wish they were dead. The other possibility of our times was that America would rule the world on the strength of its superior morality, politics, economics, power, and knowledge.

It is a new year now. In 1974 the two possibilities that have ruled our lives for so long have become wild unlikelihoods. American and Russian generals may still thumb-wrestle for hypothetical advantage, but there will not be an atomic war. Neither will there be a New American Empire imposing democracy and California on the world. The planet is aswarm with independent forces that do not accept the superiority of America and who will not have control imposed on them by anybody. Some of these forces are older and wiser than we yet recognize.

In this new year it is clear that we are entering a new era. What its shape will be, we cannot yet tell. But the old era is over.

The old era ruled our lives and our thinking for thirty years. All its factors were established by the end of World War II:

Computers. Plastics. Rocket ships. Atomic weapons and atomic power plants. The United Nations. Russian-American antagonism. The arms race. Technological superfluity.

All of us whose years of awareness have come since 1945 have grown up in a world dominated by these factors. It was as though we had been handed a particular situation and it was our fate to play its permutations out to their conclusion—atomic disaster or American triumph. We had no choice other than these. Like it or lump it. Love it or else.

The protest of the 1960's was an objection to the American Dream Machine, but it was doomed to fail. When an era has crystallized, alternatives are unimaginable. Hate their two choices as they might, the protesters of the sixties could not imagine any others. They still believed that their most likely futures were nuclear hell or America squatting on the face of the world.

The imagined universe of science fiction during these same years was a reflection of the hopes and fears of the new era. The great fear was Atomic Armageddon. The great hope was that the men of Earth might stride forth to conquer the stars.

These hopes were first expressed in the pages of the Golden Age *Astounding*—in exactly the same period of time in which our modern world crystallized itself. They were the basic assumptions of the superman stories of A. E. van Vogt, of the Future History stories of Robert Heinlein, and of the Foundation stories of Isaac Asimov. If no sf writers during the past thirty years have matched these three in importance, it is because Asimov, Heinlein, and van Vogt have held the patents within which a generation of science-fiction writers have labored.

The writers of the Campbell *Astounding* set forth the outline of our future. We would establish colonies among the stars. We would dominate alien races. We would found galactic empires. And we would explode through the entire universe. The heroes of this world to come were technocrats, secret agents, and team players—the analogs of all the bright young Americans who expected to rule the postwar world.

By the end of the 1950's this sf scenario of the future had become gray, trivial, and unpromising. Heroes revealed fatal fallibility. The virtues of human rule of the universe seemed questionable.

In the 1960's, just as there was reaction to the assumptions of American life, so was there reaction to its science-fictional image. Writers sought color. They wrote of lost colonies and of the dropouts of Galactic Empire. They wrote, too, of the exotic landscapes that might survive the nuclear firestorm, of holocaust as the wellspring of magic. But like the political and cultural protest movements of the time, the science fiction of the 1960's was an evasion rather than a true alternative to the mainline future that had been set out in the Golden Age *Astounding*.

When an era has crystallized, there are no alternatives. This can be seen in the stories that J. G. Ballard wrote during the 1960's. His inert inner landscapes of the imagination are an expression of Ballard's hatred of the postwar universe of sterile plastic. But his stories offer no alternative to the Future History of Heinlein and the others. They offer only exaggeration of sterility, ennui, and death.

All the abortive revolutions of the 1960's failed at the end of the decade. Rock music heroes discredited themselves or died squalidly. Weathermen went underground. Dissenters were prosecuted in public show trials. The counterculture went into seclusion. The American Monster won a final victory in the election of Richard Nixon, who is the living symbol of the Postwar era and all its assumptions.

Since 1969 the typical science fiction story has been able to envision little besides disaster. The common story of the period is an account of final extinction in the near future resulting from a willful abuse of technology.

The most successful writer of the past few years in science fiction has been Barry Malzberg. Malzberg has been overheard to say, in the spirit of these years, "Paranoia is science fiction." And in his stories of insane astronauts, such as his novel *Beyond Apollo*, Cape Canaveral and Future History meet in some ultimate disaster of the spirit.

But science fiction is not inevitably paranoid. Not all writers have succumbed to the fear and loathing that result from being trapped by a choice between the unsurvivable and the unendurable. There have been some few stories in these past years that see a new and wholly different world lying just before us.

Examples of these new stories are R. A. Lafferty's "When All the Lands Pour Out Again" and Fred Pohl's "The Gold at the Starbow's End"; Jack Dann's "Junction" and our own "When the Vertical World Becomes Horizontal." Listen to the titles of these stories. They are portents. They bid farewell to yesterday's tomorrow.

They speak of the new time that we have now entered. For here it is 1974 and suddenly all our long-held assumptions no longer obtain. It is a new springtime season.

The old crystallization that held us in thrall has been shattered. We have entered a new era. Change is upon us once again. For who could have dreamed that the American economy of abundance would now be plagued by scarcity? Who would ever have suspected that a crisis in the supply of energy would already be transforming the great American machine? Who would have thought only a few years ago that the political trials of the Nixon Era would all fail, every one, and that Richard Nixon would himself be on trial? All the discredited young men of the Nixon Administration—technocrats, secret agents, team players—are our former heroes in discard.

All is fluid now. The old situation, the old era, is no more. The new era has not yet become fully apparent.

In a period of fluidity there are opportunities for all those who can perceive them. For those who strive to cling to the hopes and fears of yesterday, the times will be profoundly disturbing. But for those who can grow, these will be times of unparalleled adventure.

Revolutions are now under way throughout the sciences—in astronomy and physics, geology, anthropology, archaeology, and psychology. The details are unclear, but it is already certain that when the revolutions are complete, we will have completely revised our ideas about the nature and history of the universe, about the emergence and evolution of life on this earth, about the origins of man and the length of his existence, about the intellectual abilities and achievements of prehistoric man, and about the nature and capacity of the human mind.

We are likewise entering a period of radical international readjustments. The bases of world finance and of world trade will be redefined. The arms race will be abandoned as an expensive anachronism. World controls on population growth will be established. It will be demonstrated that the United Nations is no longer an instrument of American foreign policy. The UN will grow in effectiveness and change in function.

Within fifteen years we will all be living in ways that are presently unimaginable to us. All the priorities of American life will be altered. There will be new goals in education, new styles of life. We will become masters of the American machine rather than cogs within it.

This new season of change might be likened to the 1860's, the decade that saw the rise of corporate capitalism and of European imperialism, the decade that set the crystal that was the early twentieth century. It is also like the 1930's, the period of the Depression and the New Deal, the time in which American values were last rearranged.

Science fiction, the ideal reflection of the world around us, will also change. All our former assumptions, the assumptions of the 1940 *Astounding*, will be abandoned. We can no longer write seriously of Nuclear Cataclysm or of Terran Empire.

We might take note of the fact that we are living now in the days that were imagined as the beginning of Future History. That future is now, this very moment. But when we look about us, we do not see Heinlein's rolling roads. We do not see van Vogt's Slans. We do not see Asimov's positronic robots. The future of 1940 is now, but this now is not the world that was dreamed in 1940.

The last period in science fiction that was like the one we are now entering came during the 1930's. Hugo Gernsback had founded *Amazing Stories* in 1926, in the last days of the crystallization of the 1860's. *Amazing* reflected that world. It was a sister magazine to popular science magazines. The future it expected was populated by young Tom Edisons. Its heaven was a utopia of backyard inventions. Its hell was devolution—the collapse of civilization and return to skin-clad barbarism. The other planets of our solar system were envisioned as being likewise utopic or barbaric. Their populations were either just like us, or they were monsters with a taste for human flesh. This sf world was laid down by Jules Verne and given its classic expression by H.G. Wells.

After 1930, however, all was different. There were new magazines. With the appearance of *Astounding* in 1930, sf took on the racier style and size of the pulp magazines. It no longer seriously pretended to be popular science. During the 1930's the number of science fiction magazines grew. As late as 1937 there were only three. By 1940 there were seventeen.

There were new editors—in particular, F. Orlin Tremaine and John W. Campbell. With their encouragement new writers entered the field. The assumptions and matter of sf changed radically. Before 1930 there was "scientifiction." After 1930 there was "science fiction."

Such writers as E.E. Smith, John W. Campbell, Jack Williamson, and Stanley Weinbaum began producing stories with strange premises and stranger conclusions. They provided the basis from which Heinlein, van Vogt, and Asimov eventually elaborated a new conception of the future. With Smith and Campbell we traveled to the stars and beyond the bounds of our own galaxy. With Williamson we penetrated new dimensions.

The planets of our solar system were colonized. With Weinbaum we discovered that aliens need not be either humanlike or monstrous.

With all this exciting possibility there was no point to writing the familiar old-fashioned style of story about wearing a sweater and bow tie and living in a utopia of chuff-chuffing inventions. It was more creative and exciting to imagine being an explorer of alien realms, or an asteroid miner, or an outlaw of the spaceways.

Just so, as of this springtime of the mid-seventies that we are entering, will sf once again be made wholly new. Just as E.E. Smith's *Skylark* once went forth to discover the universe, so we need to send new starships of the imagination forth to take account of a new world. These ships will not find an empty universe to be strip-mined and subjugated. Instead they will find a universe filled to the brim with the new, rare, and different. It will contain standards by which to measure ourselves—alien races with different abilities, some less advanced than we, some more advanced. This universe will be the ideal reflection of the new multiplex Earth we are now awakening to.

The key words of this new time are *synergy* and *ecology* and *evolution*. The era will be a time of liberation, unfolding, maturation, creativity, and growth.

What the actualities that wait locked in these words may be we do not yet know. We must discover these things for ourselves, and it is an exciting prospect.

The new sf will help us to understand and direct our new lives in the years immediately ahead. It will be more popular in appeal than it has ever been. There will be new magazines and new forms of magazines. There will be new editors and new writers. Sf will excite you as it has never excited you in all your years within the Great American Machine. It will amaze, astound, and delight you as you never dreamed possible. It will scratch forgotten itches and satisfy unrecognized thirsts. It will aid in the remaking of your minds and your lives.

It is time to say good-bye to yesterday's tomorrow and put it out of mind.

Good-bye. Good-bye.

The good-byes are now all said.

A new tomorrow is waiting.

RECONSIDERATION

IN READING OVER these predictions—written in a moment of exaltation at the peak of Richard Nixon's final days—a series of reactions occurs to me.

First is a certain embarrassment when I compare the intense optimism of this essay with the actual darkness of the times we have been living through and hoping to survive. The general renewal of life and culture I hoped for has yet to take place.

But second is a realization that I wasn't wrong in seeing change in the making. The revolutions in the sciences I spotted then have only accelerated. The concern with brute-force technology and its consequences for Mother Earth have become everybody's concern. And the appearance of the Internet gives us promise of new human connection and organization.

Perhaps the greatest puzzle is the degree to which politics-as-usual has lagged behind imagination and the appearance of new realities. How could we have dreamed in 1974 that in this new century the idiots who rule us would still be wrangling over whether "America would rule the world on the strength of its superior morality, politics, economics, power, and knowledge"?

It may seem that yesterday's tomorrow has come back to bite us in the ass and we're all doomed to live out a 1940's science fiction story. In the long run, however, I think that seeming will prove to be as local and limited as the seemings of the Watergate crisis.

In the conflict between imagination and politics, it is imagination that leads the way and politics that eventually—if only with the greatest reluctance—follows.

Farewell, yesterday's tomorrow. The sooner you're gone, the better. Welcome, new ways of living and becoming fully human. You can't come too soon.

More Titles from Phoenix Pick

Poul Anderson
The Burning Bridge $3.99
Security $4.99

Paul Cook
The Engines of Dawn $7.99
Fortress on the Sun $6.99

Andre Norton
Key Out of Time $5.99
Voodoo Planet $4.99

Frank Herbert
Missing Link & Operation Haystack $4.99

John W. Campbell
The Ultimate Weapon $4.99

Lester Del Ray
Police Your Planet $5.99

www.PhoenixPick.com

Phoenix Pick - Great Science Fiction at Great Prices

Being Released Soon!

Multiple Award Winner, L. Neil Smith
Tom Paine Maru (fall 2008)
The Venus Belt (winter 2008)
The Crystal Empire (winter 2008)

From A. A. Attanasio's Acclaimed Radix Tetrad
Arc of the Dream (fall 2008)
Last Legends of Earth (winter 2008)

(Prices as of 9/15/2008 and subject to change without notice)

CPSIA information can be obtained at www.ICGtesting.com
Printed in the USA
BVOW09s1015240214

345830BV00002B/240/P